just until

just until

Joseph Moldover

MARGARET FERGUSON BOOKS
HOLIDAY HOUSE · NEW YORK

Margaret Ferguson Books
An imprint of Holiday House Publishing, Inc.

Library of Congress Cataloging-in-Publication Data

Names: Moldover, Joseph, author.
Title: Just until / a novel by Joseph Moldover.
Description: First edition. | New York : Margaret Ferguson Books,
2024. | Audience: Ages 14 and up. | Audience: Grades 10-12. | Summary:
"Seventeen-year-old Hannah must choose the impossible—put her
nephews into foster care so she can stay true to her dream, or
take them on and lose everything she has worked so hard to
achieve"—Provided by publisher.
Identifiers: LCCN 2023034662 | ISBN 9780823456192 (hardcover)
Subjects: CYAC: Family life—Fiction. | Family problems—
Fiction. | Interpersonal relations—Fiction. | High
schools—Fiction. | Schools—Fiction.
Classification: LCC PZ7.1.M63965 Ju 2024 | DDC [Fic]—dc23
LC record available at https://lccn.loc.gov/2023034662

ISBN: 978-0-8234-5619-2 (hardcover)

For Leah, as always, with love.

And in memory of Alessandra.

1

I squint against the wind and steer my bike into the snow-plow's fading tracks. The top of the hill doesn't seem to be getting any closer; the harder I fight, the more I'm pulled back. There's nothing along this stretch of road apart from endless trees and a crumbling stone wall, and while you can usually smell the ocean if the breeze is blowing from one direction or the dump if it's coming from the other, right now my face is frozen solid and I can't smell a damn thing.

The message from my father said to meet him at Sol's Diner, that it's important, and that everything is fine. Which, translated, means that everything is decidedly not fine. And of the infinite varieties of not-fine, the ones most likely to drag me out into a snowstorm have to do with my sister. I stand and lean into the pedals.

The headlights appear before I hear the engine. They strike the back of my glove and I look over my left shoulder to see a red SUV coming out of the snow and gloom, wipers on, going too fast. I shift to my right and don't stop as it slows beside me and the passenger window slides down.

"Hannah Lynn!"

I turn, look into Brittany O'Neal's incredulous face, and pedal harder.

The car keeps pace on the incline. I see, out of the corner of my eye, that one of Brittany's friends is driving. At least two fellow members of our Evans Beach High School class of 2014 peer out from the backseat.

"Hannah, what on earth are you doing?"

I grit my teeth. "Just out for a ride," I say, though I doubt they can hear me.

The SUV shimmies and I involuntarily jerk the handlebars, sending the bike into a fishtail and almost lose it in a snowbank.

"Sorry, sorry!" Brittany calls, then turns to say something to the driver, who laughs.

"Happy New Year, Hannah!" the driver yells. The truck speeds up, effortlessly cresting the hill and disappearing, leaving me with fresh tracks in the snow. I follow them all the way to the Portland city line.

The ride from my hometown of Evans Beach to the Portland waterfront is easy in good weather. Pleasant, even. I used to bike it all the time, before I was able to drive. I'd head into the city—what passes for a city, in Maine—and prowl the thrift stores, grabbing pieces I'd seen in photos of my mom from the nineties. A belt here, a scuffed-up pair of Doc Martens there. I'd wind up at Sol's Diner and spend whatever change was left in my pockets on fries. They'd usually comp me a soda; sometimes it pays to be the daughter of a local legend.

But this ride sucks, and I don't make it to Sol's until 6:40. Dad's message said to meet him at six but that was before my car wouldn't start and he didn't answer his phone when I called for a lift. I throw my bike into a snowbank and go inside, soaking wet and with every extremity numb. I scan the rows of stools and booths. Mostly lobstermen. Sol's is an institution, but it's a local institution. Set just over the city line separating Portland from Evans Beach, right on the water. There are times, during the warmer months, when the smell from fishing boats unloading on the dock outside is almost overwhelming. It's good for keeping tourists away.

Sol Jr. leans across the counter. His father, the original Sol, was okay. He made a decent omelet. Junior is the shitty knockoff version. He takes his time doing what he always does, undressing me with his eyes, which takes a little extra effort given the number of layers I have on. "Did you swim here, Hannah?" he asks.

I clench my fists and try not to visibly shiver. "Shut up, Sol. I'm looking for Dad."

He shrugs, gestures to a group of men eating their dinners—my father not among them—and retreats to the kitchen.

"Come here, honey." A gentle hand on my back guides

me away from the counter. "You're freezing and wet. I'll get you hot tea." The waitress, Sonya, brings me to a corner booth and helps me out of my coat before heading to the back, pausing to switch the channel from the news to a game show. She winks at me and smiles.

One of the more irritating changes Sol Jr. made when he took over the diner was to install a TV above the counter. I generally despise television, but if there's any sort of trivia show on, I'm slightly less annoyed. "John Jay," I mutter, settling into the booth and staring at the televised image of a contestant who apparently believes that Benjamin Franklin was the first Chief Justice of the Supreme Court. Snot is starting to pour down my face and I dab at it with a paper napkin. I can't stop shivering.

"Here you go." Sonya takes a steaming mug off a tray and places it in front of me. She sets the tray down on the table and takes a pair of clean dish towels from it. "I stuck these in the microwave." She wraps one around the back of my neck and drapes the other over the top of my head. They're hot.

"Sonya!"

Sol Jr. is calling and Sonya smiles at me apologetically. "Drink," she says as she heads to the kitchen.

I do. The tea, flavored with lemon, burns my tongue. The warmth, behind my neck and over my head and in my throat and belly, is almost more than I can take. Rocking bath and forth in my wet clothes, I look down into the mug.

"Oh, my goodness! Hannah? Hannah, that is you, isn't it?"

I look up. The woman is coming right toward me, smile plastered to her face, eyes wide. "It's me," I admit. "Hello, Ms. Harper."

"What are you doing, sitting here by yourself, all soaking wet?"

I take the dishcloth off of my head. "I'm meeting my father."

"Ah, Larry!" Her face resolves into the mask of pity, compassion, and totally creepy lust that middle-aged women always seem to get when they think of a widower. "I haven't made it to church for the past several weeks. How is he?"

"Dad is fine, Ms. Harper." I wait a beat and then make myself do it. "How is Jessie?"

"Wonderful! She just scored a 1450 on her practice SAT!"

"That's...a number."

"I'm not bragging, of course. It's all due to that new tutor on Oakland Road. He has a PhD and he's brilliant. I mention it in case you were looking for test prep."

I shrug and look over Ms. Harper's head at the TV. "Wabash, Indiana."

"Excuse me?"

"It was the first city with electrical power. You were saying something about tutoring?"

She smiles. "You know, I haven't seen you for a while, Hannah. Jessie said you quit the track team."

"I needed more hours."

"Hours?"

"At work. At the DPW. With my father."

Now Ms. Harper stares at me for a very long moment, the smile fading into a look approximating horror. Above the counter, the same man who was stumped by John Jay is wrestling with the location of Costa Rica.

"Hannah."

"Ms. Harper."

"This is your junior year. Your most important year. You need to…study, and do some test prep, and build your resume. Jessie's interning at a law office in Portland. The Evans Beach Department of Public Works is hardly—"

I raise my eyebrows and take a long sip of tea. Ms. Harper stops short.

"I've offended you."

"You haven't offended me, Ms. Harper."

She leans against the post by the bench and looks at me again, as if really studying me for the first time. Her face relaxes so that it looks like there might be a real human being underneath. "You look so like your mother, Hannah."

I make a concerted effort not to visibly cringe. My efforts to look like Mom are deliberate but not meant to be commented on.

"You know, your mother and I did prenatal training together at Maine Med when I was pregnant with Jessie and she was pregnant with you. Do you know what she said when I asked why she wanted to take the class when she already had a thirteen-year-old?"

I'm tempted to suggest that it was because she wanted to get it right the second time, but I shake my head.

"She said that it was time she got to spend with only you. Just thinking about you, talking about you, planning for you."

I nod, poking the lemon wedge with my spoon, holding it down, letting it float back up. Ms. Harper was a particularly active member of the flock of Evans Beach church ladies who tried to help out after Mom died. I was four and didn't know what was going on. Dad meant well but couldn't tell which way was up. Understandable, I guess. His wife was gone and my sister, Pauline, was mostly gone, too. She was a walking disaster: seventeen years old with a baby of her own, a high-school dropout, moving in with the kid's father in Portland. Someone needed to drive me to preschool and pick up groceries and I'm sure Ms. Harper and her friends helped.

Ms. Harper sighs. "I know that I must seem ridiculous, Hannah. It's been years since you and Jessie have been friends and here I am, talking about SAT scores."

I do some combination of a nod, a shrug, and a grunt. Christ, I wish she would leave. Or that Dad would show up and she would shift her focus to him. If there's one thing the man can do, it's soak up attention.

"Be well, Hannah."

"K. You too."

Ms. Harper looks like she wants to say something else but just nods, then turns and walks out of the diner.

I exhale and lean back. Where...the...fuck...is...Dad? Why isn't he answering his phone? This has to be about Pauline. My position is that my sister can have no more than two hundred dollars to piss away this time, maybe two-fifty if it's about one of her kids.

I used to come to Sol's with Dad all the time. When I was little, I sat in this booth, or one near it, and ate French fries and watched my father talk to the guys at the counter, his face thrust close to theirs, waving one hand in the air while pounding the Formica with the other. It was before Sol Jr. took over and there was no TV playing; the only sound was Dad's booming voice and whatever little bits his conversational partner was able to work in edgewise. I loved it. Most of the time they were just talking about baseball or the weather but it seemed like they were taking up the most important issues in the world and my father was standing right in the center of it all.

Pauline met us here a few times. Mom hadn't been gone that long and Pauline's son, Henry, was just a baby. She'd sit across the booth, Henry in her lap, mostly ignoring me and Dad. That was before she moved up the coast with Henry and Henry's father, Marcus, looking for a "new start." What a joke. Pauline always had problems and a change of scenery wasn't going to make a dent in them.

The door bursts open and a gust of freezing air whips inside and down the aisle. The men at the counter all turn to look. "Close that door!" Sol Jr. shouts.

"I'll close it when I'm goddamned ready." The voice comes from outside. Most of the men at the counter know it as well as I do and turn away, back to their dinners, understanding that hurrying my father works about as well as hurrying the weather but with less predictable side effects.

Then he fills the doorway. His jacket is buttoned at the chest but open below his sternum to allow full expansion to his bellows of an abdomen. An ancient hunter's cap is pulled down over his head, the ear flaps sticking straight out, fur long since worn off. He twists as he enters, something bulky under one massive arm, and as he turns to fully face me and kick the door closed behind him, I see what it is: a lobster trap.

"Sonya!" The sound waves roll down to where I'm sitting. I swear I see ripples in my tea.

"Larry." She hurries toward him, arms spread.

He stoops and kisses her cheek, then sets the trap on the counter. "Will you do these up for us?"

She peers inside. "Where did you get them?"

"The *Elise Jean*."

"Pat Armstrong's boat?"

"He owed me."

She laughs. "I'll see what we can do."

Dad grunts and starts down the aisle between the counter and the booths, his boots leaving a thick trail of dirty slush. A few men glance up and acknowledge him.

"Larry, what'd you want me to do with that trap?" Sol Jr. asks.

"It's all yours," Dad says as he slides into the booth across from me. "I brought us dinner, Hannah. Real fresh."

"I see that."

He leans across the table, bestows a kiss on my forehead, and then settles back.

"Hi, Daddy."

"How are you, baby?"

"Super. Why'd you want to meet at Sol's?"

"Let me catch my breath." He unbuttons his coat, takes his hat off, and rolls his neck, the vertebrae audibly cracking. "Hmmm." He looks at me again and frowns. "You're all wet."

"I biked here."

"Biked? Where's your car?"

"Car wouldn't start. I tried to call."

"My phone died. It's been a helluva day."

"What's going on?"

"Hold on while I just gather my thoughts." He rolls his head again and, satisfied, sets about the work of cracking his knuckles while I resign myself to waiting and look back up at the TV. "The Battle of Shiloh."

Dad twists around and looks. "Really?"

"Yup."

The answer appears on the screen and he laughs and claps his hands. "Amazing! Hey, Sonya, Hannah knew that one."

Sonya looks up from taking an order and nods.

"Daddy, please."

"You're incredible."

"I just know a lot of random stuff."

He shakes his head, smiling. Dad never gets tired of my trivia knowledge. "Stanford is going to love you."

"I told you, I don't want to go to Stanford. I don't want to live in California."

"I know. You want to go to that little place with two names in South Carolina."

"Grant-Covington College."

"Right. Sure. Well, you know I don't know schools, but they'll be lucky to get you."

I smile at him. "Thank you, Daddy." Dad always tells the guys at the DPW that I'm going to go to Stanford, even though he doesn't know anything about it other than it's a famous university. The only time he's been to California was on a road trip to play the A's during his very brief tenure with the Red Sox.

Dad looks out the window. "These storms are coming more often."

"Of course they're coming more often."

"The department will be over budget again. We didn't plan to clear this much snow."

"Well, plan on it. And we should get out here to Sol's more, too. It'll be washed away within twenty years, along with everything else along this strip."

Dad grunts. He's heard what I have to say about the coming renegotiation of boundaries between the City of Portland and the Gulf of Maine. "Let me tell you…" He's interrupted by a coughing fit that quickly escalates, his face turning an alarming shade of red, his chest rumbling. He shakes his head and slaps the table so hard that the guy in the booth behind him twists around to stare.

"He's fine," I say. "You've never heard anyone cough before?" The guy turns away. I watch Dad with concern. Sonya comes with a tall glass of water and pats him on the shoulder before moving on to a new table. He drains it in one gulp and sits back, panting. I wait for him to settle.

"Let me tell you a story," he finally says. "Art Miller, first thing this morning, Art Miller almost got himself killed."

"That sounds like something Art would do. What happened?"

Dad chuckles, risking another coughing fit. "That fool; Marty was bringing the plow out and Art walked right in front…"

"The little one, or one of the big ones?"

"Big Blue."

"Oh my God, you can't see someone walk in front when you're driving Big Blue." I've ridden along with Dad many times; it's my favorite plow.

"You sure can't, and Art strolled right out into the bay eating a jelly doughnut, not paying attention to what anyone else was doing."

"What happened?"

"I grabbed him by the collar and dragged him up onto the center island. You should've seen Marty's face when he realized what a close call it was. White as a sheet."

"What did Art say?"

"Art was mad 'cause I made him drop his doughnut!"

"Jesus, what an idiot. You shouldn't have bothered to save him."

Dad laughs and stretches an arm along the back of his seat. The guy behind him half turns again, seems to think better of it, and goes back to eating.

"You have a good day?" Dad asks.

"Yeah, it was pretty good. Until I went biking in a snowstorm."

"We'll get you a ride home. One of these characters will be heading back to Evans Beach."

"You're not coming home?"

"That's what I have to talk to you about."

I wrap my hands around the mug. It's almost empty and I wish Sonya would bring me a refill, but more people are coming in and Sol Jr. is keeping her busy. "What's Pauline done now?"

Dad lets out a long breath. "The cops found her early this morning."

Everything goes still. The voices around me seem farther away, and the question printed on the TV above the counter blurs out of focus. For years I've been expecting my sister to die. Often wishing her to. Sometimes wanting to kill her myself.

"She's at the hospital," Dad says. "She'll be okay."

"Oh."

"She was passed out in a snowbank on Deering Avenue. Another twenty minutes and she'd have been dead of exposure. They sent her to Maine Med and then went to her apartment. The boys were by themselves. No one was taking care of them."

"What else is new?"

"It was bad, Hannah. She's off the wagon, drinking again, maybe some of the other stuff, too. The electricity was off, there wasn't food. She'd gone out last night after the boys were in bed and didn't come home. The police called her caseworker to come pick them up."

I was only dimly aware that my sister had a state

caseworker. For the last few years, ever since she and her sons moved back to Portland, I've been trying to give them as little of my mental real estate as possible. "So that's what you've been busy with today?"

"Sort of."

"Sort of?"

Dad suddenly looks nervous, which is not a look I'm used to seeing on him. It's disturbing. He chews on a bit of thumbnail, pries it loose, and spits in onto the bench beside him. "You know how you always wanted to be a big sister?" he finally asks.

I stare back at him. "I have never, ever wanted to be a big sister."

He widens his eyes theatrically. "I could've sworn..."

"I don't even want to be a little sister."

"Well, there's no helping that."

"Guess not."

"Here we are." Sonya appears at our table and places steaming bowls of chowder in front of each of us. "Lobster's cooking."

"Oh, my goodness," Dad says, leaning forward to inhale the aroma and sighing in satisfaction. He reaches out and draws Sonya down, planting a kiss on the top of her head. "If you weren't married, Sonya..."

"I haven't been married for four years, Larry."

"Is that right?"

"But I'm far too good for you. Now, eat." She takes her empty tray and walks back to the counter.

Dad stirs the chowder and takes a monstrous slurp.

For the third time tonight the guy sitting behind him risks a look. I glance at my own bowl. One good thing about Sol's: Dad has a running tab that never seems to come due. He'll show up with someone else's fresh lobster and a good story about Art Miller, but he won't remember to pay the bill and he won't get to the goddamn point.

"Daddy," I say, "please just tell me what's going on."

He puts his spoon down and reaches across the table to take my hands in his. They're warm and calloused and my fists, as they form, are lost in their flesh. He squeezes gently, his energy countering what's slowly building inside me as I start to get an inkling of what is happening.

"The caseworker's supervisor, Frank, was on the junior division all-star team with me. Third base. Switch hitter. He called, right after Art almost got run down this morning. Since he's the one who knows me, he wanted to be the one to let me know about Pauline and the boys."

"All right, fine. The kids need a place to crash for a night while she's in the hospital?" I hate the idea, but knowing Pauline, there's nowhere else for them to go while things get sorted. Her crowd isn't the reliable childcare type.

"No."

"Two nights?"

"Baby, Child Services wants to take the boys from her until she can get it together."

"Is she really that bad of a mother? I mean, I know she's a bad mother, but there are lots of bad parents out there, right? They can't all have their kids taken away."

"This isn't the first time she's messed up—that's why

she has a caseworker to monitor the situation. It doesn't matter what we think about it anyway, it matters what the caseworker thinks, and he thinks that she can't keep her kids safe. Frank agrees."

It's sad, but it's been coming for a very long time. Honestly, the boys will probably be better off without my sister. "So, they're going to, like, send them wherever they go when they take kids away?"

"Yeah. Not forever, just until she gets her act together. Unless…"

I freeze. No no no no no. This is not my problem. There is no "unless." I look up and over his hunched shoulder. "J.D. Salinger," I softly say in the direction of the TV. I'd have won almost a thousand dollars if I were a real contestant.

"Hannah…"

Three hundred, four hundred dollars. We barely have that much in the bank, but she can have it. Not this, though. Not this. "You want us to take them," I say.

He nods. "That's why Frank called. It's procedure to contact family first. He wanted to see if they can come to us."

"For how long, Daddy?"

"Something like two months, maybe three. Let's say three, while Pauline gets herself together and works it all out."

"That doesn't sound something like two or even three months. That sounds something like forever."

He raises his eyebrows and gazes down into his bowl. I think about the boys. It's been about a year and a half since

I've seen them. I do the math: Henry would have turned thirteen last November, Simon would be nine. "Where's Marcus?" I ask. They do have a father, even if he's always been a piece of shit.

Dad snorts. His face, which had finally drained to a normal color after his coughing fit, goes crimson again. "Who the hell knows? Why should we care? Dead, I hope, or in jail. Last I heard, he was up in Canada. Frank said he's not an option anyway. He's got too much of a record." He digs in his coat pocket and pulls out a yellow piece of paper, unfolding and smoothing it on the tabletop. I recognize it as a roadwork order from the DPW. He flips it over, revealing his terrible handwriting, and squints at it. "They'll do something called a reunification plan," he says. "Basically, Pauline will have to do some things. Therapy, a parenting class, get a sponsor and start a twelve-step program, and then some supervised visits with the boys." He ticks the requirements off on his fingers and scrutinizes his notes for another moment. "Like I said, maybe three months."

I stare past him, watching people come in and go out the door, oblivious to what is unfolding in our corner of the diner.

"Hannah, I won't do this without your support. I need you to be on board. But if I am going to do it, I have to let Frank know so we can set the wheels in motion for..."—he squints at the paper again—"temporary kinship custody. I have to go over to his office—he's staying late, special for me—and sign some papers so they can get stamped properly or something like that. I don't really know."

"We have to decide now? We can't—"

"They have nowhere else to go. Nowhere good."

"When would they come?"

"If I go soon, they can be with us by tomorrow. The caseworker has an emergency place for them, but it's just for tonight."

"And they'd be living at our house?"

"That's right."

"What about Pauline?"

"No. She'll need to live on her own. And like I said, she'd get them back; we'd just be holding on to them for her."

"So, we're supposed to take care of her kids? I'm supposed to take care of them? I haven't had anything to do with them for over a year, Daddy. I doubt they even, like, think of me as an aunt. I don't know what I'm supposed to say here. I really, really don't."

"I'll be the one taking care of them. You'll just go to school, and work, and whatever you want to do. They won't be your problem. I promise."

I snort and look away. Dad passes his open palms over the surface of the table. He still wears his wedding ring, and it glints in the light. "Hannah," he finally says, his big voice rumbling in his chest, "I want you to understand a few things before you make a decision…"

"They're not welcome, Daddy. I mean, what the hell would we do with them? Don't you think some sort of care home would be better? There are people who want kids, they know what to do with them, how to take care of them. I don't know anything about this stuff. Plus, Simon has problems. He's in SPED classes, right?"

"SPED?"

"Special education."

Dad clears his throat. "I think he has attention problems, if that's what you mean. I said there are a few things I want you to understand, so listen for just a minute. First, if we don't take them, then the boys won't be kept together. Frank says there's no way. He doesn't have any sibling placements."

"So, they'd be separated for three months. Big deal."

"Where will they go? I mean, there are lots of great families in the system, I'm sure. Real nice people who take care of kids. But there are some that aren't that great, and there are some that are really bad. Plus, at least one of them might end up in a group home if there's no foster family available. I can't... Hannah, they're in trouble." He leans over the table and places a hand on top of both of mine. "These are your nephews. These are my grandkids. I want to help them. And your sister needs us now. She needs us to keep her boys together."

"And you need me to be on board? You need some sort of approval?"

Now it's his turn to look away. He stares out the window. "I do," he finally says.

Dad's a powerful man; when he played baseball for Evans Beach High School, he was known for his monstrous home runs. He's the only player from this town who ever made it to the major leagues. Still, he doesn't have it in him to do this against my wishes. So, I can say no and be complicit in whatever happens to those kids next. Or I can say yes, and be equally on the hook for all the inevitable shit that goes down.

"Hannah," Dad says, "this is what your mother would want…"

I'm on my feet and shooting for the door, almost knocking Sonya over. Then I'm outside, the smell of the fish and the bay deep in my nostrils, my eyes burning. The snow has let up but the wind is harsh. I reach the pier. It's empty, and the wind off the water is brutally cold. I wipe the snow from a bench and sit. The back is broken off and I lean forward, elbows on knees.

Heavy footsteps fall on the dock behind me. Dad circles the end of the bench and stands with his back to the water, shielding me from the wind. He drapes my coat over my shoulders. I look up at him. He pulls his hat more firmly down on his head, then flexes his hands. "I lost Pauline. I failed her. And Hannah, if something happens to these boys, then I believe that it will kill me. I need to step up. I need to help my grandchildren."

I lower my head, my throat constricting. It's not about the three months. It's not about the mess the boys will make, not really, though I do hate a mess. I try to wrap words around what it's really about, but the things I want to tell him slip away and the tears in my eyes feel like glass in the wind.

"Nothing will change," Dad says. "I won't let it. Not

more than it has to. There will just be more of us under the roof for a little while."

I stand, pulling my coat on, and look up again. My eyes trace the familiar lines in his ruddy face. My father is like a mountain; walking with him and holding his hand used to feel like the safest place in the world, and for a moment it feels that way again. I reach out and put my arms as far around him as I can, squeezing with all my strength. He holds me for a long moment, the smell of his jacket filling my nostrils. "All right," I murmur. I don't say it because of my sister or her boys. I don't say it because of my dead mother. I say it because it's what he needs to hear.

He finally lets me go, and we head back inside to ask Sonya to pack up the lobsters and find someone to drive me home while Dad heads off to see Frank, the third baseman.

2

Richard Greene honks his horn exactly the way I'd expect: with utter precision. Two quick toots, then a pause, then a third noticeably longer one. It's infuriating.

Dad already left to meet someone about the boys, and with my car marooned in the driveway I needed a lift if I was going to avoid a long bike ride. Wednesday and Thursday mornings I have chemistry tutoring before school, and Richard, my tutor, was the obvious choice.

There are no neighbors to bother with the early morning honking. We have woods across the street and behind our house and a cemetery on one side, though it's all filled up and no one ever comes to visit except old men who put flags on the graves for Memorial Day. A vacant lot is on the other side. Land is worth a ton in Evans Beach, even land next to a beat-up house like ours, but this lot never sold. Years ago, before I was born, there was a service station here and rumor has it that the owner dumped all sorts of gas and chemicals in the soil. I don't know if that's true or not, but I'm in no hurry to dispute it. The last thing we need is another McMansion.

I struggle into a near-perfect replica of Mom's old army jacket and sling my backpack over one shoulder, a semi-frozen waffle gripped in my teeth. My boots crunch through the snow as I cross the lawn and circle around to the passenger side of Richard's ridiculous rose-colored BMW. I look up, studying the peeling paint around the windows of our house, the dilapidated mailbox with the fading stencil of four figures (two big and two little), and the rusting remains of several lawnmowers in the side yard. With any luck the caseworker will come and check it out before signing Pauline's kids over, determine we're unfit, and I'll be off the hook.

I yank on the door handle. "Open up!"

Richard hesitates for a moment, head turned to the left, away from me, as he contemplates our front yard. I'm suddenly self-conscious; he's never been by my house before. Then he punches a button on the panel next to him and the doors unlock with a deep, unhurried, satisfying click, the sound of strong German gears. I get inside.

"Thanks." It's warm and the seats are soft leather. I pull the door closed and settle back, biting into my waffle.

"Are you going to put your seat belt on?"

"Oh, yeah. Sure." I buckle up.

"Seat warmer button is there," he says, gesturing toward the dash as he looks over his right shoulder and pulls onto the road.

"No thanks," I say with my mouth full. "Those things make me feel like my ass is going to catch fire."

Richard drums his gloved fingers on top of the wheel, leather on leather, as we shoot down the street.

"Hope you didn't have to go out of your way," I say, not because I hope any such thing but because it's uncomfortably quiet and I'm curious about where his house is.

"I live over on Marshall Street," he says.

"Oh. So, about as out of your way as it can be."

"You know where Marshall is?"

"I work for the DPW. I know where all the streets are."

"Ah. Well, no problem."

"You far enough down Marshall to be in that development by the beach?"

"That's right."

That development is ugly as anything, but I try to think of something nice to say. "It's good you have the town sewer."

"Uh—yeah?"

"I mean, rather than septic. That would be a hell of a place to have a septic field. Sorry, you probably don't want to talk about waste disposal."

"Well…"

"It's important, though."

"I'm sure it is."

"You don't want to buy a two-million-dollar house and have raw sewage back up into it."

"I think our house was 1.2 million."

"Same difference, at that point."

"Not really. Eight hundred thousand dollars' difference."

I shrug and look out the window. I hope the sewer does back up on them, but it won't. Marshall hasn't had any problems.

"Will you need a ride tomorrow, too?" Richard asks.

"Probably, unless my car decides to heal itself."

"Okay."

"Am I still better than a sick cat?" I ask.

"I told you, I'm allergic to cats."

"That doesn't answer the question."

Richard wants to get into Harvard and is maneuvering to take two extra AP classes senior year. That means that he has to get his community service requirement for graduation out of the way as a junior, and his choices were tutoring me or volunteering at the cat hospital. "It's a pretty bad allergy," he says. We ride the rest of the way to the high school in silence.

Richard and I are spending two mornings a week together because rumor has it that one day, in 1976, Andrew Carlson, our chemistry teacher, dropped a test tube. It was a very important test tube, containing a rare compound that was precious to his faculty supervisor. It wasn't the end of the world but it was the end of his job at that particular lab and of his graduate career. Instead, he got a job teaching chemistry at Evans Beach High School and in the decades since he has taken out his thwarted academic aspirations on generation after generation of innocent juniors.

This is not disastrous for most students. Some,

probably most, don't give a shit. They take their C in chem and move on with their lives. Others, like Richard, ignore the messenger and download the message, learning chemistry despite the ultra-dry presentation of non-contextual facts and the rude jibes at any student who seems the least bit unprepared. I, on the other hand, am in an unfortunate minority: my college plans require a higher grade than the D+ I am currently carrying, but my inability to stomach Mr. Carlson and his class is totally insurmountable. And so I finally swallowed my pride and emailed peer tutoring, and once I edged out the sick and dying cats, Richard and I settled into a routine of forty-five-minute sessions every Wednesday and Thursday morning in which he attempts to convey the fundamentals of physical science and I attempt to remain awake.

We arrive in the school library and sit at our usual table. Richard takes out his laptop. "All right," he says. "Limiting reagents."

I pull my laptop and a notebook from my backpack. "What are those?"

"You sat through a lecture on them last week."

"They don't ring a bell." I flip my notebook open.

He sighs deeply. "Let's begin with some definitions." Richard starts talking, scrolling through his notes, and I almost immediately lose focus. Richard Greene more or less epitomizes everything I hate about Evans Beach. Handsome, smart, unfailingly polite, and well-spoken. It doesn't sound so bad until you realize it's all strategic. His whole personality, his whole life is meticulously curated and it's about one thing: going to Harvard. Everything else is incidental. A year and a half from now he'll be in Cambridge and Hannah Lynn will be some dim memory of a strange girl who couldn't grasp the basics of chemistry.

Still, he's interesting to look at. His eyes are very, very black. I don't think I have ever seen such unapologetically black eyes. Technically, eyes aren't supposed to be black. If they look black it's a trick of the light and they're just extremely brown. I swear his are true-black, though. His hair is the same color and it's combed back from a high forehead. He has a mole just beneath his hairline. He's letting his sideburns grow.

"So, what would that yield?" Richard asks.

"You're asking me?"

He looks up. "Yes."

"Can you clarify the question?"

He blinks once, then again. "I...I can't...it doesn't get clearer. You just have to do the calculation."

"Right. The calculation." I pull a pencil from behind my ear and look at the clock above the door. We're six minutes in.

"Were you paying attention, Hannah?"

"I have to admit that I was not."

He sighs and closes his eyes, and I can see that his eyelashes are unusually long. Long, black eyelashes.

"Sorry," I say, "I have a lot going on. I had a tough night."

"Well, where did I lose you?"

"Um...the agents."

"The limiting reagents?"

"Those."

"That's the topic for the unit; what aspect..." He trails off, apparently realizing that we need to go back to the beginning. "I was talking about you with Mrs. Jenkins," he says. Mrs. Jenkins is the guidance counselor. I raise my eyebrows. "I have to," he continues, "because you're my service project and all. We meet twice a month for progress monitoring. She thinks you have a motivation issue."

"Does she?"

"Yes, she does. She says you have tons of A's on your transcript but every once in a while you just bomb a class out of the blue, and when she sees that kind of variability it usually means someone is smart but only does well in subjects they happen to find interesting."

Mrs. Jenkins is a moron. The irony is that I'm nothing if not motivated, and getting into the school I want to go to is exactly what's been motivating me all these years. "I signed up for this tutoring, didn't I?" I ask Richard. "I just can't open my brain when someone like Mr. Carlson is trying to stuff meaningless shit into it. That doesn't mean I don't care. I want good grades; I want to go to college."

"Mrs. Jenkins told me about that, too. She looked in your file and said you want to go to Grant-Covington?"

"Go Dwarf Hippos."

Richard spins his pen across his fingers, frowning. "The thing it, Hannah, I don't think Mrs. Jenkins is the world's best guidance counselor."

"No? What makes you say that?"

"Because she never followed up. Grant-Covington College closed in 1956."

"Ah."

"And they weren't the Dwarf Hippos, they were the Blue Hawks."

"So did you tell her?"

"No."

"Thanks. I don't want to fill out another one of those college surveys for the guidance department."

"I'm just curious about why you'd put a defunct college down as your first and only choice?"

That does seem like the logical question, but I don't want to answer it. "Do you have any siblings?" I ask, changing the subject.

"What?"

"Brothers. Sisters. Any of those?"

"No. I'm an only child."

"That must be nice."

"It's... fine."

"I don't really like kids," I tell him. "I don't have much of a touch with them. They never seem comfortable with me. Not that I've ever really tried. My older sister, Pauline, has two sons. Who are coming to live with me, I guess."

He raises his eyebrows. "What, like your parents are adopting them?"

"My dad. My mom died when I was four."

"Oh. Sorry."

"It's okay." Sometimes I forget that Richard's family didn't move to town until ninth grade. Most of us have been together since kindergarten, and we all know each other's stories. "Adopting means forever, right?"

"Right," he says.

"This is the opposite of forever."

"So, it's temporary?"

"Yes. Very temporary."

Richard frowns. He looks characteristically disapproving, but uncharacteristically interested. "Did something happen to your sister?"

"Yeah, she has some problems. That's an understatement, actually, but we'll just say that: problems. So, I guess this guy, a third baseman—former third baseman—told Dad that if we didn't take them, then they'd get split up in the system until my sister gets back on her feet."

"A third baseman?" Richard asks.

"That's not the important part," I say. "The important part is that these two kids are showing up tonight and I don't know what I'm going to do. Sorry, I know we're straying pretty far from chemistry."

He opens his mouth to say something but is interrupted by a call from the direction of the circulation desk.

"Richard!"

I turn and see Amity Williams coming toward us. Her chestnut hair is pulled back and she's wearing red leggings and an oversize Evans Beach Ski Team sweatshirt. She flashes a wide smile, bathing us both in her radiance, before arriving at the table and wrapping her arms around Richard's neck. "Hey, you." She kisses him just below his mole and then turns to me. "Hello, Hannah! How are you? I love your hair down like that!"

God, if only she were even a little, tiny bit hateful.

"Hi Amity," I say, pushing my hair back behind one ear. "Thanks."

"I wish I had thick, blonde hair like yours," she says, "I would always wear it down."

The thing about Amity Williams is that she was always kinder than the others. She was kind when we were six and seven and eight years old and were all friends, playing at the beach in the summer and in the snow in the winter. Me, her, Jessie Harper, Brittany O'Neal. A gaggle of girls, the mothers fussing over me because I didn't have one of my own.

Amity was sort-of kind, in the sense of not being actively hateful, when we were in seventh grade and Brittany O'Neal turned the group on me for what was literally the most ridiculous, only-in-Evans-Beach reason in the world, and just like that I was a loner on the outside looking in. She was also distantly kind when I was a weird, sad ninth grader who'd started dressing like her dead mother used to dress in the nineties. And she's being kind now that we're juniors and have zero overlap in any aspect of our lives.

Amity glances at the notebook. "Oh, limiting reagents. That unit was such a drag. I really had to dig in on that one."

It's not enough that Amity is beautiful and relentlessly positive; it's not enough that she's athletic and is co-captain of the ski team; she also happens to be smart enough to have taken chem a year before the rest of us. "That's what we're doing," I say. "We're digging in."

"Well, don't let me stop you. I have to get to the weight room anyway." She kisses Richard again. "You invited Hannah for Friday night, didn't you?"

He looks at her blankly.

"Oh my God, Richard." She turns to me. "I'm so sorry. For a good boyfriend, Richard can be a complete dimwit. There's a party at my house Friday night and you have to be there."

"I do?"

"Yes, of course you do, and if I had known that Richard was such a hopeless case I would have invited you before now. Bring whoever you want, okay?"

"Um...okay." Amity Williams has had plenty of parties over the years and I've never warranted an invitation, but maybe my role as Richard's project has bestowed some sort of weird, minimal status.

Amity smiles at me, a genuine, unironic expression of pleasure. "It's going to be so great. I'll see you there." She kisses Richard a third time, on the ear, then turns and leaves the library. We sit in silence for a long moment after she's gone.

"Well," I say, "I guess we should get back to the chemicals."

Richard nods, his eyes on my face, a slight crease between his eyebrows. "Right. This unit isn't easy. Only... Hannah, did this third-base guy say how long your nephews are going to be staying with you?"

"Third baseman, not third-base guy. Who calls it a 'third-base guy'?"

"Baseball's not my game. Did he say?"

"Dad thinks a few months. Why?"

Richard twirls his pen across the back of his fingers, faster this time. He's very nimble. I tried to do that once and threw a BIC clear across the room. "That's a tough situation," he finally says.

"Yeah, it is. I'll get through it, though."

"Not for you; for the kids."

"Oh. Sure. Them too."

"Going to a new place, not knowing exactly when they're going back. You need to make them feel like it's... I don't know, like it's home, you know?"

"It's not. Not theirs, at least."

He stares at me across the table. "I don't think you understand what this is going to be like for them."

"And you do?"

"I have a little bit of an angle on it, yes."

"So, what's your suggestion? How do you make a kid feel at home?"

He thinks for a moment. "You should have beds ready for them. When they arrive at your house, they should have a place to sleep all made up for them."

"Beds."

"Right. Each one should have his own spot, his own bed, waiting for him."

I nod. It's hard to imagine that a made-up bed is going to make much of a difference in this shit show of a situation, but I guess it can't hurt. "All right. I'll make sure they have beds ready."

Richard nods. He looks like he's about to say something else and I'm not sure I want him to. "What is your game?" I ask.

"Sorry?"

"Baseball's not your game. What is?"

"I like chess."

"Of course you do." I actually like chess myself. "So. Limiting reagents." I fold my hands on the table and do my best to focus on chemistry and not think about my father, about Pauline and her kids, or about Amity Williams kissing Richard on the ear.

3

One. Two. Three. I lift.

The couch moves, one end swinging away from the wall. It's heavier than I thought. I walk around to the other side. One, two, three. The other end moves so now the whole thing is about two feet off its footprint, revealing a bed of dust and a sticker that had been pushed against the baseboard. I bend over and pick it up. "Hello," it reads, "my name is Kevin."

"Who the fuck is Kevin?" I say to the empty room. I put the sticker in my pocket, lift one end of the couch, and slide half of a big piece of cardboard underneath. I return to the other side, get the cardboard completely under, and start to push.

I walked the three and a half miles home from school and have been working since I got here, pausing only to eat some leftover fries, microwaved and doused in the last of our ketchup. Most of the breakables have been put away. Framed pictures and table lamps packed up in milk crates and tucked into the bomb shelter, a windowless room dug into the back of the foundation that a prior owner thought would save them if the Soviets decided to drop the big one on southern Maine. The couch—one of three in our sprawling living room—is the final item.

Pauline and her kids moved back to Portland from the Midcoast when I was fourteen, leaving Marcus behind. She wanted another change of scenery, another new start. What she got was three years of bouncing from one apartment to another, one shitty job to another, one guy to another. Dad wanted to blame it all on the booze and whatever else she was putting into her system, but the times when she stopped drinking and using weren't much better. Finally, summer before last, I told Dad I was done. I didn't want to see her, I didn't want to hear from her, I didn't want to know about the slow-motion train wreck of her life. He heard me—the second or third time I told him—and I've had as little as possible to do with Pauline or her boys for a year and a half.

I reach the top of the stairs, push the couch right up to the edge, walk around and down a few steps, and consider. This may not be a good idea. Still, I'm not leaving this couch upstairs to be spilled on. It's featured in one of my favorite photos of Mom, the one in which she's holding a three-year-old me on her lap and we're sticking our tongues out at each other. She still looks healthy in the photo, and happy, and she's sitting on this unexpectedly heavy couch.

I grab the front legs and pull them toward me, stepping back and bracing myself as it begins to tilt down the stairs. I envision it sliding down on the stiff cardboard, me walking in front and controlling the rate of descent. It starts out all right. I lean in hard, gripping the banister with one hand, the other arm outstretched and braced against the end of the couch. It's entirely on the stairs now, the cardboard passing over the carpeting without friction. Halfway there. I'm going to wrestle this beast into my bedroom, cover it with a sheet, and worry about getting it back upstairs after the kids are gone.

Four steps to go. Three. My foot catches, my balance wavers for a moment, and that's all it takes. The couch moves forward and I can't stop it. I let go and jump backward, landing and falling to my left so that the couch slides by my feet and crashes into the wall of the downstairs hallway.

Lying there on my back, staring at the ceiling, I finally remember who Kevin was.

He wasn't a good friend. I'm not sure he was really a friend at all. In fact, I think he was a total dick, but apparently he got invited to a birthday party when we were kids. He moved sometime when we were in middle school. There's something about that name tag, though. I twist around and pull the sticker from my pocket. "Kevin" is written in a looping script with a winking smiley face for the dot over the i. Not Dad's handwriting, not Pauline's— she wouldn't have been helping out at one of my birthday parties anyway. I climb to my feet and inspect the couch. It's not damaged, and neither is the wall. I got lucky. I leave it where it is for a moment, go into my room, and open the closet.

Mom's clothes are on the left. Four flannel shirts, three pairs of jeans, five T-shirts. Carefully folded, slipped into thick, archival-grade polyethylene bags. Two pairs of Doc Martens on the floor, similarly situated in their own bags. Dad let the church ladies clean out Mom's things after some decent interval; this is the stuff that they missed, scavenged from the back of closets and the bottom of storage bins over the course of years, kept until the day, three years ago, when I finally fit into them.

The right side of the closet is much busier. It's the replicas; shirts and jeans and belts and boots identified in photos of my mother. The replicas are for day-to-day wear; the originals are only for very special occasions.

I crouch and open a metal box tucked beside the original boots. These are the documents, scavenged like the clothes. They are highly miscellaneous. Thankfully, Dad never cleans; there are ancient grocery lists in her handwriting, recovered from the bottom of piles in his room along with notes to herself about the vast blend of things Mom apparently had to remember to do ("get toaster repaired; patch Larry's jeans; lasagna for church picnic; find better therapist for Pauline"). And, at the bottom of the box, the postcard. The front is a beach scene with "Greetings from Cape May, New Jersey" printed in red letters. On the back:

Dearest Alessandra.

This is every bit as fantastic as I hoped! Next time you're ABSOLUTELY coming with!!!

XO ;)

E

The identity of "E" has been a mystery ever since I found this card. Now I hold it alongside Kevin's name tag and compare the handwriting. The smiley face over the "i" cinches it; it's the same as the one next to the "XO" on the card. It doesn't tell me who the author was, though. I tuck the name tag into the box alongside the postcard, close it, and then close the closet door. Intriguing, but there's still work to do.

I retrieve the cardboard, resituate the couch, and begin the difficult task of angling the whole thing through my bedroom door. In a final burst of energy, I push it across the room and up against the wall. It sticks out into the middle of the floor and is completely out of place, but it will only be here for a few months. Pauline's old room would be better for storage but it's even more packed with stuff than the bomb shelter.

I go upstairs. Dad should have been back with them by now. He should have at least called or texted. The wind is picking up again, whipping branches in the woods across the street and sending wisps of snow snaking down the asphalt. I do one more walk-through starting at the front door, trying to look at the house the way one of my nephews might, looking for something to damage. I turn left, into the living room, down to two couches. The bookshelf against the far wall is complicated. My old friends, the battered copies of the World Book Encyclopedia, line the bottom shelves. Many of the volumes still have Evans Beach Public Library stickers on their spines from when Mom carted them home from work, outdated castoffs destined for the dumpster. The photo albums are on the top shelf. I study them, thinking once again about boxing them all up and hauling them downstairs, but what are the boys going to do to a bunch of albums? I move on.

Our house is built into the side of a hill. Dad's room is on this level, behind the kitchen, while the other bedrooms and the family room are downstairs. I go back down, checking once again to make sure the plaster isn't cracked where the couch made impact, and continue on to the family room. It's where I decided to put them.

I've vacuumed and picked up most everything I can find that a kid might break. I made up the fold-out couch with a sheet and a blanket and then I inflated an air mattress and made it up, too. I decide that Richard would approve, then sit on the edge of a chair and reach for a remote, turning the TV on. I flip through until I find cartoons. Can kids watch cartoons at night? Is it okay for them to have the TV on when they're falling asleep? I study the images, not recognizing any of the characters. I turn the TV off, get back up, and resume wandering.

Simon used to have something he carried with him. A stuffed frog. Will he have it tonight? Do they let kids bring their things with them when they take them away from their mother? I return to my room and peer under the bed, pulling out dusty, long-forgotten stuffed animals. I root through monkeys and panda bears and even an ostrich before I find it: a little green frog Dad won at a carnival for me. I think he had to hit a bell with a hammer or something. I take it back to the family room and place it on one of the pillows.

Where are they? I head back upstairs to the living room, pulling my phone from my pocket and tapping the screen. I absently scroll along with my thumb until I come to an image of Amity with Richard. It's her new profile picture. I study the way his arm wraps around her waist; the way she leans into him; her knowing smile as she stares into the camera. I tap his profile and look at more photos, shots of him with his parents on vacation in Puerto Rico, surfing and sleeping in a hammock with a book resting open on his belly.

I throw the phone down, walk into the bathroom to once again inspect the sink and the edge of the toilet, and decide to go over it one more time. The smell of bleach calms my nerves and I scrub hard at the porcelain, killing any germs that might have formed since I did this an hour ago. Around and around the edge of the sink. Underneath the faucet. Nothing will change, I think in time with the brush. Nothing will change. They'll stay in the family room and go to school; between that and the after-school program they'll be away from the house most of the time. It's just until Pauline finishes the reunification plan. Three months, at most.

The bathroom is pristine. It is literally inconceivable that a microorganism could have survived on any of these surfaces. You could serve dinner on the toilet seat. I take off my rubber gloves, return to the living room, and—having exhausted all other options for procrastination—I take my laptop out of my backpack and sit down to write an email.

From: Hannah Lynn <hlynn123@gmail.com>
To: Alessandra Lynn <alessandra.lynn@gmail.com>
Subject: the shit, the fan, etc.

You're very helpful, for a dead person.

I hope you don't mind my saying that. Is there a more PC term? "Deceased individual"? "Human non-being"? "Formerly alive parental figure"?

I'll stick with dead person. I don't think you'd mind.

These emails were the only worthwhile thing to come out of 8th grade computer science. When Mr. Leonardo said we needed to practice electronic correspondence and I impulsively made you an account, I did not expect to spend years updating a ghost on my activities. But here we are.

My God, Mr. Leonardo. Mr. L used to hover behind me and compliment my prose. I don't think he ever realized I was writing to a mother who died when I was four years old. I don't think he particularly cared.

Anyway. You are quite useful because I can go six or eight (or has it been ten?) months without writing and I don't need to apologize. I can just jump back in when there is something I need to tell you, and I need to tell you something this evening. It's not something that makes me proud, but I can count on you not to be judgmental.

I was relieved, last night, when I thought – just for a moment – that Pauline had died.

My earliest and worst memories, other than losing you, are of her. Even when I was only five or six, I sensed the chaos she caused. I knew she was out of control. She'd come by the house, looking to pick a fight with Dad, leaving me to scurry down to my room with whatever volume of the encyclopedia I could grab while they roared and bellowed and stomped their way through the latest crisis. I was so glad when she and Marcus moved away, and so pissed when she and the kids came back to Portland.

Taking her boys in is a mistake. I know it is. I don't know exactly what shit will go down, and that's the point. Dad thinks, with the caseworker and the reunification plan, that things are under control. He's wrong. Nothing is ever under control when it comes to Pauline, and helping her, even just for three months, opens our door to her out-of-control.

Dad wants to save them. Maybe if I got out of bed on Sunday mornings and went to church with him, sat and listened to Reverend Jim, then I'd believe in saving people, too. But I know better. I saw you not be saved from the cancer, and Pauline not be saved from herself, and I know the truth. People don't get saved.

THAT'S what's so crushing about this: seeing how deluded Dad is. Pauline is a bucket with a hole in the bottom; pour in a pint or pour in a gallon, it doesn't matter. In the end the bucket's going to be empty and you'll have a mess on the floor. But how do you tell him that, sitting on the cold, windy pier, with a third baseman waiting for him to come sign legal papers?

I have to go. I finally hear the truck, coming down the road.

Hannah

4

I meet them in the front hall. "Boys," Dad says, "say hello to Aunt Hannah."

I've never liked that title. It doesn't feel earned or wanted. Still, I make myself smile and say hello.

Henry is the older and he looks like Pauline. The strong jawline and blue eyes, the hint of a smirk around his lips. Blond, wavy hair, just like mine. "Hiya, Aunt Hannah," he says.

"Henry, you're getting so big."

He shrugs but doesn't bother to otherwise respond, looking around the front hall instead. His brother, Simon, stares at me, shifting his weight from one foot to another. He's very slender, almost scrawny, and he looks more like his father, Marcus, with his brown hair and sharp nose.

Each boy is holding a white plastic bag. Henry puts his down under the table in the front hall, then takes his younger brother's and carefully tucks it away too. "Take your coat off," he tells Simon.

"I'm still cold," Simon says.

Henry shrugs. "All right, leave it on but don't just stand there." He takes his coat off, hangs it on a hook, and steers his brother toward the living room.

"Jeez, Hannah, it's freezing in here," Dad says, following the boys. "What happened to the couch?"

"I'll explain later," I say, "and I'll turn up the heat." I walk to the thermostat, eye it, touch it, decide not to move it. We skipped the last oil delivery.

"Who's hungry?" Dad asks. Simon brightens and Henry shrugs again. Dad turns to me. "What's for dinner?"

"What's for... dinner?"

"What did you have?"

"I had leftover French fries."

"Oh."

"And there aren't any left."

"Gotcha."

"And I used the last of the ketchup, too."

"Sandwiches!" Dad bellows. "I'll make sandwiches." He marches out of the living room, through the adjacent dining area and into the kitchen like a man taking command of a battleship. "Simon!" he calls. "Come pound some chips for me." Simon scampers after his grandfather.

"Don't ask me what they're pounding chips for," I say to Henry. He doesn't respond. I look at the plastic bags underneath the front hall table. They're not even half full. I wonder whether they let him pack his most precious things himself, or whether some caseworker went into Pauline's apartment and selected the items they thought he should have. Maybe there's a state checklist: underwear; toothbrush; socks.

"Hannah, where's the peanut butter?" Dad calls.

"Look in the cabinet above the microwave," I reply. Henry and I listen to the sound of Dad rummaging in the other room. "This is crunchy!"

"I always buy crunchy."

"Oh." He sounds crestfallen. I've done the grocery shopping ever since I was ten years old, when I rode my bike to the IGA and back with bags carefully draped from the handlebars. If he wanted smooth peanut butter he could have bought it himself.

Henry has settled himself in Dad's armchair. "How're you doing over there, Henry?" I ask, still hovering in the doorway between the front hall and the living room.

"Fine."

"You going to watch TV?"

"Yup." He picks up the remote and points it at the screen. Nothing happens.

"You want help?" I ask.

"I can work a remote."

I watch as he tries again. Nothing.

"You need to turn the cable box on first." He ignores me and continues to click. I walk over to the chair and snatch the remote from his hand. "Like this." I point it at the TV, turn on the cable box and then the set, and toss it back into his lap.

He stares up at me for a long moment, his face inscrutable. "Thanks, Aunt Hannah."

I sit on the couch across from him as he flips through the channels. This is extremely awkward. I did not expect it to be this awkward. I expected them to have questions, or to need things. This would be easier if they needed things. "Do you need anything, Henry?" I ask.

"Nope."

"Ah."

He settles on an old cartoon. I sort of feel like it's for younger kids, but what do I know? I scroll through my phone, wishing I knew a magic trick or a good joke or something that would lighten the mood.

"Sandwiches!" Dad bursts from the kitchen with Simon right behind him, so close that he is at high risk of being stepped on. He drops a platter of food into the middle of the dining table, beaming. "These are Grandpa Larry's signature sandwiches! Peanut butter with Marshmallow Fluff and crushed potato chips."

Simon sits in a chair, seizes a sandwich with both hands, and sinks his teeth in, the crunch of the chips audible across the room. Henry rises and languidly makes his way across the living room and into the dining area, taking a seat at the table. Once everyone is eating Dad returns to the kitchen for drinks. "Water or milk?" he calls.

"The milk is bad," I say.

"I put it in my coffee this morning."

"That was a mistake." I go into the kitchen and look over his shoulder. Apart from the possibly lethal milk we have a container of OJ with about a millimeter of liquid at the bottom. "I'll get them water."

By the time I bring the boys their drinks Simon is on to his second sandwich and Henry is on his third. "Since when is PB and Fluff and chips your specialty?" I ask Dad.

"C'mon, I always made these. I made them for your eighth birthday at Roller Kingdom."

"I didn't have an eighth birthday party at Roller Kingdom."

"Sure you did. That little boy broke his wrist."

"You're probably thinking of one of Pauline's birthday parties."

"Oh." Dad turns to the boys. "I made these once for the fellas on the Sox when we got in late for an away game and the hotel restaurant was closed. You know who loved them?"

"Who?" Simon asks.

"Jim Rice."

They both stare at him in blank incomprehension.

"Come on...Jim Rice? One of the greatest left fielders of all time. The man is in the Hall of Fame!"

Nothing.

Dad turns to me. "We have a lot of work to do."

The boys finish their sandwiches and drain their glasses. Henry drifts back to the easy chair. Dad takes the plates to the kitchen and whistles as he does the dishes.

Shouldn't they go to bed? I never had a bedtime, or if I did it was too long ago to remember. I take my phone out and google *what is a good bedtime?*

The results come back:

What is a good bedtime for a four-year-old?

What is a good bedtime for a five-year-old?

What is a good bedtime for a six-year-old?

I decide to use Simon's age and click on the nine-year-old option.

The American Academy of Pediatrics recommends that nine-year-old children sleep nine to twelve hours per twenty-four hours in order to maintain optimal physical and mental health. I glance at the clock. Shit, we're already running behind. "Guys," I say "you should probably go to bed."

Henry doesn't even look at me. Simon seems mildly troubled. Dad is still whistling in the kitchen. "Do you want me to show you where you're going to sleep?" I ask. Simon nods. Henry shrugs. "Grab your bags and let's go downstairs." They follow me into the family room. "Here are your beds," I say.

Henry has pajamas in his bag but Simon does not. Neither has a toothbrush. So much for a state check- list. I give Simon a pair of my old sweatpants, which fit with the drawstring pulled taut and the legs rolled up, and then I fish around in the bathroom drawer for some of the free toothbrushes the dentist gives out at every cleaning. While they're brushing, I run back upstairs to get a couple of glasses. When I come back down Simon and Henry are still brushing, their mouths foaming with toothpaste.

"That's probably enough," I say. They both stop and look at me quizzically. Am I supposed to tell them what to do? "Rinse and spit." Henry takes the glass and sips. "Sorry, sorry, I mean spit and then rinse and then...um, I guess then spit again." They eventually get it right, though both glasses are coated in toothpaste by the time they're done. I look at the toilet, seeing that one of them has peed all over the back of the seat. It's a physical effort not to make an immediate run for my bucket and bleach spray. Instead, I lead them back into the family room.

"I'm thirteen years old," Henry tells me. "I don't have a bedtime."

He also apparently doesn't know how to brush his teeth effectively, but I decide not to press the point. The boys examine the air mattress, bobbing on it and experimenting with the pump. Simon picks up the frog I left on a pillow and I realize that I was remembering him as a younger child and that nine is probably too old for a stuffed animal. "You used to have one of those and, um…" I trail off. There's no frog in his plastic garbage bag, just random assorted clothes like someone dumped a drawer into it, and a picture book with the cover torn. "I don't know if you still like frogs."

He studies it gravely.

"Do you want to give him a name?" I try. "He was mine, but I don't think I ever gave him a name. What was your other frog named?"

"Mr. Frog." Simon's lower lip is set, as though he's determined not to cry over the memory of his stuffed animal.

"Let's give this guy a name," I say. Simon doesn't respond.

There's a long moment of silence, and then Henry speaks up. "Herbert," he says.

"Herbert," I repeat. There are worse names for frogs.

Simon seems pleased. He smiles. "Yup. Herbert."

It's settled. Simon lies down on the air mattress. "I'm gonna go back up and watch TV," Henry says.

"I don't want to be alone," Simon tells him.

"You're not alone. Aunt Hannah is here."

"I'm here," I say, "but I'm not here, here. I mean, I'm not staying in this room."

Simon looks at Henry.

"You don't need someone in this room," I tell him.

"Don't tell him what he needs," Henry says. He walks over to the couch and sits, looking around the family room. "That TV work?"

I nod.

"Okay." He gets up, grabs the remote, and sits back down. "We're good," he says without looking at me.

I should feel relieved to be dismissed, but I don't. "Well, Grandpa will come down to say good night, but I'm going to turn off the lights, and, uh...well, maybe I'll leave the hall light on so you have a bit of light, but you can tell me if it's too much? And also if it's too little? Like, I can probably find a lamp or something to put in here if you need more light. Not that you need light. Everything's fine."

They both ignore me.

"Good night," I say. I go out into the hallway, turning off the family room light, head to my room, and sit on the edge of my bed. The TV is playing too loud in their room, some sort of cop show with gunshots and sirens, and the rest of the house is dead silent by comparison. Minutes go by. I decide to check on them one more time and then try to get some sleep.

Henry is sitting on the couch, watching TV. Simon is lying curled on his side, turned toward his big brother. He has one arm stretched out with his hand resting on the couch cushion, not quite touching Henry's leg. I retreat to my room and close the door.

Did it help that there were beds waiting for them? I think about texting Richard but decide that it's pathetic. Another moment goes by, and then I hear Dad saying good night to the boys. I should go talk with him, see if his buddy the third baseman gave him any more information, tell him that he needs to take the kids to see a dentist. I should remind him to set them up with the after-school program—we both called out of work this afternoon and we can't keep doing that—but I am suddenly very, very tired.

Mom's college T-shirt, the one original garment I allow for daily wear, is folded under my pillow and I quickly undress and pull it over my head, studying myself in the mirror. It used to hang down to my knees but these days it's way too short for me to make a breakfast appearance in front of the boys. I fish out an old pair of track shorts and pull them on. Better.

The "T" is flaking off of "Tufts" and a fading blue elephant looks back at me from the front of the shirt, his face barely visible after decades of washing. It's no dwarf hippo, but it's the honest answer to the question on Mrs. Jenkins' stupid guidance form. I could share it with Richard

Greene and it would make more sense to him than a long-defunct college in South Carolina. I won't, though. Richard understands chemistry and he may even be able to help me wrestle a B from Mr. Carlson. One thing he doesn't understand, though, one thing that no one in this town understands, is that my dreams aren't meant to be shared.

I turn off the light and crawl into bed.

5

1:56 AM: Henry has some sort of weird nightmare. He's screaming, but not really awake. I have no idea what to do. Dad and I stare at each other. Simon is frightened. Henry doesn't wake up, but eventually stops.

2:39 AM: Simon wets the bed. It takes me a long moment to figure out what's happened. He stands in my room like some slender ghost, holding the frog, not speaking. It's the smell that clues me in. I find him dry clothes.

3:28 AM: Henry has another episode. Dad doesn't wake up this time, but Simon does. I sit next to Henry until he stops. I drift off myself, and wake up when I slide off the couch and land on my ass.

5:02 AM: Simon wants a snack. I give him crackers.

5:28 AM: There is literally no point in trying to sleep again.

"Ms. Lynn."

My head comes up and my eyes snap open. My whole body jerks, and my notebook and pencil fall onto the floor. "Sorry," I say, "what's that again?"

"Mrs. Jenkins is here for you," the teacher says.

I get up and walk across the room and into the hall. The teacher closes the door behind us. "I received a call from the lower school," Mrs. Jenkins says. "There's a situation with some boys who say they know you."

"Oh," I say, "they must be my…nephews." The word feels strange in my mouth.

"Are they living with you?" the guidance counselor asks.

"Yeah, as of yesterday, and just for a little while. What's the problem?"

"The lower school has been trying to reach your father but he's not picking up."

"Sometimes he's tough to reach at work."

The counselor looks at me.

"He works for the DPW."

"Yes, I know."

"Look," I say, "I don't know what you want me to do."

The classroom door opens and Richard steps into the hall, scanning first the guidance counselor and then me. "Can I help you?" I ask.

"Getting some water." He brushes by and walks away.

I turn back to Mrs. Jenkins. "The administration at the lower school is asking for you to come over," she says.

"Me? Why do they want to see me? I'm just their aunt." I look up and down the otherwise empty hallway, shifting from one foot to another. "Look, I don't really know these kids. They literally showed up last night. Before that..."

"They need you to go over there."

"I don't have a car today," I tell her. "Mine won't start..."

"I can drive you," a voice says.

We both turn to see Richard, walking back toward us.

"Are you kidding?" I ask.

"No. I'm no good at kidding."

Mrs. Jenkins nods. "Good. It's settled then. Remember to sign out." She pivots and briskly walks away, trying to escape before I can come up with another reason that this should not be my problem. I look back at Richard. "Why?" I ask.

"Why what?"

"Why are you helping?"

"The lower school is two miles away. I'm offering you a ride."

"What about history?"

"My least favorite class. Disconnected facts, pointing in no particular direction."

"Now you know how I feel about chemistry."

"Except I'm still getting an A in history."

I'd like not to hate him, but he makes it hard. We retrieve our backpacks and five minutes later we've both signed out and are driving away from the high school. "You look tired," he says.

"Thanks."

"You're pale, and there are big bags under your eyes."

"Really, you know how to make a girl feel special."

Richard picked me up this morning but I closed my eyes so I could rest on the ride to school and then begged out of our tutoring session, claiming a headache. "I think what you're doing is called a kinship placement," he says after a moment.

"What's that?"

"Remember yesterday, when you were trying to explain how the kids were with you? Whether they were being adopted? I looked it up last night, when I was supposed to be studying history. Temporary placement with family during a period of hardship is kinship care."

"Yeah, that sounds like something my dad said." "Kinship" seems like an old-fashioned term. It doesn't sound at all applicable to my relationship with Pauline or her kids. "Why are you looking my family up?"

"It's an interesting situation. More interesting than the Peloponnesian War."

"That's what I want under my senior picture: 'Hannah Lynn: more appealing than a sick cat, more interesting than an ancient war.'"

He laughs. It's a nice sound and it makes me realize that I don't think I've heard Richard laugh before. We drive on in silence and after another minute we pull into the lower-school lot. I open the door and step out of the car when it has barely stopped moving. "Thanks for the ride."

"You want me to wait here?"

"No, it's fine." I slam the door and walk away.

"You're welcome," Richard calls through the glass

before pulling away from the curb. Whatever. I didn't ask him to drive me.

The boys are sitting on a bench outside the main office. Henry looks bored and Simon looks worried. "You both in trouble already?" I ask.

"We're not in trouble!" Simon protests.

"I'm kidding. Don't wander off." I go into the office. "Hey Principal Stanley," I say. "It's good to see you again."

Principal Stanley does not look like it's good to see me. "We have a problem here," he says by way of greeting. "I'm not at all sure how anyone could think that it's acceptable to drop off two unregistered children without waiting to make sure all of the paperwork was in order."

I blink. "It's me, Hannah Lynn," I say.

"Yes, I remember you, Hannah."

"My dad is Larry Lynn."

"I understand that. We've been trying to call him."

"These are his grandkids, Pauline's sons."

"Oh yes, I remember Pauline quite well." There's something in his tone that I don't like.

"Your father dropped these boys off this morning and completed their registration paperwork but did not wait until we had the opportunity to make sure everything was in order. And it is not."

Principal Stanley is standing behind a counter with the school secretary at his elbow. He's shorter than I remember, and balder too. There are two equally thick piles of papers in front of him and the secretary glances at them and then back at me, raising her eyebrows.

"Paperwork?" I ask. "This is about paperwork?"

"Yes, we called you over because this paperwork needs to be complete," Mr. Stanley says, "and until it is you need to take these boys home."

I blink. "Um, you know I go to the high school, right? I'm seventeen years old. I'm not the one responsible for them."

"Well, your father isn't answering his phone and your sister is apparently…out of the picture?"

"Principal Stanley," I say, "you were always really great about things when I was here, you know? Remember when Dad forgot to send a check for me to go on the trip to Aquaboggan, and you let me go anyway? We'll get all the paperwork done, it's just that Dad was in a hurry this morning or he probably would have waited. He's overseeing a repaving project over on Kennedy."

"This is not a trip to Aquaboggan," he says. "Two children from a challenging background are not simply dropped off on the doorstep for me and my staff to manage." The secretary makes a slight noise to punctuate the sentiment.

"A challenging background?" In that moment, all at once, I see it. I am one hundred percent sure that a pair of well-dressed kids brought in by a typical Evans Beach mother who didn't finish the paperwork would nonetheless be greeted with open arms. These two, on the other hand, were dropped off by my father, who was probably hustling to get coffee and get the crew on the road, and they look about as un–Evans Beach as you can get. "What paperwork is missing?" I ask. The piles on the counter are covered in Dad's messy handwriting.

The secretary presents two identical forms, blank with "Nursing Office—Medical History" printed at the top.

"Were those in the packets?" I ask, gesturing at the piles.

The secretary is silent, but her eyes shift to Principal Stanley. He clears his throat. "That was an—uh—oversight," he says, "as they were not included in the packets your father completed, but nonetheless they are mandatory. They must be completed before a child can be enrolled."

"I know what mandatory means," I say. "How was Dad supposed to fill out a form he wasn't given?"

"He could have waited while we went through things," Mr. Stanley says. "He could answer his phone."

I should have had Richard wait, we could have driven the forms over to Dad. I drum my fingers on the counter, turning the situation over in my mind.

Principal Stanley stares at me. "They can't stay," he says.

"Let me just think for a moment…"

"There's nothing to think about. You need to take the boys. Your father can bring them back tomorrow, if the medical forms are completed, and then we will process and place them appropriately."

"What am I supposed to do until then?"

"Take them home."

I want to tell him that the whole fucking problem is

that they do not have a home, but he turns and walks back to his office, leaving me facing the secretary.

I go back out to the hall and let the door swing closed behind me. The boys are still waiting on the bench. I walk across the lobby to the front door and take my phone out. The call to my father goes straight to voicemail: "Hey, this is Larry. Leave a message unless you're a Yankees fan...in that case, go screw yourself." It beeps.

"Hi, Daddy," I say. "Call me when you get this. I'm at school with the boys. We have a situation and you need to come in and sign some more things. I don't know what to do. Just...give me a call when you get this, or come to the school." I hang up and put the phone in my pocket.

"Well," Henry asks from the other side of the lobby, "are we going to school, or are we going back to your house?"

I want to tell him that I don't have a working car and even if I did the last thing I am ever going to do is spend a day at home entertaining the two of them. I think for a moment, then turn back to the boys. "You're staying here," I say. "Come on." I cross the lobby and start down the hall before looking back. They're still on the bench. Henry is watching me warily; Simon is watching Henry. "Come on," I say again. This time, they follow me.

"They gave us teachers?" Simon asks, hurrying to catch up.

"Um," I say, "they're working on it."

The hallways of the lower school bring back memories I'd rather not recall. Seventh grade, for example, when

Brittany O'Neal decided that I was emphatically not going to be remaining in her orbit. We pass the music room and glancing in I see the exact spot where I was sitting when she first announced, theoretically speaking to Jessie Harper but in reality issuing a proclamation to the entire grade, that my dad and I were poor, that I was pathetic, and that our house was disgusting.

In the most Evans Beach way possible, it was all about high-end real estate. Brittany's mom owns the Sunflower Café on Route 77. It's not what they live on; her dad is some sort of broker or consultant or something, but her mom takes the café really seriously. It's pretty much the opposite of Sol's: neat, tidy, well-ventilated, with a wide variety of teas and smoothies. It also has an ocean view and the only thing between it and the water is a parking lot belonging to the DPW. That lot was empty when Mrs. O'Neal bought the café but equipment began to accumulate over time and she complained about it, a complaint that eventually landed on my father's desk. In typical Dad fashion he was not particularly sympathetic to a family that had lived in Maine for fewer than three generations and played a role in bringing chai lattes to the community. He parked Big Blue in the center of the lot, right in the middle of Mrs. O'Neal's ocean view, and he left it there.

The feud escalated. More complaints to the town. More equipment parked between the Sunflower Café's patrons and the Atlantic Ocean. Mrs. O'Neal called it an eyesore. Dad called her an eyesore. It did not go well. At some point Brittany absorbed enough negative energy directed toward the Lynn name that she decided to take the battle to our generation, and by the time she was done shit-talking me the dispute was resolved (the equipment moved to another lot, though at Dad's glacial pace) and I was an outcast. There was no one around to tell me what was happening, or how to act, or what to do. I ran into their contempt like a bird crashing into a window and then I lay there on the ground, wondering what was going on, and by the time I got myself back up the rest of seventh grade had received the unmistakable message that Hannah Lynn did not belong. Some of them joined Brittany's offensive and others, like Amity, simply assumed a position of sheepish neutrality. In the end, though, it didn't really matter whether they participated or not. They all moved on.

"Here we are," I say.

The boys look around. "This is just a hallway," Henry says.

I nod. "The west hall. I'll text the location to your grandpa. He'll get the message at some point and head over, round the two of you up, and finish the paperwork.

"You want us to wait here?" Simon asks.

"Look," I say, "there are seats between the pillars, right against the window."

"Those aren't seats," Henry says, "they're big windowsills."

"Well, you can sit on them. I used to sit on them." It's where I went when I was no longer welcome in the cafeteria, or much of anywhere else. I'd make myself as small as

I could, wedge myself between the pillars, and eat whatever lunch I'd brought from home.

Henry walks over to one of the windows.

"It won't be for long," I say. "You can hang out. Do you have phones you can go on?"

Simon shakes his head. "We don't have phones."

"Oh. Well, talk to each other, then. Just don't be loud."

There doesn't seem to be much more to say. I don't like the way Henry's looking at me, so I nod in a manner that I hope is both firm and reassuring and then I turn and hurry back through the school, not pausing when I get to the lobby, accelerating through the doors.

The wind has picked up and for a moment I think about calling Richard. I take my phone out, see that my father still hasn't tried to reach me, and text him the boys' location. Then I start walking in the direction of the high school. I cross the parking lot to the road and head east along the shoulder. There's not much traffic and the plows have pushed the snow from Tuesday's storm far off to the side, leaving a hard-packed salt-studded crust for me to walk on. Dad will show up. Henry and Simon will be all right. It's not my problem. They're not my problem.

The wind cuts right through my jacket. I duck my head and push my hands as far into the pockets as they will go, continuing on in the direction of the high school, leaving the boys behind as quickly as I can walk along this icy, empty road.

6

I have high hopes for dinner. Kids like pizza. Everyone likes pizza. You can't go wrong with pizza. We do it twice a month and it's one night when I try not to worry about Dad's cholesterol and carb intake. We usually get a large; I have two pieces and he eats the rest save for one slice, which he puts in the fridge for the morning. I love cold pizza for breakfast.

The day did not go well. Dad eventually got his messages and went to the school. He found the boys in the hallway where I'd left them and made a minor scene in the office about having to return for some forms he wasn't given in the first place. Things sort of righted themselves after that; the boys went to their classes and then to the after-school program. Dad had gone back to work and then picked me up from school and took me to the DPW with him. Less than half an hour later, though, he got a call to come back for the boys because Henry had been in a fight. I got a ride home from one of the guys when my shift was over and picked up pizza on the way. The day had been terrible but at least dinner could be fun.

Dinner is a disaster.

Henry and Simon go at the pizza like wolves on raw meat. They pile slices on their plates, jealously guarding them from each other. Dad glances at me uneasily. "Now, boys," he says, "there's more than enough to go around."

He's right. They're soon stuffed full, and there's still three-quarters of a pizza in the last box. That's when Henry grabs two slices, sticks out his tongue, and slowly licks them. "Mine," he says, dropping them onto the grease-stained paper plate in front of him.

"Write your name on it," Simon says.

"You write your name on yours, idiot."

"Henry!" I say, horrified by the licking. "Simon's not an idiot, and what do you think you're doing with that pizza?"

His face colors, as though he's just realizing that what he's done is strange. Instead of answering he rises from the table and takes his plate into the kitchen. I hear him putting it into the fridge.

The evening devolves from there. Simon and Henry wind up fighting over the remote. Henry wins, giving his little brother a hard shove. Simon tumbles, hitting his knee on the edge of the end table and I wait for him to cry or ask for help but he doesn't even look at me, just crawls away.

"Do you guys have homework?" Dad asks.

They both look at him blankly. Simon shakes his head.

"Shouldn't they have some homework?" Dad asks me.

"I don't know. Maybe they get a night off because they're new."

He looks worried. I kiss him on the top of his head and he wraps an arm around me and pulls me in for a hug. I squeeze him back and then go to my room for some quiet.

It lasts about fifteen minutes. First Simon is screaming, then Henry is shouting over him. I run back up the stairs and burst into the living room, arriving as Dad emerges from his bedroom. Simon is sitting on the floor. His hands are cupped over his face and his nose is bleeding.

"What the hell happened here?" I ask.

They both look at me. Neither says anything.

"Henry, you hit him?"

Nothing.

"Well, Simon didn't do it to himself."

Henry shrugs, impassive.

Dad peers at the bloody nose. "Dammit, Henry, what did you do that for?"

"You should send him to time-out," I say.

"Go to time-out," Dad tells Henry.

"Why? My mom never has us do time-outs."

"It's your punishment for hitting Simon," I tell him. "Go down to the family room and leave the TV off until Grandpa tells you you're done."

Henry shrugs, walks past me and Dad, and goes downstairs.

"Simon, come here," I say. "Let me see your nose." I take him by the arm and lead him to the kitchen where I can see under the bright light. "It's not bad. It's just a little swollen. Here." I give him a wad of paper towel to stop the bleeding and then make a cold pack with ice and a ziplock bag. "Just hold it on there and it'll stop in no time. And try not to bleed on anything else."

"You'll be fine," Dad says from the doorway. "You just have to learn to hit back."

"No, Dad, that's not the lesson," I say. I turn to Simon. "You have to get Grandpa if Henry is being rough with you. Now go sit at the dining room table and hold that on your face."

Simon leaves and Dad says, "I should give Henry a paddling."

"You can't do that."

"That's what my old man would have done to me, for sure. I never had boys; you and Pauline never hit each other."

"Well, I don't think you're allowed to spank them." I open the fridge. Henry's two licked pieces of pizza are sitting on a plate. I scan the shelves. "Where's the leftovers?"

"I don't know."

"Didn't you put them away?"

"I was gonna do it later."

I go into the dining area between the kitchen and the living room. Simon sits with his face lowered over a blood-spotted placemat, dutifully holding the ice pack to his nose.

The grease-stained boxes are still there, but when I look inside, they're empty. "Who finished all the pizza?" I ask.

"Are you still hungry, baby?" Dad asks me.

"No, I just want to know what they did with the food."

"Maybe they threw it away or something. Tried to clean up."

I return to the kitchen and open the trash can. No pizza.

"It's not a big deal..." Dad begins.

I march back. "Show me where you hid it."

Simon looks up at me, face blank.

"Right now!" I yell, the force of my own voice startling me.

He leaps to his feet, eyes wide.

"Move."

Simon goes to the bookshelf and pulls a photo album down. Two folded pieces of pizza are stuffed behind it, sandwiched between a pair of the cheap, thin paper plates the restaurant gave us. I take them out. "Let me see that."

It's an album from the year before Mom was diagnosed. Tomato sauce is smeared along the edge of the pages. I whip around and before I know what's happening I've brought my hand up and even though a part of my brain is watching the scene and is saying "you're not going to hit him, not really, he's a kid and there is no way you are actually going to hit him," I feel myself swinging and Simon cries out, ducking and turning away.

Someone else is yelling, too. Out of the corner of my eye I see Henry hurtling across the room, face red, fists up, coming right toward me.

Then Dad is between all of us. "That's enough," he bellows.

Everyone freezes. My hand is still far enough from Simon that I can tell myself I had no intention of making contact.

"There will be no fighting in this house," Dad says. "None. No one is hitting anybody else ever again." He looks at Henry, who still seems ready for action, and then he turns to me. "Hannah." He takes the album from my hands. "This will wipe away."

"Where's the rest of it?" I say. "The rest of it! There was more fucking pizza…"

Simon hurries to pull food from under the couch.

"Is that all?"

He nods.

"Is that all?" My voice rises.

"Hannah, go do your homework," Dad says. "I just walked away for a second but I'm here now. Go."

Christ, I hate it when he tries to act like a parent. I stand for a moment, looking at the tomato sauce along the edge of the photo album, looking at my father, a man who didn't know how to raise me or my sister and is now going to try his hand with another two kids. Then I turn and walk from the room.

There's no way I can study. I take a replica of Mom's thickest sweater from my closet and let myself out the back door. I stand with my back against the house. No one's taken care of the yard in years; the grass hasn't been mowed and seasons of leaves are composting where they fell. Our old playhouse, Vine Cottage, is listing to one side. It's cold, but for the first time in days there's no wind. I pull the sweater on and then I close my eyes and, as I've done so many times before, I try to conjure her image.

I've studied every picture of Mom I can find, burned

them into my memory. I used to pore through the albums, trying to see whether I'd missed her in the background of a group shot. One more look. One more glimpse. An expression I hadn't seen before; a haircut I didn't know she'd had. A shirt, a torn pair of jeans I could imitate. Anything.

The image I choose tonight is from the sauce-stained album. She's holding me in it, walking along the seashore. Wind is blowing her black hair to the side and she's carrying me on her hip. She's wearing a loose dress, sleeveless, reaching nearly to her ankles. She's looking above the photographer and to the left but I'm looking up at her, one hand resting on the side of her neck. I try to place myself in the picture, try to recall a moment I was far too young to remember. The feel of her sun-warmed skin, the way she smelled when I pressed my face to her shoulder.

My phone vibrates. I open my eyes and pull it from my pocket.

Richard: You coming to the party tomorrow?

He's probably with Amity. I'm not going to her party. What would I talk about? Henry licking his pizza? Pulling back to haul off on a nine-year-old? I thumb a response. Nah pbly not.

Dots wave on my screen as he composes what seems to be a lengthy response. I wait, but in the end he just texts "ok." He and Amity are going back to doing whatever they were doing.

The screen door bangs open beside me and Dad comes out. He's not wearing a coat and he claps his hands together, the noise echoing in the trees beyond the yard, then he blows into his palms.

"I wasn't going to hit him," I say. I know it's a lie. Apparently I am someone who can wish that her sister was dead, who can want to inflict harm on a nine-year-old.

"Hannah," Dad says, "there's nothing you can tell me about how angry a kid can make you that I don't already know."

"As your child, I appreciate that."

He grunts. "It was never you."

"I know." His fights with Pauline were epic. If we had had neighbors, they would have called the police. "I feel bad for scaring him."

"I know all about that, too. Simon's all right, though."

"I doubt it. His mom's not around, he's here with half-a-garbage-bag full of belongings, his brother punched him, and his aunt almost hit him again."

Dad nods, still studying the woods, his breath emerging in great clouds as he speaks. "I called Reverend Jim this afternoon, let him know what's happening. He was really supportive. They're going to drop off some donated clothes tomorrow, and probably some hot suppers."

"I hate that."

"It's what the church is there for. They're happy to help."

"I don't want their help."

Dad finally turns to me. "You're crying," he says, reaching out and wiping one side of my face.

"Am not."

"I know when my girl's crying."

I shake his hand away and rub the side of my face with a sleeve. "You weren't there today, Dad. At the school. I couldn't reach you."

"I got there eventually. I forgot to charge the phone last night and it wouldn't turn on."

"You can't do that now. Someone might need you."

"I know, I know. I have to get used to that. I guess they're not like you, eh? You always solved your own problems."

"Yeah, they're not solving problems. They're causing them."

Dad lets out a long exhalation. Then he turns and starts to pace back and forth, cracking the knuckles on one hand, then the other. "Why didn't she call me if she needed money?" he finally says.

"She was drinking."

"She always called before."

"Maybe she didn't want to do it again. It's not your fault, Daddy."

He shakes his head. "That's the thing about being a parent, baby. In the end, there's no one else to blame." He turns and leans against the house beside me. "Your mother was so damn competent. Anytime someone was sick, someone needed something, she knew exactly what to do. And when it was just me, I know I let you down. I know that I fell apart for a while. I know I've never been on top of...anything." He takes another deep breath, holds it a second, then lets it out. "This is a second chance," he says.

"For the boys, and for me. I know they have problems, but we can turn things around."

"Turn things around? This isn't the Sea Dogs in July, Daddy. This isn't about getting some long relief and maybe making the playoffs. People don't get 'turned around.' Not in three months, anyway."

"We'll see. I'm going to get them set up with some stuff. I want them to talk to a counselor, and the caseworker told me about a group Simon should do to practice social skills. You mentioned the dentist and they probably need physicals too."

"Sounds like a lot of appointments. Who's going to drive them?"

"I will. I'm owed some favors. The guys will cover for me. The point is, I'm going to do better. I'm going to try to be a good grandfather."

Someone screams inside the house.

"Sounds like it's time to start doing better," I say.

He squares his shoulders and turns to me. "We're gonna get through this. They need us, and they need each other. And in a few months everything will be back to just the way it was." Dad leans over, kisses me on the cheek, and goes inside.

I'm shivering, but I decide to stay outside a little while longer. I go back to my spot against the wall and close my eyes, alone with the pictures in my head.

7

Friday night comes and I find Dad in his room, standing in front of the glass case where he keeps his Red Sox memorabilia.

"What are you doing?" I ask.

He turns, baseball in hand. "Thinking of selling."

"What do you think you can get for that?"

"Couple of hundred."

"Really?"

"Sure. Fisk, Yaz, Jim Rice." He tosses it in the air, catches it, and replaces it in the case next to his jersey and bat. The entire 1980 team signed the ball for him when he got sent back down to the minor leagues.

I walk into the room and sit on the edge of his cluttered desk. "We need the cash that bad?"

"Not yet, but I'm guessing we will."

"For what? Doesn't the state help out with the kids?"

"They do, but sizing things up, I'm not sure it's going to be enough. I called their caseworker, Ben, about counseling for the boys, but the place he mentioned has a year-long wait-list. I called someone else, here in town, and they can get them in but they don't take insurance. Stuff like that."

"Oh."

"Two kids, two hours a week, two hundred dollars an hour. That's…"

"Forty-eight hundred dollars for three months."

He grins. "You were always faster than me."

I shrug.

"I won't touch the college money," Dad says.

"I didn't say you were going to."

"I just want you to know."

The college money is the result of a small life insurance policy Mom took out when she first had a child. It's been sitting in the bank for the thirteen years since her death, waiting to be used.

Something falls over in the living room and I hear raised voices, an argument starting over who exactly is to blame.

"I was thinking of going out tonight," I say.

"Really?"

"Yeah. I was invited to a party."

"A party?"

"Don't sound so surprised."

"No, but—you don't go to parties. I thought maybe kids don't have them as much as they did when I was in high school."

"They still have them; I just don't go. I want to get out, though."

Dad nods. "You should." Something else is knocked over. He closes his eyes and takes a deep breath. "Have fun," he says, eyes still closed.

"I won't be out late. Can I take your truck? My car will be in the shop until tomorrow."

"Sure. Yeah. Have a good time."

I slide off the desk. "See you," I say, and leave the room.

I arrive late. Amity's mother is the president of Portland Savings and Trust. Evans Beach has some rich families, people who work in Portland or who commute to Boston or even New York, a few who don't seem to work at all, and I don't know how people's bank accounts match up to the Williamses', but their house is easily the nicest. "Nice" being a euphemism for a gaudy display of gratuitous wealth, siphoned out of the New England economy via the legal but highly immoral mechanisms of modern finance and, God willing, destined to be swept out to sea by a superstorm sometime in the next couple of decades.

Still, people seem to be having a good time.

There's a huge garage, more of a hangar, sitting across a broad expanse of grass. Music and screams come from inside and I walk toward it. Kids are going in and out, laughing, calling to each other. I stick to the dark edge of the lawn and trust that they won't be able to see me with the light behind them. I edge a little closer.

Inside, there's a beach volleyball court; piles of sand, teams in swimsuits knocking the ball back and forth, huge glowing heaters with fans so that no one will feel the need to put on a shirt in the twenty-degree weather. I've never played beach volleyball and I don't feel like starting now, so I circle back and let myself in the front door of the house.

I immediately know that I've made a mistake by coming. The foyer is crammed with people, all of them shouting and no one listening, most clutching those oversize red plastic cups. A few of them glance up but no one seems to register my presence. I know pretty much everyone at Evans Beach High—there are only about a hundred and twenty people in my class—but I don't recognize a lot of the people at this party. Someone has a Grandview Prep sweatshirt on; Amity must be pulling kids from all over the greater Portland area. I guess she's just that popular. I find myself again wishing I could hate her.

I wander from room to room, hands in pockets, feeling like a pathetic ghost chained to an indifferent haunting. I nod to a few kids I recognize. How many high school parties have they been to together, I wonder. How much have I missed?

I could just slip out and leave. I don't want to go home, but I could drive to the DPW and see who's working the night shift, have some coffee. It would be comfortable. Not like here. I turn back toward the door and as I do a guy pivots in the opposite direction, his hand colliding with my chest, his drink showering both of us.

"Oh shit," he says, laughing. "Oh shit." He transfers the cup to his other hand and licks his fingers. Two girls he's been talking to are in hysterics. I look down at my shirt, which is now covered in a bright red punch that reeks of liquor. "Sorry," he says, almost as an afterthought. One of the girls takes his arm and leads him, wobbling, away.

I'm wearing a random T-shirt and a replica flannel. The plaid matches a shirt in a photo of mom circa 1995. If this was one of Mom's originals the kid would be swallowing his own teeth right now. "Fuck off," I half-heartedly call after them, but my voice is lost in the noise of the party. No one else has noticed the spill, no one else notices the red puddle on the floor. I'm sure the Williamses have a housekeeper. I start toward the door.

"Hannah!" The squeal is at such a high decibel, with such a degree of frenzy behind it, that there is no way it is not alcohol-enhanced.

"Hey, Amity."

She emerges from the crowd on my left. "I'm so glad you came!" Amity throws her arms around me, exuding punch from every pore, and then steps back. "What happened?"

"Some guy spilled his drink."

"Oh no, oh no…"

"It's okay. I was just…"

"Come with me." Amity takes my wrist and marches me back into the heart of the party. Towed in her wake I get a taste of what it's like to be noticed. People turn, nod, call out. Brittany O'Neal peers out at me from the crowd, her face unsmiling. Amity acknowledges them but doesn't break her stride and soon we're heading up a wide flight of stairs to the far quieter second floor. "Come in," she says, opening a door.

I go in and look around, telling myself not to compare even though I know it's unavoidable. When I get home tonight, I'll look at my stained rug and see the lush white carpet I'm standing on now. I'll pass my chipped mirror and see her full-length one with a scalloped frame, presently hanging to my right. I'll lie down in my single bed with a wire-enamel frame and plywood base and wonder how soft the king-size mattress in front of me must be, fantasize about the pile of down pillows and the thick comforter.

Amity pulls a Princeton T-shirt from one of two large dressers on the far wall. "I think this will work." She underhands it across the room. "My dad got it for me when we toured, but I've decided to apply early to Cornell."

I hesitate, not knowing what to do. Do girlfriends change in front of each other? I study the shirt, rub the cotton between my fingers, and wonder whether I should ask for directions to the bathroom.

"Where are you applying?" Amity asks.

"What, for college?"

She giggles. "Yes, for college!"

Would Richard have told her about Grant-Covington? A funny story about crazy Hannah Lynn? "Uh—I'm not sure yet," I say. "Probably someplace small. Or, like... bigger."

"Do you want to stay in New England? Go south? West Coast?" She reels off the possibilities with the ease of someone whose family has always been, and always will be, able to afford a plane ticket.

"Oh, I don't…I mean, I want to get out of Maine, that's for sure."

Amity nods. "Makes sense." She walks to the window and looks out. "Look at him." I walk over and join her. I can tell that there would be an amazing ocean view in the daytime. "Just look at him," she says again.

We're side by side in the window, looking down on a broad patio with a full-size in-ground pool and a huge octagonal hot tub. The pool must be well heated; it's full of people and I can see steam rising against the lights. The hot tub, on the other hand, has only one person in it and I know that he is the one Amity's referring to. Richard seems completely oblivious of the kids splashing and having chicken fights in the pool. He has his head back, eyes closed.

"I just hope he doesn't get hurt," Amity says.

"What, in the hot tub?"

She laughs. "No, silly, with applications next year. He's applying early to Harvard. He wants it so bad—he always has. Both of his parents did Harvard College and then Harvard Med, and he's determined to do the exact same."

"Well, he seems to get pretty good grades…"

"He has a perfect GPA and great extracurriculars, but that's not enough. Maybe not even with two parents who are alums. My mom has actually been helping them structure some donations."

"To what?"

"To Harvard!"

"Oh. Right."

Amity's voice drops into a confidential register. "Honestly, Hannah, I'm not sure it's going to be enough. Mom says you need to approach the seven-figure line just to get on the radar, and she's not sure how far they can stretch."

"They're both doctors."

"Yeah. I'm not sure how well doctors really do, though."

"Well, there are lots of other schools if Harvard doesn't work out."

"No. Not for him." She turns to me. "Of course, he has safety schools, but haven't you ever wanted something so badly that you can't imagine a future without it?"

I know exactly how Richard feels, but I just shake my head. "He'll be fine," I say. "He seems pretty tough."

"Richard? Oh, no. Richard might seem tough. 'Remote,' maybe."

"Yeah, remote."

"He's not, though. He's very sensitive."

"If you say so. He's just my chemistry tutor."

"He's sensitive. It just takes a while to see it. He's like an iceberg; there's this bit on the surface that's dark and strong and gorgeous, but then there's all this other stuff underneath."

I don't think of icebergs as dark, strong, and gorgeous, but I'm not particularly interested in continuing the conversation, so I say the first thing that comes to mind: "Doesn't it cost a lot to heat that pool?"

Amity looks at the pool, then at me, then back at the pool. "To heat it?"

"Yeah, the electricity. The volume of water; the DPW looked at heating the town pool so it could open earlier in the spring and stay open through the fall, but that increased revenue was totally wiped out by the cost."

Amity chews her lower lip and frowns. "I...don't know."

I guess not every seventeen-year-old handles their family utility bills. "It doesn't matter," I say, "it was just a stupid random thought."

"It must be terrible for the environment," Amity says, "the electricity use, I mean. I never even thought of it. I'm going to tell my parents to close it for the winter, right after this party."

"Oh..."

"Thank you, Hannah," she says. "I love the way your mind works. It's so...practical. Do you know how many people have been in that pool and no one has ever, to my knowledge, considered the energy implications?"

"Wow," I say.

"Yeah. Wow." She sighs. "It's too bad we haven't spent more time together. I've always liked you."

She is definitely drunk. "Yes," I say. "I also...yes."

"Why did we stop hanging out?"

"Oh, I don't really...I mean, it wasn't exactly a mutual decision..."

"You're so tough. Tough and practical. Oh! You know what would be absolutely perfect for you?"

"What?"

"UPenn."

"UPenn?"

"The University of Pennsylvania. It's a great school, Ivy League, but it's in West Philadelphia. We drove through on the Princeton trip. Smart but totally real, totally gritty. Authentic, just like you. You should look at it!"

"Yeah. Uh, maybe. My dad wants me to go to Stanford."

"Oh, tough choice!"

"Though I don't think he's ever been to Stanford. He just played the A's in a weekend series. He hit a sacrifice fly."

"Well," Amity says, "did he ever play the Philadelphia baseball team?"

"No. The Phillies are National League."

She shrugs. "It will all work out, Hannah. I know it will. Things always do. Now get changed and let's go back to the party."

I step away from the window, shed my flannel, and peel the stained T-shirt over my head as I try to remember which bra I put on this morning and pray that it's not one of the tattered ones. Glancing down I see I'm in luck. I quickly pull her shirt on.

"Just toss that on the floor," she says, "I'll get it cleaned and bring it to school."

I awkwardly drop the stained shirt. Amity looks out the window once more and turns back to me, critically studying the shirt for fit and then focusing on my face. "You're so pretty, Hannah, and you don't even have to wear makeup."

I feel my face color. When was the last time someone called me pretty? "Thanks," I say. Am I supposed to return the compliment? "Um...you're..."

"I'm so glad you came," she says again.

"Me too." I pull my flannel, which only has a few spots of punch, back on over her T-shirt.

"You ready?"

"I maybe could use another moment." I sort of want to stay here in this room, just me and Amity, talking about whatever it is girls talk about, including how pretty I am.

"No worries, hang here as long as you want." Amity steps forward, gives me a hug, and bounds from the room, leaving me alone. My phone rings and I take it out and look at the caller ID. *Pater.*

"Yeah, Dad?"

"Hannah, where's the cough medicine?"

"Why?"

"Simon's coughing."

"I don't think we have cough medicine."

"We must. Remember when you were real sick and wouldn't stop coughing and Doc Kerbel gave us that stuff that fixed you up?"

"That was when I was, like, eleven. And I think that was an antibiotic."

"Do we still have it?"

"No. Put Simon on."

There's a pause at the other end of the line, and a shuffle, and then Simon's voice. "Hi, Hannah."

"Hi, Simon. What's wrong?"

"I'm coughing."

"I don't hear you coughing."

He coughs.

"Okay, that was one."

He coughs again.

"Do you feel sick?"

"A little."

"What feels sick?"

"My...legs."

"Your legs are sick?"

"I think so."

I sigh. "Simon..."

"When will you be home?"

Why does he care when I'm coming home? "I won't be out late," I tell him.

"After my bedtime?"

"Yeah."

"Where are you?"

"Simon...can you just..."

He coughs, declaratively.

"Okay, Simon. I'm going to tell Dad, Grandpa, about some medicine that I think will make your cough and your legs all better, and then when I get home, I'll check in on you and...yeah. That's it."

"Okay."

"Okay."

"You want to talk to Grandpa again?"

"Yeah, put him on."

"Okay."

There's another shuffle and then Dad comes back on. "What'd you think?"

"You know those lemon lozenges I like when I have a sore throat?"

"Yeah?"

"Give him two of them. They're in the medicine cabinet, behind the Band Aids."

"That'll help the cough?"

"Yup." I hang up and walk back over to the window. I literally cannot imagine why Simon would give a shit where I am. I mentally inventory the things I've done for him this week: a) give him a toothbrush and an old stuffed frog; b) drop him off in a random school hallway; and c) shame and terrify him for hiding pizza. He should be thrilled Aunt Hannah is taking the night off.

Below, Amity emerges from the house and runs across the patio. She crouches down beside the pool to talk to someone, laughing and splashing them with some of the expensively heated water. I stand in her window, wearing her shirt, wondering whether things could have been different. I told her the choice to go our separate ways wasn't mutual and I meant it. I meant that it wasn't mine, it was about Brittany O'Neal and her ridiculous mother and her café's ocean view, but that wasn't right. That was bad but it didn't have to be forever. Amity and I could have reconnected, we could have been friends. Jessie Harper too, probably. The problem was me: Brittany's taunts opened something up that I didn't know was there, like a cyst I'd been carrying inside me ever since Mom died and Pauline left. I felt different, and alone, and by the time I was big enough to put my mother's clothing on like armor it was too late to make amends and make up with anyone. The decision was mine all along.

Amity reaches the hot tub and quickly peels off her sweater and jeans to reveal the bikini she's wearing underneath. She slides into the water next to Richard, wrapping one arm around his neck and whispering in his ear. He laughs and shakes his head and then she whispers something else and now he nods.

I turn away from the window and leave the room, heading back to the party below. I wander for a moment and start to relax into my invisibility. People seem even looser than before, louder, less aware of what's going on around them. The current of the crowd brings me to the kitchen, a massive space with a marble island in the middle. Someone is ladling punch into the red cups and passing them around, and a guy next to me presses one into my hand. I raise it to my nose and inhale. "Alcohol," in the World Book, was noted to be associated with a wide variety of short-term effects including reduction in anxiety, memory loss, and somnolence. All three sound good to me right now. I take a sip.

It's awful; it has to be the juice from the deformed offspring of some unfortunate liaison between a pineapple and a grapefruit. I almost spit it out and look around in amazement at people pouring this shit down their throats. Still...somnolence and memory loss. I try again.

My phone vibrates. Dad: better but still coughing. I shake my head, ruing the limited power of placebos, dump my cup in the kitchen sink, and make my way to the door.

I let myself into the house as quietly as I can, then trip over something dark in the entryway. Cursing under my breath I flip on the light to find three huge Hefty trash bags on the floor. I open one up and peer inside. Random clothes, toys, battered books. It takes me a moment to realize that Reverend Jim must have dropped all this off after I left. It looks like crap. Why people feel that castoffs need to be boxed up and delivered to the needy under the guise of charity, I will never understand.

Dad's asleep in his chair, a recap of today's sports news playing softly on the TV. He must have passed out in the fifteen minutes it took me to get home. Henry is stretched out on the couch, also asleep. This has been one hell of a week. I go downstairs and look into the family room. Simon isn't sleeping; he's tossing and turning, Herbert clutched in his arms. I go in and sit on the edge of his mattress. He looks up at me, chewing the edge of the stuffed frog's ear. "Your cough gone?" I ask.

He nods and chews.

"You shouldn't bite him," I say. "I mean, maybe he'll bite you back while you're sleeping."

Simon releases the ear and his eyes widen. That was probably the wrong thing to say. It's possible that I'm really, really bad at this. "That's not going to happen," I clarify. "He won't bite you. He's stuffed. Nothing will bite you. Nothing's going to bite you while you sleep."

Simon looks at me silently.

"So…you're having a hard time relaxing?"

He frowns.

"Right." I have no idea what to do. He would quite literally be better off if I hadn't come by.

"Hannah?"

"Yeah?"

"When is my mom coming back?"

"Oh. Gosh, Simon, what did they tell you about it?"

"What did who tell me?"

"Anyone. Like, the caseworker, or Grandpa, or…anyone."

"Grandpa said she needs a break. He said she needs to 'get her act together.'"

"Yeah, that's right."

"I don't know what that means."

"Well, it means she has to stop drinking, for one thing. And…all the other stuff. And she needs to talk to someone. Like, a therapist." Dad said the reunification plan included therapy and starting a twelve-step program. I try to remember what else. "She's going to see you," I say. "She's going to visit, and the caseworker is going to come and supervise."

"You mean Ben?"

"Yes, I think so."

"When are they coming?"

"I'm not sure. Soon, I hope."

"What does it mean that he's going to supervise?"

"He's going to watch her. Make sure she's being a good mother."

"One of the people who came into our apartment said

she wasn't. A cop. I heard him tell another policeman that she's a bad mom."

"He said that?"

"He said she's a 'shit mother.'"

"He might not have been a very nice policeman. But, you know, she was supposed to be taking care of you…"

"She was! She was taking care of us!" Simon's eyes are wild and fierce and he struggles up in the bed so that his face is level with mine. "Don't you say she wasn't taking care of us! Don't you say she's a bad mother."

"All right…all right, Simon…all right. God, just…stop."

His chest is heaving and his lips are working, as though words are forming behind them but they can't line up in the proper sequence to come out. Not knowing what else to do, I reach out and rub his back. After a moment his breathing slows. "Who's on the mailbox?" he asks.

"What?"

"The little people. They're on the side of the mailbox. There are four of them."

"Oh, those. Those are just stupid stencils. They're old."

"But who are they?"

"Simon," I say, "I'm exhausted. Maybe you can just go to sleep?"

"I can't."

"Yes, you can." I don't mean to snap at him, but I do. I look up at the ceiling and shake my head. "Everyone else is sleeping. You're tired. I'm tired. I'm…" Tired. Sad. Angry. Lost. I'm lonely, even though our house suddenly has twice as many people in it. On the other side of town, the party is going on without me. Maybe Amity and Richard are still in the hot tub. Maybe they went up to her room, Amity relieved to find that I was gone. "You can go to sleep," I tell him. "You will go to sleep. It's impossible for you not to. And you will stay in this bed until you do." I get up.

"Hannah?"

"Yeah."

"Are you going back out?"

"No. I'll be in my room. But don't come bother me."

I can hear him breathing. "Okay," he finally says. His voice sounds small and faraway. It occurs to me that he might be crying but I carefully avoid looking down to check. I walk to the doorway, then pause. "Grandpa, Grandma, me, and your mom," I say.

"What?"

"We're on the mailbox. Our old family."

"Grandma died."

"Yeah."

"I never met her."

"No."

"Mom told me once that she would have loved me."

"Yeah. I guess she would have."

"Are you going to fix it?"

"What do you mean?"

"The mailbox. Like, make it new. What the family looks like now."

I should have covered Mom and Pauline with a fresh coat of paint years ago. Just me and Dad, receiving bills and junk mail, day in and day out. "Maybe," I say, "someday."

I leave before he can say anything else, retreat to my room, and shut my door. I place the boots in the closet, followed by the flannel and my jeans. I toss Amity's Princeton shirt in a corner, intending to wash it and return it to her at school. Then I take Mom's college T-shirt from under my pillow and pull it on.

There's a little tear by the hem I hadn't noticed. I should mend it, just a few stitches. I've done it before. Mom would have had no idea, buying it as an incoming freshman at the Tufts University bookstore, that this shirt would be seeing nightly use thirty years in the future. I'll buy a new one, someday soon, when I make my own way to Medford, Massachusetts.

All these years, I've been following in her footsteps. I'm like a little kid struggling to catch up with an adult walking ahead, and no matter how hard I run I can't close the gap. When I get to Tufts, though, things will be different. I'll be eighteen, walking the paths she walked when she was eighteen. I'll ask to be placed in the same dorm. I'll be sitting in the same classes, maybe even with some of the same professors.

Mom didn't get to finish college. She met Dad, got pregnant with Pauline, and with her own family back on the West Coast and never that close to her anyway, she decided to drop out and move up to the little town in Maine where her kid's father came from and where he thought he could get them both jobs, him at the DPW and her at the library. They got married at the town hall and settled down in a house that working people could still afford in 1982. They tried to raise Pauline, who was wild from the start, and thirteen years later they got a surprise in the form of yours truly, baby Hannah. Then, a few years after that, Mom got a less cute surprise when she went to the doctor to check on a lump in her breast.

Mom left college, came to this town, and never left. I'm doing the opposite. I'm leaving Evans Beach, going to the school she went to, and finishing what she started.

From: Hannah Lynn <hlynn123@gmail.com>
To: Alessandra Lynn <alessandra.lynn@gmail.com>
Subject: yesterday

I know you're not sitting on a cloud.

That's what religious people think, right? That dead people are up above the clouds, looking down and watching everything happen from thirty thousand feet?

Presumably with binoculars and x-ray vision so you can see indoors.

It's been three months since I wrote, since the boys got here, and things have been very busy. I don't particularly want to write about it at the moment; I need a break from thinking about Pauline and the boys. What I do want to tell you about is something that happened yesterday that I keep replaying in my head, even though it wasn't all that important. And since I'm not under the delusion that you were watching it happen, I'll write it down.

I had tutoring with Richard. He started out as my chemistry tutor but we've experienced what I believe people in the military call "mission creep," meaning that we've moved beyond chemistry.

It's not what you think. He's still with Amity and they show no sign of letting up, not that I want them to or care one way or another. Perhaps a topic for another email (or not). No, what happened was that yesterday, midway through our session in the library, Richard asked: "What do you want to study in college, Hannah?"

"I'm not even in one yet, and I have to decide what to do once I get there?"

He smiled. "I'm not going to ask where you want to go. We can just keep saying Grant-Covington."

"Go Dwarf Hippos," I said.

"Go Dwarf Hippos."

I should tell you that Richard Greene is starting to grow on me.

"It doesn't have to be super-specific," he said. "Just in general, what do you think you want to do? STEM? Humanities? Pre-law?"

I shrugged. "I guess I'm a blank slate."

"But you know about everything!"

"I know a little bit about a lot of things."

"All right, so of all those things, what do you really care about?"

I sat there, Mom, and I thought about all those blue volumes. The World Book Encyclopedia you brought home from the library with the worn and bent spines, the hours I spent poring over the glossy pages. I learned about everything, but what did I care about? I ran through the alphabet in my mind, searching for something meaningful.

A...Agriculture; Anarchy; Animals.

B...Banking; Black Jack; Botany.

C.

"I care about climate change," I said. "In the sense that I am perpetually pissed off about it."

"Cool," Richard said. "Totally STEM, though there's a business angle too. Amity's mom consults on responsible investing funds."

We spent the rest of the hour talking about colleges: small liberal arts versus big research university; party scene versus lack thereof; northeast versus south versus midwest versus west coast.

"All right," he finally said. "I'll email you later."

"With what?"

"Your matches. Amity has a college counselor and she uses this program to find best-match schools."

"You don't have to do that," I said.

He did it anyway. And do you know what was at the top of my list? That's right. He emailed and when I clicked on the link Tufts' own Jumbo the elephant was looking back at me.

I hate that his damn system worked. But do you know what I did? I emailed him back and told him that was where I'd wanted to go all along, and he was under no circumstances to share that information with anyone else. It makes him the only person who knows about my dream, and for some reason that feels good.

To be continued...

Love,

Hannah

8

Just until Pauline pulls herself together.

It's April—the three month mark—and she is not pulled together. Dad has hushed phone calls with Ben, the caseworker, back in his room and I've overheard enough to know that Pauline's having a hard time with therapy. She's passed her drug tests but missed twelve-step meetings. She never enrolled in the parenting class. What had been weekly phone calls to the boys have tapered off. There were supposed to be supervised visits but Ben cancelled those when she didn't stick with the plan, and Henry and Simon have stopped asking when they're going to see their mom.

Ben comes by but I rarely stick around. I don't like being evaluated, and though he tries to be nice, there's no way around that feeling as he looks at us and our house and then makes notes in his file.

The boys, meanwhile, never miss a therapy session. Dad makes sure of that. I pitch in when I can, but he has to leave work early at least twice a week for those appointments and sometimes more if he needs to meet with the teacher to talk about Simon's learning problems. No one but Larry Lynn would get this much slack at the DPW.

Dad wanted to stay late at work to catch up on some things so I said I'd get the boys from after-school and go to the grocery store to get a missing ingredient for dinner. That's why on this Tuesday night, when I'm already feeling worn out from the week, we are shopping for green beans.

Pauline may be floundering, but Dad is pulling things together. Last month, he put up a big white dry-erase board in the kitchen. He screwed it right into the wall above the counter and announced that predictability is critical and we would therefore be planning out and writing down the week's meals every Sunday night, charting them on the board with necessary ingredients and anticipated cook times in separate columns. I didn't want to tell him that's what I've done in my head for years.

Dad has been reading a lot of books. They're piled on his bedside table, highlighters in a Red Sox mug nearby. Behavior management, attachment theory, learning disorders, special education, self-efficacy. The meal schedule is not an isolated phenomenon: the week before he hung the dry-erase board, he gave me a handout on the ABCs of behavior (antecedent-behavior-consequence), and the week after he decided that we're going to eliminate red food dye and processed flour from the family diet because they're supposed to affect a person's ability to concentrate or something.

Which brings me to the beans. It's Tuesday, and we're having a whole wheat pasta casserole with steamed carrots and beans for dinner, but somehow the beans didn't get written in the ingredient column and so they weren't purchased when Dad went to the store last weekend, and God forbid we swap Thursday and Friday and have fish tonight.

"I'm going to be in aisle five," I tell the boys. "Get some green beans and meet me at the register."

"What's in aisle five?" Simon asks.

"Don't worry about it. Just get good beans, none of the prepackaged ones."

Henry and Simon head for produce. I watch them go, then make my way to aisle five.

Chips. Pretzels. Soda. Oreo fucking cookies. Every single thing here has been processed, dyed, and then processed some more. It's glorious. I walk down the aisle, running my hand over swollen bags of chips, distended by salty air, promising a "massive crunch." I want a massive crunch. I deserve one. I yearn for it. That, and chocolate. Dad's been doing a carob thing, trying to get us to eat frozen bananas covered in the chocolate substitute instead of ice cream.

Fuck carob. After the boys leave I am never, ever putting that shit in my mouth again.

"Screw you!" The shout comes from the far end of the store, and it is unmistakably Henry. People are shouting. I run toward them, dashing past aisles one through four to reach produce.

Henry is standing with Simon behind him, and before

him a boy is sprawled on his back, his nose bleeding. A half dozen other shoppers are watching from a distance. "What the hell is going on?" I ask.

Simon turns to look at me while Henry keeps his eyes on the kid in front of him. "It's nothing," he says over his shoulder.

"Bullshit," I say, advancing on them, "what is this?" I vaguely recognize the boy as a freshman.

"My brother works here," the boy says. "He's gonna kick your ass."

"No one's ass is getting kicked," I say. No one else's ass, at least. "Henry." I step into his line of sight. "Tell me what's going on."

"Are these your kids?" a nearby woman asks.

"No, these aren't my kids," I say. "Do I look like I'm old enough to have kids?"

"I meant, are they your brothers or something? Are they your responsibility?"

I don't have time to draw her the family tree, so I default to "mind your own business." The woman draws in her breath and turns away.

"He called me a retard," Simon says.

I turn. "Shut up," Henry tells him.

"Don't shut up," I say. "He called you that?"

"I couldn't read the word right and he heard me sounding it out."

"What word?" I ask, but then I look at the sign he's pointing to. "Pears." Yeah. It should be p-a-r-e-s, or something like that. English is so damn stupid. "You hit him for calling Simon the r-word?" I ask Henry.

A woman from the florist section of the store has handed the kid a wad of paper towels and he's sitting up now and applying them to his face. "I don't need to talk about it," Henry says.

"Who said anything about what you need?" I ask. "I just want to know if I should hit him again."

The boy on the floor and the woman from the florist stare at me, but before anyone can say anything else there's a shout from the other end of produce: "Hey!" We turn to see a guy, maybe twenty years old, lumbering toward us. He's dressed all in white and his apron is bloodstained. He's wiping his hands on a rag. He must weigh at least 250 pounds. "Who fucked with my brother?" he asks.

Of course, I think. Of course this kid's brother is Greg from the meat section. He comes to a stop in front of us and tosses the rag into the bin with the pears, clenching two massive fists.

"This kid and his re...his brother," the boy on the floor whines.

Greg looks down at him and then up at Henry. "Is that right?" he asks. "You hit my kid brother?"

I step between them. "You need to take, like, two big steps back," I tell him.

"Who the hell are you?" Greg asks. I open my mouth, but then he answers his own question: "You're Hannah Lynn!"

"Uh—yeah."

"Your dad is Coach Larry."

"Sure is."

"Grandpa is a coach?" Simon asks.

I glance back. "He was. Sort of. Like, an honorary coach."

Greg nods. "Head coach for the whole league, yeah. What a great guy."

Dad was head coach of the Evans Beach Little League for years. It didn't actually mean anything; it was a position they created just for him. He led the annual parade in his old Red Sox jersey and cap and tirelessly signed autographs, told stories, and dispensed advice for generations of players who thought they'd follow in his footsteps to the big leagues (but stick around for longer than twelve games). As far as I know there were no obligations to actually perform the functions of a coach. All of the attention, none of the responsibility. It was perfect for him.

"Hey," the kid on the floor says, "he hit me." He sounds concerned that he's being forgotten.

Greg looks at him, then at Henry, then back at me. "These kids with you?"

"They're my nephews."

"You're Coach Larry's grandkids?" Greg asks.

Simon and Henry nod in unison.

"You play ball?"

They shake their heads.

"Aw, you've got to play baseball!"

"Maybe we'll get them started," I say.

Greg nods in satisfaction, his work here evidently done. He looks down at his little brother. "Don't fuck with

Coach Larry's grandkids," he says. They he turns, grabs his rag, and makes his way back to the meat section.

My father is sorting through papers when we get home. "Go put the groceries away," I tell the boys. "Simon, do the dishes, and Henry, start some water for the pasta." They head into the kitchen and I join Dad on the couch, peering over his shoulder. He's flipping through worksheets and quizzes, his grease-lined fingernails tracing comments written in red ink: "incomplete," "redo," "see me."

"This is Simon's work?" I ask.

"His teacher sent a packet home yesterday but I didn't get a chance to look at it." He scrutinizes a math quiz. Simon only completed three of the fifteen problems. "I don't think he knows the things a kid his age should know." He speaks quietly so that the boys won't hear from the kitchen.

"He's supposed to be getting extra help."

"Okay, but—do you think there's something seriously wrong with him? You were always ahead, Pauline was always behind. I don't know what's normal."

I sigh and rub my forehead. "I mean, I never saw him all that much but he always seemed behind. His life's been kind of crazy and I'd understand if he'd missed some things, but I think it's more than that. I think he kind of learns slowly."

"Mmm." Dad nods and cracks his knuckles. "What should we do?"

"I really don't know. Maybe you should talk to Simon's therapist."

It's often my answer, these days. There were things I did know on the night I gave Dad what passed for my approval. I knew that things would be hard. I'd seen enough of the boys to know that they could be rude, and hyper, and general pains in the ass. I was ready for them to break things, or try to, which is why I went to such pains to hide anything precious. I was ready for them to be messy, to leave the milk on the counter, to make a mess in the bathroom.

And general messiness with milk on the counter is, in fact, how things have looked to the outside world when it stops by. To the caseworker. To Reverend Jim, when he's dropped off more donations. Although, to be honest, it's gotten a lot less messy lately. Along with the meal-planning board in the kitchen, Dad has installed systems of bins and charts that sort of function to keep the boys' things in order and their lives on track. There are evenings when I look at the color coding and plastic tubs and think that if Dad had done even half this much when I was a kid and it was just the two of us, then my life would have been very, very different.

Behind the scenes, though, it's not so tidy and I rarely know what the right thing to do is. Behind the scenes, Henry has a temper that makes him punch holes in the plaster downstairs, holes that I spend my Sundays patching while Dad takes the boys to church. Behind the scenes,

Simon seems to be hopelessly overmatched by his school-work. And once, behind the scenes, Henry peed in the wall.

It was a month ago, early March, and I was studying for a massive chem exam. There were three punched holes that I knew of, two in the family room and one in the hallway, all of them associated with a meltdown Henry had over having to finish his homework when a particular show was on. I put off patching the holes until the exam (I got an A-), and then I put it off for another week, and then I started smelling the urine.

Simon had been hiding food. I knew it, Dad knew it, we tried unsuccessfully to talk to him about it. Dad said the therapist told him that it had to do with Pauline not always having enough for them to eat. What we didn't know, during those weeks when I neglected the repair work, was that he was putting food in the walls. And there was something else we didn't know: that Henry had, more quietly and subtly, been hiding food of his own, and that Simon had discovered this and helped himself to some of his big brother's stash.

Henry found out about this, and he decided to obey Dad's ban on fighting in the house and not pound on Simon. There was no ban, however, on urination. Henry found out where Simon was putting his food and peed in that hole, drenching his supply. It was, to be quite honest, a fucking weird thing to do, but it was somehow not that surprising. Henry has a way of carrying on like a normal kid and then something happens and there's a flash behind his eyes, something that seems almost primal, and all bets are off. It's been happening less, and in fact there haven't been any new holes in the wall in recent weeks, but he hit a kid at school a week and a half ago and he wouldn't tell anyone why, even when he was offered fewer days of detention. And it happened tonight with Greg's brother at the store.

The landline rings, interrupting our examination of Simon's schoolwork. I get up and grab it from the table in the front hall. "Hello?"

"Hello, Hannah."

I glance over my shoulder. "Hey," I respond. "What do you need?"

There's a moment of silence on the line. "Is everything okay?" Pauline says.

"Yeah," I say, "all good. We're just late getting dinner started."

"Are the boys around?"

"They're helping in the kitchen and then they need to get started on their homework. That's late too; Dad's schedule has them getting started thirty-five minutes ago."

Pauline chuckles. "I don't remember any schedules from when I was a kid."

"Well, a lot of things have changed. Do you want to talk to the boys?"

"I don't have time tonight, but I need to talk to Dad."

"All right. I'll get him."

"Hannah?"

"Yeah?"

"How are they?"

I lower my voice to make sure they don't hear me from the kitchen. "They're fine. They're good. Why don't you look into coming to see them?"

"I will, soon. I just have to get clearance from my caseworker."

"I don't think having visits cancelled is good for them."

"I'm not the one making the decision."

"Still. You need to follow the plan so you get cleared to come."

There's a long moment of silence on the other end of the line. I think she might have hung up. Then: "Don't tell me how to raise my kids, Hannah."

I want to remind her that she's not raising her kids, that our father is the one raising them and that—contrary to Dad's initial promise—part of the burden is also falling on me. But that seems counterproductive, since taking responsibility for Henry and Simon is exactly what she needs to do, so I bring the phone to Dad and then I go to the kitchen to check on the boys.

Henry is leaning against the counter, reading a copy of To Kill a Mockingbird. Simon is rinsing dishes in the sink. "Good book?" I ask.

"It's okay. Didn't you read it?"

"Nah, I think I skipped that one."

"They let you do that?"

"No. But I faked it at school, and Grandpa wasn't really paying attention at home."

Henry shrugs and goes back to his book. I open a box

of whole wheat pasta and dump it into the boiling water, giving it a stir with a wooden spoon. I look at the boys out of the corner of my eye.

I can see the little differences. They're both flossing and brushing religiously without being reminded. Henry's cursing less, based on a "profanity-reduction program" Dad has him on. He helped me patch the hole he peed in, pouring a whole container of deodorizing powder in first. His face was red and he looked like he'd die of shame the whole time we were working, but he did it nonetheless.

For a moment I let myself wonder what will happen when they go back to Pauline. Where will they live? Where will they go to school? Will she make them do their homework? What will she give them for dinner? Then I catch myself. They're not my problem. They're not my responsibility. I need to focus on my own life. On work. On chemistry class.

On finishing a whole wheat pasta casserole with steamed carrots and green beans.

9

I pick at the blister on my thumb until it pops. The pus
oozes down onto my palm. I watch in fascination and then
rub it against the paper napkin beside my cereal bowl,
slurping some disgusting, cardboard-like health flakes and
chasing it with black coffee. Volume T of the World Book,
its spine cracked and reinforced with packing tape, is
propped open in front of me. I've reread the Titanic article
for the fourth or fifth time and am thinking about back-
tracking to Tinnitus when a noise on the stairs surprises me.

"What are you doing?" Henry asks.

"I have work this morning," I say. "Now that it's
springtime, there are lots of projects. I get paid extra for
weekend hours."

He comes into the kitchen. "Is there more coffee?"

"No."

Henry peers into the empty glass carafe on the coffee maker. I have a sudden image of him smashing it on
the kitchen floor. Instead, his shoulders sag and he turns

away. He looks exhausted. Henry's screaming episodes, what the pediatrician identified as night terrors, have faded to once or twice a month. He still sleeps like crap, though. "You should go back to bed," I tell him.

He shrugs, leaning against the counter and passing a hand over his face. He needs a haircut; his blond hair is sticking up in all directions and as his eyelids flutter I think that he looks very, very young. Henry is thirteen; when I was his age, I was taking care of a lot of things around the house. I could change the oil in the truck; I could unclog a drain; I could get on the phone and convince the power company to leave the lights on until our check cleared. Henry, I'm now realizing, does not know how to use the coffee maker.

"Working on Saturday must suck," he says. "Don't you get cash for having us here?"

"I've always worked," I say, ignoring the comment about money. "I did a little babysitting when I was younger, though I wasn't good at that. When I turned fourteen, I got a work permit and worked at the grocery store sorting bottles people brought in for redemption; that was before there was a machine to do it. The DPW is way better than that."

It's true, I do like working at the DPW. I also like contributing to the monthly bills. Mom and Dad bought this house shortly before Pauline was born. They used the last of Dad's baseball money as a down payment and tried to make a go of it from there. They did okay, but after Mom died it was hard on one salary. So money has always been tight, but with the extra expenses and fewer work hours, we're dipping into the college fund.

"What are you going to be working on?" Henry asks.

"I'm finishing a ditch; there's a drainage problem over on Hutchinson Drive. I was working on it earlier this week." I hold up my hand with the oozing thumb.

Henry stares impassively at me for a long moment. I can't tell what he's thinking; frankly, I never can. "Can I come?" he finally asks.

"What, to work?"

"Yeah."

"Sorry, it's not bring-your-sister's-kid-to-work day."

He turns his attention to the empty coffee maker.

"What would you even do, anyway?" I ask. "Do you know how to do anything?"

"I thought you could show me," Henry says.

Show him what? How to use a shovel? Where to put road cones?

"All right, eat some breakfast and get dressed," I say, surprising myself. "You won't get paid, but Simon has his social skills group this morning and Grandpa's going to be out with me. You'll get some exercise and it will be better than sitting around here by yourself. Wear long pants and a hat, your hair looks like shit. We'll leave as soon as Grandpa and Simon are up."

A bit over an hour later we've dropped Simon off at his group and arrived at the worksite. I've set up cones and lowered myself into the portion of the ditch I've been working on. "Basically," I tell Henry, "we need to square this off, lower that side by about a foot, and then extend the whole thing down to be level with the curb."

Dad is supposed to be supervising but he's on a coffee run. It would be faster if he would just go to the Sunflower Café, but he'd rather die and that means he's driving all the way to the Dunkin' in South Portland, where he'll wind up critiquing spring training with the old guys spending their Saturdays in plastic chairs reading hard copies of the *Press Herald*.

Henry looks at the work ahead of us, shovel in hand. "That seems like a lot."

"Good thing I brought you. Get down here."

"What's going on over there?" Henry points to the far end of the ditch, where a cluster of buckets are arrayed against the dirt wall.

"Stay away from those. There's some sort of seepage. The town engineer has to come look at it on Monday, but it's pretty nasty. We're working this end today."

Henry frowns. "It looks like a grave."

"Trust me, graves aren't this big."

He jumps down.

"Start over there," I say. "Sooner we get started, the sooner we get done."

He attacks his section, wielding the shovel like some sort of weapon in a fight against the earth. Stabbing, pulling dirt up, again and again. I watch him out of the corner of my eye as I work on my own section. It takes a while to learn how to pace yourself. His shoulders and back will kill him tomorrow the way he's going at it, using nothing but muscle to drive the shovel down, no real rhythm, no momentum, no use of his body weight. Leave it to a boy to turn a simple job into an epic competition with himself.

Predictably, Henry runs out of gas. He leans against his shovel and looks at his palms. "Do you have gloves?" he asks.

"Grandpa will, when he comes back."

Henry hoists another shovelful of dirt. "Are you tired?" he asks.

"Nope."

"Me neither."

"Good."

"Why are we doing this?"

"Runoff. If you came over here after a rainstorm, you'd see a few inches of standing water. We get more rain than we used to and the system isn't up for it. It isn't safe."

"So, this is going to fix that?"

"Not by itself, but we're going to use this ditch to lay pipe for a runoff drain."

"You're going to do that too?"

"I might help. It depends."

Henry stands straight, stretching his back, and peers out of the hole and across the road. "Those are some big houses."

"Yup."

"I mean, Jesus. Look at them."

I stop shoveling and stand next to him, peering out of the ditch. "Yeah. They're massive."

He's silent for a moment. His jaw is set, the way I've

learned it is when he's getting mad. "It's fucked up," Henry finally says.

I nod. "I know."

He turns to me. "You do?"

"Yeah, I do. I really do." I think about some of the places he must have lived, the way the caseworker described Pauline's apartment to Dad. I know what he's feeling. "Here's the thing, Henry: there are a million things that will make you feel small. Start giving them real estate in your head and pretty soon there won't be room for anything else."

We're interrupted by the sound of a truck rolling up alongside the worksite. A door slams and a moment later Dad is looming over us. "Break time?" he asks.

"It is now," I say.

Henry and I hoist ourselves up on the edge of the ditch. Dad hands each of us a coffee and crouches down, knees popping. "You're making good progress," he says, engaging in his minimalistic version of supervision.

I nod. Henry looks pleased.

Dad sips his coffee and looks at Henry. "One of the guys at Dunkin' asked me whether you're playing ball this spring. Any interest?"

"Are you still coaching?" Henry asks.

"Coaching? Nah, I haven't been head coach for years. I can give you some tips, though. I think I still remember a few things."

"Were you a good ballplayer?"

"He played in the big leagues," I say. "Everyone who plays in the big leagues is good."

Dad smiles. He picks up a handful of gravel and sifts it between his fingers. "I was as good as I could be," he says. "I wasn't as good as I wanted to be."

"Do you think I could be good?"

"Yeah," Dad says, "I think you have the makings of a ballplayer. I'll look into it. I know the guy who runs the town leagues." Dad stands, groans, and rubs his lower back as though he's the one who's been digging. "Time to get back to it. I shall return."

I grab gloves for Henry from the truck before Dad drives away, nominally to file some paperwork at the office but more likely to grab a short nap in the shade. Then we get back to work.

Henry has renewed momentum, and this time he doesn't stop. I smile as sweat pours down my face. I love this. The musty smell of dirt merging with the odor of my own straining body. My aching muscles. The visible, tangible evidence of hard work: a ditch growing deeper, a corner cut off square. I feel the pieces of the world sliding into place. I feel happy. I feel generous, even toward the kid across from me who, along with his brother, has so upended my life over the last several months. "Henry," I call, "how's school going?"

"Fine."

"Dad says you're actually doing pretty well."

He pauses. "Actually?"

"Well," I say, "it doesn't sound like you were exactly killing it in your old schools."

He spits to one side and digs in again. "Those were shit schools. At least here I can concentrate."

"That's good."

"Good while it lasts."

"How're you getting along with people?"

He hesitates before he responds. "Fine."

"They're probably different from the kids in your old schools."

"People are people."

I straighten my back and lean on the shovel. "Cut the bullshit, Henry. I know how kids in Evans Beach can be. I've lived here all my life."

He glances up as he lifts another shovelful. "I said, they're fine."

"All right." I go back to work. "Who do you like?" I ask after another moment.

"What do you mean?"

"I mean, who do you have a crush on?"

"Fuck off."

"Aw, Henry, we've come so far on the fucking profanity." He laughs. The sun is beating down on us. "Come on, tell your aunt Hannah."

He laughs again and shakes his head. "Yeah, sure, there's a girl in social studies."

"Name?"

"Olivia."

"And?"

"And, she's cute."

"And?"

"And nothing. That's it."

"Well, you're a bad boy with a mysterious past who's

new in town. Irresistible. Jesus, I'm surprised she's not throwing herself at you already."

I've worked my way around the section I'm digging out so that my back is to Henry, and after a moment I realize that he hasn't responded. I stop and turn to him. He's standing with the shovel in hand, gazing off to one side.

"Henry?"

He shakes his head. "It's not as easy as that."

"What isn't?"

"Olivia."

"I was teasing you."

"They know I'm different."

"Yeah." I glance up. "Is that why you hit the kid at school?" I ask. "Was he giving you shit?"

Henry's quiet for a long moment and I don't think he's going to answer. "You know what fumigation is?" he finally asks.

"Uh...yeah, sure. Like, gassing insects and stuff. The town outsources to a fumigation company for the mosquito problem out along the soccer fields."

Henry nods. "It was April Fool's Day, the day I hit that kid."

Of course it was. I'm a complete idiot. "What did they do, Henry?"

"They set up like they were fumigating my locker. Taped it off and sprinkled baby powder and put up a notice with a poison sticker." He jabs his shovel into the ground so hard that he struggles to pull it back out.

"Because they think you've got an infestation?"

"That's the fucking joke. Get it? Because I'm poor. I'm dirty, gross. My mother's a junkie. I have fleas. It's hilarious. They all know, Hannah. It's a small town. Everyone knows everything."

"Yeah, I get that. So, you hit the kid who did it?"

"One of them. The others ran away."

"Why didn't you tell the principal? He would have gone easy on you. You were provoked."

Henry snorts. "No one's going easy. The principal hates me."

"That's not true."

"It doesn't matter. I'll be gone soon, anyway. Back to Portland, or wherever Mom moves us next. No one cares. Yesterday I stayed after class and asked my math teacher for help. She said my next school will probably have 'less challenging curricula' and I shouldn't worry about it."

I shouldn't have brought any of this up. I don't know what to tell him. "Time to get back to work."

We pick up our shovels.

"Oh…my…God."

Henry and I both turn. Brittany O'Neal is standing beside the ditch, looking down. She's wearing running shorts and a sports bra, her six-pack glistening below it, her legs tan and round. Henry stares up at her, his mouth open a full inch. I nudge him with my elbow. "Hi there, Brittany."

"Hannah, what are you doing?"

I raise my shovel and rest it on my shoulder. "What does it look like I'm doing?"

"Are you, like, digging an actual ditch?" Her voice is incredulous, delighted.

"Water won't run off into a virtual one."

"Oh, thank God you're doing something about the water! My Range Rover doesn't have any trouble with it but I worry about my father in his little Miata."

"You live near here now?"

"Right over there. We moved a few years ago. I guess you weren't coming over anymore."

"Well," I say, "it's your lucky day. Glad we could…"

"I knew you were working for the town but I had no idea you were actually out digging ditches!"

I tighten my grip on the shovel. "Yeah, among other duties."

"I guess I never really look down when I go by a worksite."

"We need to get back to it, so…" I half turn away.

"Sure, sure, I just…I have to." Brittany tugs her cell phone from a strap on her upper arm and swipes the screen.

"What are you doing?"

"I have to document this."

"Absolutely not."

"Please, I just…" She raises the phone.

"You're going to take a picture of a child without his parent's consent. That's a federal offense." I have no idea whether that's true and strongly suspect it is not. Nonetheless, Brittany hesitates.

"I'm not a child," Henry says.

"Shut up," I tell him.

Brittany smiles sweetly and shuffle steps to her left, crouching a little bit so that the picture will just be of me. "Per-fe…"

The mistake she made was coming within reach of my shovel. The blade shoots out and neatly clips the phone from her hand, sending it sailing into the far end of the ditch. Brittany doesn't have time to cry out, not even time to move. She's left in a half crouch, her empty hand held out in front of her as though pantomiming the act of taking a picture. A moment passes in which none of us move. Then Brittany slowly straightens. "Hannah," she says, "please get my phone for me."

"Why don't you come down here and get it yourself?"

Brittany smiles and turns to Henry. "Would you hand me my phone?" she asks in a soft, patient tone.

Henry leans his shovel against the wall of the ditch and trots down to where her phone has landed. I watch as he scoops it up, blows dirt off, turns, smiles, and drops it into a bucket full of foul-smelling muck. It lands with a plop. "Oops," he says.

Brittany stares at him for a long moment, then turns back to me. "People are going to hear about this," she says.

"Yeah, just be sure to tell them what you were doing within three meters of an active public works site. You're supposed to be behind those cones."

Brittany flips me off, turns, and heads toward her over-sized house. "You're a loser, Hannah," she calls. "Always have been, always will be."

Henry dissolves into laughter. "Holy shit," he says, "what a piece of work."

"Always has been, always will be," I say.

He peers down into the bucket. "Should I?"

"Leave it." I walk over to him. "You know, Henry, some of the crap those kids are saying to you, about being infested or whatever, it's not so different from what kids said to me when I was a little bit younger than you are now. Actually, Brittany was sort of the ringleader. I never had the right clothes. My hair was never right. There were a few months when Dad hurt his back and wasn't working and I had free lunch. You know how many kids in Evans Beach get free lunch? Not many. They called me poor."

"I know poor. You're not poor."

"We were, for Evans Beach."

"But your dad was Coach Larry."

"Middle school girls don't give a shit about the 1980 Red Sox."

"Did they ever fumigate your locker?"

"They were never that creative. They insisted I had lice, though. They told each other not to touch my hair, not to sit where I had been sitting."

"That blows."

"That's Evans Beach. That's why I'm leaving."

Henry nods, then pauses, listening. "What's that?"

I hear it too. Brittany's phone ringing, deep in the bucket.

"Is that—a horse?" he asks.

"I think so. Brittany does equestrian."

We listen to the neighing coming from the bucket, and this time we both break down laughing.

The work goes quickly after that. We finish by 12:15 and close the site down. I call Dad, who has gone to pick Simon up from his social skills class. He returns, and Henry gets into the back seat with his brother, who peppers him with questions about the ditch before stopping mid-sentence with a gasp. I twist around to look. Henry has peeled his gloves off, and his palms are bloody. "Jesus, Henry, why didn't you stop?" I ask.

He shrugs. "Didn't want to leave you shorthanded."

"Yeah, but that must hurt like hell."

"They're just blisters. When will the pipes go in?"

"Monday, I think. That's why we had to get this done."

"So, it was important?" he asks, looking out the window as we pull away.

"Yeah. It was important."

He doesn't say anything else as we drive back to the DPW and park. We all get out and Simon runs ahead with Dad. "Come on in," I tell Henry. "I'll get you fixed up. There's a first aid kit with plenty of bandages, plus we need to clean those out."

"I'll take care of it myself when we get home."

"It's easier to let someone help. Come in. There's coffee. There's always coffee. I mean it's terrible, we use the leftover to fill potholes out on Route 77, but it is coffee."

Henry is standing with his back to the truck, leaning against the passenger-side door. He looks down at his damaged hands. "Yeah," he says. "All right. I could use some more coffee."

I take him inside.

10

Another three months pass. Three more months during which Pauline edges forward in her reunification plan, making enough progress that a supervised visit has finally been scheduled. Three months during which school ended and the boys went into the town rec summer program. Now it's July, it's hot, and several things have become very evident.

#1: Richard Greene was an outstanding tutor.

I finished junior year with a B in chem, and alongside my usual A in history, a B+ in math, and an A in English, my GPA cruised into the range reported to be typical for Tufts applicants.

#2: Throwing money at therapists works.

Dad sold his signed ball for a few hundred bucks, which probably covered about one and a half sessions with the therapist who doesn't take insurance. We had to go even deeper into the college fund; Dad has a notepad on his desk with meticulous debits against the account and he swears he'll pay it all back. The upside is that the plaster is increasingly safe. It's been many weeks since Henry punched a hole; the boys are sleeping better; and there are signs that they're making something along the lines of friends, particularly Henry. They're getting better at helping with dinner. Is it the therapy? Is it Dad's dinner schedule? Is it the carob? It better not be the damn carob.

This is not to say that things are perfect. The mice, in particular, have been the pits. There must be caches of food I missed, now sealed up inside of the walls. I screamed at the boys the first night I found rodent shit in my blanket. Then I scrubbed the floors and walls with bleach and put out traps. Nothing really worked. In the end, I pitched a small tent on my bed so that I can zip myself inside at night and try to ignore the noises in the walls.

Basically, the boys are doing pretty well and the mice are thriving.

#3: Henry can hit a baseball like a motherfucker.

Dad signed him up for the Babe Ruth League and taught him the basics in the backyard. They stay out there practicing until the sun goes down. Henry loves it and Dad says he's a natural.

It's perfect weather for a ball game. Even the mosquitos know enough to stay away. It rained yesterday and the air is crisp and dry, the base paths packed firm and neither dusty nor muddy, the white lines freshly drawn. You can smell the ocean a half mile away.

Simon's pants are at risk of falling down. The kid is so thin that it's impossible to cinch them tight enough. I jog over to him and examine the situation. He's wearing an official Evans Beach Raiders uniform just like the bigger kids and the belt only goes so tight. I used an awl to make a fresh hole last week, but I see that I needed to go another inch in. "Just keep a hand on your belt, Simon," I say. "Not when you're grabbing a ball, but in between plays, tug 'em up, okay?" I smile and wink at him.

Simon nods. He's far too young for the Babe Ruth League that Henry's playing in. He wasn't able to keep up in Little League and he hated the Challenger League, which is the one for players with special needs. The coach of Henry's team, at Dad's request, made him the ball boy and now he stands a few paces in from the right field line. "Henry's up next," he says.

I turn to home plate. Henry's uniform fits him perfectly as he walks up to bat. I look over at Dad, who is camped out in a folding chair near third base, his old glove tucked beneath his seat.

"You have to move, Hannah," Simon tells me.

"Sorry, buddy. Stay awake out here." I jog down the first base line and as I pass behind the backstop Henry is digging in, holding one hand out like the Sox players he studies on TV. "Go get 'em, Henry!" I call. He doesn't look. Nothing can break his focus when he's playing. I continue on, toward third base and Dad. The pitcher throws and I hear the ball hit the catcher's mitt and the umpire's crisp "strike!"

"Inside!" Dad bellows. The sound doesn't so much cascade through the air as split it open, echoing off the dugouts and the distant trees. Parents on the visiting team's side freeze and stare. They're not used to the massive guy on the third base line. The crowd on our side, in contrast, is accustomed to it, as is the umpire.

It takes a solid thirty seconds for the pitcher to regain his composure. Then he slowly winds up and hurls the ball at Henry, who swings and misses.

"Strike two!"

Now the parents on the other side get loud. Dad leans forward. "Easy, Henry!" he calls.

Henry should lay off the third pitch but he doesn't and he makes contact, sending it looping above the shortstop's head and dropping into shallow left. Dad struggles up from his seat, roaring approval as Henry races to first. I sit down in my butterfly chair next to his.

The next two Raiders strike out. The cleanup batter walks, moving Henry to second, but the fifth hitter leaves him stranded by lining to short. They head out to the field, Henry to his position at second base. I dig around in our cooler for a soda and glance at Dad. He's studying Henry's positioning with an intensity I never see from him under other circumstances, and as the inning gets underway his focus never wavers.

"Hey, Daddy?"

No response.

"Daddy?"

"Hmm."

"Did you call the doctor?"

"What's that, baby?"

"The doctor. You were supposed to schedule a follow-up visit because of the new medication he put you on."

"Yeah."

"Yeah, you did it?"

"Hold on…"

I stare at him, feeling my jaw clench. "Daddy!"

He looks at me and blinks. "What, Hannah?"

"You need to go and see the doctor again."

"All right. I'll call first thing Monday." He smiles at me, reaches over and pats my hand, and then turns back to the game. Evans Beach gets the third out and the players run in to the dugout. Dad cups his hands around his mouth. "Henry!"

Henry stops, mid-stride, his head snapping around and then he pivots and runs toward us. "Yeah?" he calls as he crosses the third-base line.

Dad grunts as he pulls out his glove and heaves himself up from the chair. "Look at me, now," he says, dropping into a low crouch, glove up like he's about to make a play. "Watch my feet."

Henry folds his arms and watches carefully as Dad demonstrates the way he wants him to move laterally for a ball hit to his right and then pivot for the throw to first. Then Henry turns so that he's facing the same direction and imitates. Dad watches approvingly, offers a few more comments, and then slaps him on the back. "Go get 'em."

Henry nods, grins, and runs toward the dugout. Dad drops into his seat, chest heaving. "Damn knees." His knees are the only things he'll admit are messed up. Dad is a battleship plowing through the water and nothing ever stops him. In the last few months, though, I've noticed some cracks in the hull. He's slower getting up, slower getting down, and it takes him a while to get going in the morning. The coughing fits come more regularly, his face stays redder longer, and there are times at night when I come upstairs to the kitchen and I can hear him back in his room, his breathing labored.

"Hi, Hannah."

I twist around in my chair. "Richard! What are you doing here?"

Richard is standing behind me in shorts, sandals, and a tank top. He's holding a leash and a black Lab is sitting in the grass next to him. The dog's tongue is hanging out and she's looking around. Richard is looking at me. "I was walking Lucy," he says. "I saw you sitting over here and wanted to say hi."

"You were walking way over here? Marshall Street is two and three-quarters miles away."

"Two and three-quarters, huh? That's precise."

"I've told you, I work for the DPW."

"Oh, HELL NO," Dad bellows, evidently feeling that he has a better view of the first base line than the home plate umpire and that a ball hooked foul. I feel my face color.

"Dad," I say, "this is Richard Greene."

Dad, becoming aware of Richard, gets to his feet and

holds out a massive hand. "Larry Lynn," he says, "pleased to meet you." Richard's hand is swallowed up and I can see the muscles in his shoulder stand out as he struggles to keep up with Dad's handshake. "You're a friend of Hannah's?"

"He was my tutor last year," I say.

Dad frowns and turns to me. "You had a tutor?" he asks. "You're so smart."

"Hannah is smart," Richard says. "She's smarter than I am. She just needed some help with chemistry."

"Out!" the umpire shouts, and Dad's attention snaps back to the game.

"So, you're going to keep on walking?" I ask.

Richard pauses again. "I thought I might rest a little and watch. I walked two and three-quarters miles, you know?"

"Oh. Okay." We stand in silence for a moment while Dad studies the infield and the dog looks first at me, then at Richard, then back at me. "We could go sit over there," I finally say.

"Over where? The hill?"

"Yeah. I mean, you can see the game pretty well." The hill behind left field is also possibly far enough away to take the edge off whatever stream of abuse Dad is preparing to unleash on the umpire or the pitcher or the opposing manager.

"Sure," Richard says, "let's go."

Richard, Lucy, and I make our way down the left field line and up the hill, where we sit. We can still hear Dad when he critiques an attempted tag at second base for the shortstop, the ump, and everyone else assembled around or near the field.

"Your father's a character," Richard says.

"He is that."

"You didn't tell him you were being tutored?"

"I probably mentioned it about a dozen times. Dad's not always focused. He has a lot going on."

"You still have your sister's kids?"

"For now, yeah."

"Which ones are they?"

I point out Henry and Simon. "There, by second base, and over there, the ball boy."

Richard watches the game for a moment. "Do you mind if I ask you a question?"

"I guess not."

"Why are they with you to begin with?"

I exhale, realizing that, while the boys aren't a secret, I've never explained their situation from beginning to end. To anybody.

"You don't have to say," Richard says. "It's your business."

"No, I don't mind. It's just…a long story."

"I've got time."

"All right," I say, "we'll see how far we get." Lucy puts her head down on her paws and I lean forward, running my hands through her fur as I talk. Richard sits very still and listens, his eyes not moving from my face, even when the crowd below us cheers or Dad levels another high-decibel accusation at the umpire, who by this time is probably thinking about a career change. Richard listens as my mom gets sick and as Pauline starts skipping school and hanging out with older guys; he listens as Pauline gets pregnant and Mom goes to hospice and dies faster than her doctors thought she would; he listens as Dad falls apart and for all intents and purposes stops being a parent, and as Pauline stays away for longer and longer periods of time and eventually just stops coming back (unless she needs money). He listens as I hold things together until Dad gets back on his feet. Finally, Richard listens as I describe the boys coming to stay with us last winter and three months becoming six months. By that time, it's the top of the ninth and there are two outs. Lucy rolls over and lets me stroke her belly.

"She likes you," Richard says.

"She's sweet."

"Not for everyone. Lucy is short for Lucifer."

"You named your dog Lucifer?"

He laughs. "She was a rowdy puppy."

Lucifer murmurs as I rub her belly. "I've been talking too much," I say.

Richard shakes his head. "Not too much. It's an incredible story."

"I don't know if I'd call it incredible."

"You're the teller, the audience gets to decide."

"How's Amity?" I ask.

"Probably fine," Richard says. "I haven't seen her in a while."

"No? Why not?"

He shifts his weight to one side and plucks a tuft of grass. "Anthony Russo."

"I'm not familiar."

"Anthony Russo is from Freeport. He goes to Yale. He'll be a sophomore this fall."

"Okay."

"He got a perfect score on his SAT and he does very high-priced coaching on the side."

"Got it."

"They're spending a lot of time together."

"Didn't she already take the SAT?"

"Yeah."

"Ah."

"He's an econ major," Richard says. "He speaks four languages. He has his own boat. Amity's been on it with him all summer."

"He sounds like a complete prick."

"That's kind of you to say. He's probably a great guy."

"No," I say, "Anthony Russo is a prick. Here's another story for you. He's going to graduate from Yale in three years and he's going to sell his boat and move to New York. He's going to get a job at an investment bank and he's going to work ninety-hour weeks and have a meteoric rise to partner. He's going to have an incredible apartment in Manhattan and a place on Long Island, and he's going to get a new boat, way bigger and nicer than the one he has now."

"I'm not sure this is making me feel better," Richard says.

"Anthony Russo is arrogant," I say. "Anthony Russo

doesn't play by the rules. He thinks ethical guidelines are for other people, and he cuts corners and gets greedy and eventually the SEC catches on. One day Anthony Russo shows up at his office and federal agents are waiting for him. They've been tapping his phone, and his assistant, who hates him, is testifying. They put Anthony Russo in handcuffs and walk him out of his big, beautiful office in Midtown Manhattan and into a black SUV and they take him away. The house on Long Island gets sold, and the boat gets sold, and Anthony Russo, now friendless and penniless, goes away for a long, long time."

"That's...that's a lot."

"I'm the storyteller, you're the audience, remember?"

"Well, I love that story."

"I thought you would." My eyes drift back to the field. "Wait a minute...that's Henry coming up to bat." There's a player on first and another on second. I look at the scoreboard. It's the ninth inning, the Raiders are behind by two runs, and there are two outs. "Holy shit," I say, processing the situation on the field. "Holy shit."

"What?" Richard asks, frowning at the scene below us.

"This is...Henry is the winning run...just wait. Watch."

Henry swings, hard. "Strike one!" the umpire calls. Everyone is standing up and cheering. Henry shakes his head and digs in. The pitcher glances at second and then throws again. This time Henry doesn't swing but the umpire calls out: "streee—ike two!"

"Bullshit!" I yell as loud as I can. "That was outside!"

Lucy stares at me but my voice is lost in the noise; the fans are going nuts now.

Henry steps back for a moment, taps his cleats, and glances toward third base where Dad is sitting. He pauses, nods, then steps back in. I'm on my feet, clenching my fists so hard that my nails are cutting into my palms. The next pitch is going to be right down the middle. I know it, Henry knows it, everybody knows it. This guy is throwing fire and he wants to end the ballgame.

The pitch is actually a bit inside but it doesn't matter. Henry swings smooth and he swings hard, and I know he's done it as soon as I hear the solid crack of the bat on the ball. It sails overhead, arcing against the summer sky, impossibly high and impossibly far, and when it comes to rest beyond the left field fence I finally turn away and see Richard looking up at me, a bemused smile on his face, and I realize I've been screaming. "That shit doesn't happen in chess, does it?" I ask.

He laughs. "No," he says, "it doesn't."

The crowd is roaring below us, and over it all I can hear Dad roaring "THAT'S MY BOY!" Henry is circling the bases, one fist in the air, two other Raiders running and dancing and shouting ahead of him.

"Sonya! Get us your best table!"

"Sol's doesn't have a best table," I say.

"Boys," Dad announces to the usual assembly of

lobstermen at the counter, "my grandson is a star. Sonya! We're here to celebrate!"

Sonya comes out from behind the counter. "Well," she says, grabbing a pile of menus, "maybe he'll be able to hit left-handed pitching better than his gramps."

Dad barks with laughter. One of the guys at the counter raises his mug in recognition and Dad slaps him on the back so hard he almost falls off his stool. Sonya leads us down the aisle between the counter and the booths to the back corner. Henry follows in his dirty uniform, then Simon, then Dad. Richard, Lucy, and I bring up the rear. Sol Jr. peers out of the kitchen at the dog, realizes she's with Dad, and goes back to work.

Dad insisted that Richard and Lucy come. Two months ago, even six weeks ago, it would have completely horrified me. I wouldn't have allowed it. There would have been too many permutations and combinations of ways in which Henry and Simon could act up and humiliate me, too much out-of-control and aggressive and frankly weird shit they could pull. The chances of a normal meal with a guy they didn't know would have been basically nil. Now, I'm willing to say it's 40/60.

And so Richard squeezed into the back seat in between the boys while Lucy rode in the truck bed with Henry's baseball gear and an assortment of junk Dad has accumulated from the DPW. I gave him every out I could, telling Dad that Richard probably had somewhere he needed to be and that Lucy was only midway through her walk, but Richard didn't take the cue and now he's sliding into the booth next to me while Lucy settles in the corner with a bowl of water Sonya brings from behind the counter. Then she sets menus down, plus paper placemats and a cup of crayons. "Congratulations, Henry," she says.

"Thanks."

Simon reaches for the crayons. I look around Sol's. The scarred wooden floor. The TV playing above the counter. The smell of fish and diesel in the air.

"I've never been here before," Richard says.

"You've never been to Sol's?" Dad asks. "How can you never have been to Sol's?"

"Not everyone comes to Sol's, Dad," I tell him. "Richard didn't grow up in Evans Beach."

"Where are you from?" Dad asks.

"We used to live in Freeport," Richard says. "We moved to Evans Beach when I was in ninth grade."

"What do your folks do?"

"They're both doctors at Maine Med. I hear you used to play for the Red Sox?"

Dad shrugs modestly. "I was in the Sox organization. Twelve games in the big leagues. You a fan?"

"I'm thinking of becoming one, after the game today. You're a great player, Henry."

Henry smiles at Richard. "Thanks."

Dad launches into a monologue on Henry's strengths as an infielder and his natural power as a hitter. Richard listens politely, Henry with barely suppressed pride. Simon is occupied with the crayons and the back of his placemat and after a few minutes I lean over for a closer look. "Holy cow, Simon, that's really good!"

He covers the drawing with both hands. "It's not ready yet!"

"No? It looks…amazing."

"Let me see," Dad says.

Simon sighs, apparently resigning himself to people who don't understand art, and holds up the place mat.

"Is that…" I say.

"Me?" Dad finishes.

Simon nods.

It is, in the profile that reflects Simon's positioning relative to Dad. He's done it with the black crayon and some gray shading. "Simon," I say, "it's so good. I mean, I can't believe it. It looks just like him."

"I look sad," Dad says.

"I drew you how you look," Simon says. He sets the placemat back down and starts shading beside the eyes.

I watch his hands. The more attention I've paid to his schoolwork, the more convinced I am that he isn't getting enough help. Math, reading, social studies: none of it comes easily for him. Writing is torture. But this…this seems effortless. "Did you know Simon could draw?" I ask Henry.

"Yeah, he's always been good at drawing. Better than good. He just doesn't like to show anyone."

"Does your mom know?"

"I used to try and show her. I don't think she really got it."

Sonya returns to the table. "Everything good?"

Dad nods. "Great."

We place our orders. Sonya ignores a few regulars at the counter who are trying to get her attention in order to bring our drinks out right away. I notice that Dad's iced tea is in an extra-big glass.

"So, you're in Hannah's grade?" Henry asks Richard.

"I am," Richard says.

"Where do you live?" Simon asks.

"Marshall Street."

"Is that one of the nice streets with the big houses?"

"Simon..." I say.

"It's okay," Richard says. "I guess the houses are pretty big." He turns to Dad. "What do you think about Hannah maybe heading to Boston?"

Dad frowns. "Boston?"

"To college. Tufts."

"Her mother went there!"

"Did she?" Richard asks. "You didn't tell me that."

I shrug. Now I want Richard to shut up. "Doesn't really matter."

"Sure it does, that's legacy."

"You want to go to Tufts?" Dad asks.

Richard turns to look at me, brow furrowed, probably wondering why my own father doesn't know anything about my college plans. I feel my face color.

"I was thinking about it," I say. "Maybe applying. Richard did some work with me, in tutoring, just sort of thinking about where I might want to go to school. Like, what might be a match. He used some kind of system."

"Where's Boston?" Simon asks.

"It's in Massachusetts."

"Do you have to fly to get there?"

"No, you drive."

"So, you'd come back and visit a lot?"

"Yeah, sure. If I get in. Weekends, sometimes, and I'd be back for Thanksgiving."

Dad puts an arm over the back of the booth. "Hannah's mom was going to Tufts when we met," he tells Richard. "The Sox had just sent me back down to the minors and let me tell you, I thought it was the end of the world. I mean, getting called up, that was the best thing that ever happened to me. Up to that time, that is." He glances at me. "Having my girls was better. But at that point, yeah, I'd been to the top and then, twelve games later, it was over."

"What happened?" Richard asks.

Dad shakes his head. "It's just baseball. They needed something else. Like Sonya said, someone who could hit some left-handed pitching. Plus, I was a second baseman and they needed to make room on the roster for more relievers. It just didn't line up. I could have stuck around, they might have called me back for a few games if someone got injured, but in my heart I knew that I wasn't going to consistently play at the major league level."

I've heard this many times before, but Henry is listening with rapt attention. "What did you do?" he asks.

Dad looks at him and laughs. "What did I do? I went to a bar, my boy. I walked until I found a bar in a restaurant with no TV to show me the Red Sox game, and then

I sat down and I had a drink. I had a few. And there, at a table in the corner, was the most beautiful woman I'd ever seen, trying to do her homework."

I glance at Richard, worried that he's bored, but his eyes are on Dad and he's nodding along. "Did she recognize you?" he asks. "I mean, as a ballplayer?"

"She did not," Dad says. "Alessandra was not a baseball fan. She ignored me for about an hour while I aired my grievances to the bartender and then she got up and came over and said: 'Excuse me, I couldn't help but overhear that the Red Sox just sent you down to the minor leagues. In fact, everyone in the bar couldn't help but overhear. Probably everyone on the whole street. And I know you think it's a tragedy of epic proportions but I have a paper due on a truly epic tragedy, The Oresteia, in just under twelve hours, so if you would keep your voice down I would dearly appreciate it.'" Dad throws his head back and laughs, slapping the table.

"What happened then?" Henry asks.

"Well," Dad says, "I was sick of hearing myself talk at that point, too. I was sick of analyzing my batting stance and wondering if I would have been better as a third baseman. So I took my beer, and I went over to her table, and I asked her to tell me about that book she was writing a paper on."

"The Orest-something?" Henry says.

"Oresteia," I tell him. "It's a play by Aeschylus."

Dad nods. "And to this day, I have no idea why she did. She should have told me to hit the bricks, but she ordered a glass of wine and told me about the play, and a bunch of others, and no one said a word about baseball for the rest of the night." He smiles. "I have no idea when she got that paper done." There's silence in the booth for a moment, and then he looks at me. "You should go to Tufts," he says. "Your mom loved it."

"Well," I say, "Richard's program did match me up with it, so maybe it's a good idea." I neglect to add that I have been determined to go for the last ten years.

"Or that one in South Carolina," Dad says. "You could go there, too."

Richard almost chokes as he takes a drink.

"We'll see," I say, nudging him in the side.

"Where are you going to go to college?" Henry asks Richard.

"I want to go to Harvard," Richard says.

Dad whistles. "When I was in the minors, we played an exhibition game against the Harvard varsity squad. Smart guys. They couldn't play worth shit, but smart."

Sonya arrives with the food. She sets her tray down and distributes the plates. "More tea, Larry?" she asks, leaning over his shoulder to peer into his glass.

"Yes, please," he says, and it occurs to me that once I leave and the boys go back to Pauline he'll be all alone and maybe that's not the best thing. The idea of my dad on a date is appalling to me, but on the other hand he shouldn't spend the rest of his life with the guys at the DPW. Maybe he could get a dog, I think, looking at Lucy resting in the corner.

Sonya returns with Dad's refill and an empty plate, which she sets down in the middle of the table. Dad and the boys take their burger buns and toss them onto it, leaving the patties naked on their plates alongside the side salads they've substituted for fries. I hesitate for a moment, then do the same. Richard looks on, eyebrows raised.

"We're…um…sort of reducing highly processed flour," I tell him. "It's basically a health thing Dad's trying with, you know…us. We should probably just order them without the buns, but we like the ritual."

"Hyperactivity," Dad says around a giant wad of salad he's stuffing into his mouth. "The brain-gut connection. Peptides leak right out of the gut and inflame neural tissue."

"Let's not talk about gut leaks during dinner," I say.

"Well," Richard says, "neither of them seems hyperactive, so I guess it must be working." He takes his burger off of the bun and tosses the bread onto the pile. Dad washes his salad down with half a glass of tea, stifles a belch, and nods his approval.

Silence falls over the table. The boys demolish their food. Sonya circles back to check on us a few more times. "I thought this was a celebration," she says as she's clearing away empty dishes. "You all have gotten so quiet. Come on, what's dessert going to be?"

The boys perk up and turn to Dad. "Let's see," he says, patting his chest pocket for reading glasses and looking at the menu. "I'm thinking grapefruit and brussels sprouts."

Henry rolls his eyes but Simon seems concerned.

"How about beets?" Sonya asks. "I think we have a beet casserole in the back. Should I stick a candle in it and bring it out?"

Simon shakes his head, frowning.

"All right," Sonya says, "I guess you'll have to order off the menu. What are you thinking?"

"Ice cream!" Simon tells her.

"Oh," Henry says, "can we do the trawler? Please can we get the trawler?"

Sonya turns to Dad, eyebrows raised. Sol's trawler would be the biggest departure from the food plan imaginable, but this is clearly a special occasion. He rubs his forehead, glances at the boys, and grins. "We do have an extra stomach tonight. We'll have the trawler, just no ice cream with red dye in it."

"So that's like, cherry?" Sonya asks.

"Cherry, I guess," Dad says. "Probably some of the others. Do you want me to come look?"

"You'd better."

Simon gets up to let Dad slide out of the booth. Sonya leads him to the kitchen and Simon sits back down. I take the opportunity to look at the drawing again. "It really is good, Simon," I say.

"I'm sorry he looks sad."

"Like you said, you have to draw what you see."

"It's funny," Henry says, peering over, "I don't think of Grandpa ever being sad but when I see it on Simon's paper, I know it's right. It's like the drawing is truer than his actual face."

"Do you think it means he really is sad?" Simon asks.

"Well, he's sad sometimes," I say. "Everyone gets sad sometimes."

"But really sad," Simon says. "Like, sadder than he should be."

"I don't know. How sad should he be?"

"We should do something to make him feel happier," Simon says.

I look over at Lucy. A dog may definitely be in order.

"You can't stop the people you love from being sad," Richard says to Simon. "All you can do is stick around until they get through it."

"Like a storm?" Simon asks.

"Yeah, like a storm."

"He'll be better when we're gone," Henry says. We all turn to look at him.

"What do you mean?" I ask.

"When we go back to Mom. He'll be less stressed. You guys can go back to eating whatever you want."

"You think he'll be better off without you?" Richard asks.

"I know so."

Richard looks as if he has something more to say, but Dad and Sonya return to the table bearing a trawler. "It turns out that damn dye is in near everything," Dad says. "We had to do it with vanilla, butterscotch, and rum raisin."

"We'll make it work," Richard says, distributing the spoons Sonya sets down.

"Good luck, all," she says.

"I don't know, Dad," I say after Sonya has gone. "Do you think we can do it?"

"We can if we work together," Dad says.

A trawler is a long plastic dish, vaguely resembling a boat, with twenty-two scoops of ice cream in a glorious, multicolored extravaganza. This one is a bit monochromatic but the overall impression is the same: it's enough ice cream to kill a horse.

"This isn't a problem for hyperactivity?" Richard asks.

"Total myth," Dad says as he pops a spoonful of vanilla into his mouth. "Sugar doesn't cause hyperactivity."

It does cause high blood pressure, I think, but then I decide to enjoy the moment and not think about Dad's metabolism.

"You know a lot about this stuff," Richard says.

"He's done some reading," I say.

Dad shrugs. "I've tried to figure things out."

"Have you had one of these before?" Simon asks me.

"Nope."

"You did," Dad says, "once. On Pauline's birthday. You were too little to remember."

"That's cool," Simon says. "We never really do ice cream on our birthdays."

"What about cake?" Dad asks him. "Your mom gets you cakes, right?"

Simon shrugs. "Sometimes. Sometimes we do stuff for birthdays. She did a good birthday for Henry. I remember it."

"What good birthday?" Henry asks. "I don't remember any good birthday."

"The one with the piñata!"

"Oh."

Dad and I look at each other, then at Henry. "She got you a piñata?" I ask.

"Yeah. It was...just random," Henry says. "I think she got it from a party store or something and hung it up in the living room and gave us a bat to hit it."

"Seems like a bad idea," I say.

"We weren't blindfolded or anything, and there wasn't much else in that apartment for us to hit. The thing is, though, that no one understood that it had to be filled with candy first. So, the stupid horse was hollow and it was impossible to break because it was so light. Like, every time we hit it, it just swung away, and then when we finally broke it..." He trails off, and shrugs.

"It was an empty piñata?" I ask.

Henry nods.

"I just liked hitting it," Simon says. "I liked that we all did it together, all three of us, and that was what was fun about it."

I glance at Richard but he's keeping his eyes on his food. "Less talk, more eating," I say. "There's a lot of ice cream here."

We do it. It's hard to believe, but we do. Sonya checks in on us and expresses her amazement and encouragement. By the end I think that the bananas might be spared, but they are not. They are not, in fact, really recognizable as bananas, given how much sugary milk they have absorbed, but they are devoured nonetheless, and in the end we all sit back in the booth, stunned and content.

"None of you looks really...good," I tell them.

"Neither do you, but we did it," Henry gasps. "That's all that matters."

Several of the guys from the counter come by the table to congratulate us on finishing a trawler and, secondarily, Henry for winning the game. Dad thanks them and puts the meal on his tab. He finishes off his iced tea, which Sonya has topped off a few more times than is necessary, gets up, and makes his way down the aisle, a boy on each side of him. He towers over Henry but leans on his shoulder.

I watch Simon and Henry go and marvel: the boys made it through a dinner out with a stranger and his dog, and they acted like relatively normal people. They were even, in their quirky ways, cute and charming.

Richard and I slide out of the booth and Lucy gets to her feet. I take the place mat Simon was drawing on, carefully fold it, and tuck it into my back pocket. "When do they go back to their mom?" Richard asks.

"There's a whole reunification process. She had to take a parenting class and go to therapy. It's taken a while; sort of two steps forward, one step back, but she's finally doing better and she's coming over next weekend. It will be the first time they'll see her since January, so it's sort of a big deal. She'll visit us and a caseworker will be there. Then they'll visit her and the caseworker will monitor that, too, and then eventually they'll be able to stay with her on their own."

We walk out of Sol's and join the other three in the parking lot. "Hannah," Dad says, "you think you can drive us home?"

"Sure."

"Thanks. I could, I'm just tired."

"No problem."

Richard and the boys climb into the back seat and Dad starts to walk around to the passenger side.

"Daddy?"

He turns. The streetlamp outside of Sol's highlights the crevices in his weathered face, making him look even more like Simon's drawing. "Yeah, baby?"

"Are you happy?"

He grins. "Of course I'm happy. You make me happy."

"Because if, you know, you ever wanted to get a dog or something, that would be fine. Or even…maybe…go on a date?"

He blinks, then laughs. "What in God's name are you talking about?"

"I'm just saying, it would be fine with me."

He snorts. "A dog." He shakes his head and walks over to the passenger door. "I like this Richard," he says.

The other three are inside the truck and presumably can't hear. "Yeah," I reply. "He's all right."

We get into the front seat and I pull out of the lot, heading back to Evans Beach.

11

Simon's drawings on the name cards are impeccable but his spelling is not. Each one of us is shown in profile, completely recognizable. Me, Henry, Dad, and Simon himself. I circle the table. "I have a second H in my name," I say.

"Sorry."

"It's okay, I can fix it." I lean over and look at the card beside my own. "Mom." The sketch of Pauline captures her jawline and the wave of her hair. I pick it up for a closer look, then swap it with Henry's so that she's sitting between Dad and Simon.

"What time is it?" Simon asks.

"I don't know," I say, "what time is it?" I point to the clock on the wall.

"You know I don't like that kind of clock."

"The little hand is pointing..."

"Just tell me!"

He's on edge. We all are. "It's twelve after one, buddy."

"She was supposed to be here at twelve thirty."

"I know." I suppress the impulse to quiz him on how late that makes her.

"When will she be here?"

"Any minute, probably." I walk over to the big picture window and look down the road. Simon's pacing is killing me. "Do you want to go check on Henry? I think he's downstairs. I'll call as soon as she gets here."

"Okay, Hannah." Simon heads for the stairs. When he first came I worried that he wouldn't follow directions; now I worry that he'll do anything someone tells him to.

A car rolls to a stop in front of the house and I straighten my back, stomach clenching. It's an old blue sedan I haven't seen before and the driver is on the far side, visible only as a silhouette. She waits for a long moment, then turns off the engine and slowly gets out.

The first thing I think is that she still resembles our mother. Pauline rests her hands on the roof of the car and gazes across it, looking at the house. Her eyes drift across the façade until they come to rest on me, framed in the window. I start to raise my hand in greeting and then stop so that I'm just awkwardly flapping my arm at my side. For some reason this makes me angry. "Guys," I call, "she's here."

The house, which had been uncharacteristically still, springs to life. Simon is running up the stairs and Dad is rumbling out of his room and down the hall. "Henry," I call, "come on."

"He's coming up soon," Simon says. "Where is she?"

"Outside."

Simon pulls the front door open and looks at his mother. She's come out from behind the car and freezes, looking back at her younger son. Then she starts up the front walk like a woman on a tightrope, or maybe someone walking the plank on a pirate ship. She makes it halfway and then Simon comes free from whatever is holding him and shoots down the path, throwing his arms around her. Pauline's eyes go wide and she rocks back and forth, hesitating with arms raised as though she doesn't know what to do. Put them around your kid, I think. Wrap your fucking arms around the son you haven't seen in almost seven months. "I'll check on Henry," I say.

Henry is in the family room, sitting on the edge of the air mattress. I look around. The place is a mess; the labeled plastic bins for their clothes have not been in use recently. T-shirts and sneakers and socks litter the room. It occurs to me that Ben the caseworker may take a look around and that we probably should have cleaned up, but it's too late now. "Henry," I say, "your mom is here."

"I know," he says. "I heard."

"Don't you want to come up and see her?"

He nods but doesn't look up.

"This must be weird," I say.

"How does she look?" Henry asks.

"She looks the same as she always did," I say. "She's your mom. She's upstairs. We need to go say hi to her. There's some lunch."

Henry nods and looks around at his makeshift home, maybe reflecting on the day when he'll have to pack up and leave with his mother. "All right," he says. "We'll go up together?"

"Yeah, we'll go together."

He stands and we make our way up to the front hall and then into the living room. Pauline is sitting on the couch by the window and Simon is sitting next to her, close but not too close, and Dad is in the chair across the room, sitting on the edge. Pauline turns to us as we enter. "Henry," she says, "you've gotten so big."

He nods and looks over his shoulder at me. Why is he looking at me? Am I supposed to confirm that he is, in fact, growing?

Pauline follows his gaze. "Hi, Hannah."

"Hi, Pauline."

"Dad says you're working at the DPW."

"Yeah."

"And you're done with school?"

"No, I'm about to start senior year."

"Oh."

I wait for the college question, but it doesn't come. We're all still for a long moment, an image of a family, and it feels as if we stay still, don't move or say anything, then the illusion can be preserved, but Dad brings his hands together like a thunderclap and looks around. "Carrot cake!" he cries. "There's nothing wrong with a backwards lunch. Henry and Simon helped me make carrot cake, and we should eat it right now." He stands, Simon stands, and just like that the room is in motion. Dad gets Simon to help him bring the cake to the dining room table along with a big, machete-like knife that he insists on using for such occasions. Henry hangs back, hovering near the doorway between the living room and the front hall with his hands in his pockets. Pauline stands, finds her balance, and circles the living room. "Didn't we used to have another couch in here?" she finally asks.

"Yeah," I say, "I moved it, so…yeah. Anyway. You heard that Henry's playing baseball, right?"

She looks at Henry. "Just like Dad."

"He's good."

Pauline raises her eyebrows and shrugs. Henry says nothing. She glances at the photo albums on the shelf, one still stained with pizza sauce, but doesn't reach for them.

"And Simon's taking art classes. He drew the pictures on the name cards."

Pauline briefly looks around as though wondering where said name cards would be, then pulls her phone out and taps it. I look at Henry, who avoids my eyes and departs for the bathroom. Simon and Dad return to the kitchen to get plates and forks.

"When does Ben come?" I ask.

Now Pauline looks at me. "Who?"

"The caseworker. He's supposed to supervise this, right? Make sure you're on the road to being a mom again?"

Pauline tucks her phone back in her pocket. She's silent for a long moment, shifting her weight tentatively from one foot to the other as though she's on unstable ground. "You have no idea, Hannah."

"I have no idea about what?"

"You have no idea what this year has been like."

"I know what this year has been like over here, Pauline. It's been all about taking care of your kids."

"Is that what you think? That I wanted to dump my kids on you and Dad?" She looks out the window at her car, silently shaking her head.

"Cake is served," Dad announces, returning from the kitchen. "Come and get some."

Pauline walks toward the table, stumbling slightly as she passes me. I lean toward her. I can smell her breath and her old, familiar shampoo. "Make a big deal," I whisper. "About the drawings." Then I turn away and walk out the front door and into the yard.

It's hot, for Maine. It's hot for anywhere. I'm wearing cutoffs and a T-shirt, and I think about changing into an even lighter tank top but I am not going back. I peer inside and see everyone milling around the carrot cake and then I pick my way across the front yard. The car Pauline arrived in is unlocked and she can't see me opening it from the table where she is hopefully saying something nice to Simon. I open the door and look inside the glove box but there's nothing but a few papers and a tire gauge. I glance at the registration—some guy named Doug—and close it back up. Nothing in the pocket behind the passenger seat. I circle around and open the back door on the driver's side, crouching down in the street and peering underneath the front seat. There it is. I reach in and pull out an almost empty bottle of whiskey, holding it up to the light and inspecting the remaining liquid.

It's the kind she used to drink. The mint on her breath is what she used to cover it up. Her unsteady step in the living room, the pause before she spoke, the glazed look in her eyes. I've seen her like this before.

I could throw the bottle away, heave it into the woods. She's not drunk off her ass. Everyone has lapses. This visit to see me and Dad and her sons after all these months, it has to be hard for her. So what if she had a drink? People drink.

I look up the street one way and then the other. This is bullshit. Pauline has plenty of problems, but they're her kids. They're her responsibility, not mine. Not Dad's. I know all this, have known it since the evening they arrived, but looking at the liquor bottle I know something else, too: it doesn't matter who should take care of them, what matters is who can. And, when I ask myself that question, I am faced with an answer I would not have believed back in January.

Twelve games with the Boston Red Sox. Forty-two at bats. A .203 major league batting average, two runs batted in, one walk. Assistant Supervisor for the Evans Beach DPW, honorary coach of Little League, king of Sol's Diner. For the immediate future, my father, Larry Lynn, is the best chance these kids have got.

Dad probably thought he was doing me a favor, that night at Sol's, making it a team decision and giving me some control over my destiny. What he was really doing was giving me responsibility. He was giving me this moment on a blazing hot street with a mostly empty bottle of liquor in my hand. I tilt it one way and then the other, feeling the weight shift, and I know that it is inevitable. They could get through this visit; they could get through the next, and an overnight and maybe even a month or two back together, but as long as Pauline is drinking, then sooner or later something will happen and one of the kids will get hurt.

Ben will show up soon. He'll need a place to park, and our little driveway is full. He'll pull in behind Pauline and he'll walk past her car to get to the front walk. He'll glance in the passenger-side window as he goes by. I duck back into the car and tuck the bottle into the console between the front seats where it will be perfectly visible as he approaches the house. Then I close the door and hurry away.

The fence has never done justice to the graveyard. The oldest stones are from the early nineteenth century. I don't know how many there are but hundreds of lives have come to rest here over the two centuries it was accepting new customers. And all around it, a crappy chain-link fence. I enter through one of the three gates; it creaks loudly as I open and close it.

There's a gravestone that has always fascinated me. I wander for a moment before I find it. A couple, both of whom lived into their eighties. He died before she did, but only by ten months. Their names and dates are etched near the top, and below them an inscription: "We had it all: friends, children, grandchildren, good times with lots of laughs, and love." Did they compose it together, I wonder. Maybe in their final years, looking ahead to their own inevitability, they also looked back and they wrote this down. Can it be true? Do people really make it to the finish line filled with love and satisfaction? Do they look back with gratitude instead of looking ahead to the years stretching away that they will not be present for, as my mother must have done?

I hear the crunch of gravel from the direction of my house. Someone has pulled up behind Pauline's car. There's a pause and then a car door slams. I stand very still and listen, resisting the urge to run back, to undo what I did, not because I want to protect Pauline but because I know what it will mean. It will mean the boys will have months, possibly many more months, staying here while their mother tries to work things out. It means that my father may need to handle them, alone, when I leave at the end of next summer.

I look at the gravestone for another moment. Then I turn and walk away.

12

"I'm Bethany, and I'm going to be walking backward, so tell me if I'm about to step in a hole!"

There's scattered laughter. I want to push the girl into a hole myself, but then again it's the second time today I've heard that line. We walk slowly, falling to the back of the crowd as the tour begins.

It's a gorgeous September day, the first real day of fall. The sky is crystal and blue, the air is crisp, and there's just enough of a chill to warrant one of my best flannels (identical to one Mom was wearing in a rare college-years photo).

Richard picked me up early, bringing donuts for the boys. After our dinner at Sol's, his route for walking Lucy shifted and he comes down our street several times a week. It's a long walk but he says that Lucy likes the exercise. He stops at our house and lets Henry and Simon throw sticks for her to chase. We sit on the grass and watch them. Sometimes we talk about college-application essays, and sometimes we talk about Henry's baseball games and Simon's art classes, and sometimes I talk to him about Pauline.

We haven't seen her again in the two months since her visit. The caseworker spotted the bottle, just like I knew he would, and there were consequences, just like I knew there would be. The whole reunification plan had to begin again.

Richard and I drove south this morning and by the time we reached the Piscataqua River Bridge we were deep into a debate about the Lord of the Rings. We both have strong feelings; his is that it is the greatest story ever set to paper and mine is that it is stupendously overrated and far inferior to Lloyd Alexander's Chronicles of Prydain. The conversation grew heated, and before we knew it, a sign was welcoming us to Cambridge, Massachusetts, established 1635.

Richard has visited Harvard before, with his parents, but he's never been on a tour. I was more or less indifferent, and honestly the guide—a junior majoring in applied mathematics—rubbed me the wrong way. It was fun, though, to watch Richard's face. He tried to act chill, but every once in a while his excitement would break through and I could see just how badly he wanted to be there.

We got lunch in Harvard Square, sitting side by side on a bench eating sandwiches and drinking coffee. Then it was back to his car for the short ride to Medford and the Tufts tour, which was delayed for almost an hour when the guide failed to show. "Sorry," I say as we finally set out. "I know we were supposed to be on the road by now."

"It's cool. Maybe we get dinner before heading back?"

"Okay." Getting dinner together sounds good. A day that started with an unexpected surprise keeps on getting better.

Richard was grinning when I opened the door this morning. He brought donuts, but also a gift bag with a bow.

"What's this?" I asked.

"Just a little something I got for you."

"Why're you getting me a present?"

"Can't I do something nice for a friend?"

I opened it and held it up, and then I laughed and he laughed and I went back inside to put it on, and now I'm wearing it underneath my flannel: it's a plain white T-shirt, and printed on the front are the words "Grant-Covington College, home of the Dwarf Hippos, disbanded 1956."

"What kind of food do you like?" he asks as we follow the guide out of admissions at Tufts.

"I don't know. Anything, I guess."

"Mexican?"

"Sure, Mexican is good."

The group winds its way through two academic buildings, the library, and the gym before getting to the part I've been waiting for. "All right," the guide says, "let's take a look at where you would be living if you came here." She pivots so she's walking frontwards and sets off briskly in the direction opposite to the one I'd expected her to go in.

I quicken my step and push my way to the front of the crowd. "Excuse me," I say, "I thought we were going to see Carmichael Hall."

She shakes her head. "Nope, we're going to another one today."

"But the office said Carmichael..."

She glances at me out of the corner of her eye. "They're setting up for an event in Carmichael," she says. "But we're going to see a very nice room in another hall that will give you a good sense of our residential arrangements."

I slow my pace, letting the guide cruise ahead, a long string of hopeful high school students and their parents trailing behind until it is just me and Richard, standing in the middle of the path, watching them go. "What's wrong?" he asks.

"They're not going to Carmichael. Carmichael is back that way." I point in the opposite direction.

Richard frowns and taps his phone, bringing up the campus map. "Well, we can find it on our own."

"Finding it isn't the point. I want to go inside."

"One thing at a time. Let's go."

A short walk later I am looking up at Carmichael Hall while aggressively chewing my left thumbnail, pulling a corner of it loose. The building is gorgeous, the brick and white façade wrapping around into two spacious wings and a cupola with a Tufts-blue dome sitting on top. This is where I want to be living, one year from today. Right now, though, I just need to think of a way to get inside.

We followed a girl as she walked up to an entrance and swiped her pass to open it, but she looked back over her shoulder inquisitively as I hurried to get the door and I backed off, pretending I had a message on my phone. The last thing I need is a campus security incident report the fall that my application is finally being considered.

As much as I've yearned to get away from Evans Beach, as much as I've wanted to start again someplace else, I haven't spent much time away from home and I've never been this far on my own. If Dad were here, he'd march up to the door, make some sort of proclamation, pound someone on the shoulder and offer a random but charming comment about the 1980s Red Sox infield, and then we'd be inside with a few new friends as a bonus.

"Excuse me," Richard says to someone walking by, "my sister and I were on a tour earlier today and she thinks she left her cell phone in one of the bathrooms."

"Oh, sure," the guy says. He swipes his pass and holds the door for us. We enter and look around the lobby.

"Where are we going?" Richard asks.

"This way." I walk toward the stairs and start up. "Why do we have to be brother and sister?" I ask as we reach the second floor.

"Why not?" he says, raising an eyebrow. "We might just look like different sides of the same family."

I shake my head. We exit on three and I look around. The hall is quiet; most of the doors are closed. I walk past 312, 311, 310, running a finger along the wall, Richard trailing slightly behind. Then I turn the corner and we're there: 305.

"This is it?" Richard asks.

"This is it."

I knock on the door, having no idea what I will say if

someone answers, but they do not. I gingerly try the handle but of course it's locked, and I wouldn't go into someone else's room even if it wasn't. I'd just take the smallest of peeks inside. Instead, I rest my palm against the door and close my eyes.

This is where Mom lived her freshman year; one of my oldest pictures is of her and a group of friends standing right in this spot. This is the door she opened on her first day of college. I wake up every day in the house where she spent most of her adult life, but that is a mixed space. Dad, Pauline, even Henry and Simon have a share of the memories there. But this...this will be just me and her. Soon, I promise myself. I'll be here soon. Less than a year.

I must look like a total freak. I made Richard wait for the tour, then leave it and lie his way in here so that I could stand in silence with my hand on a closed door. I'm scared to look at him; I expect him to be rolling his eyes but when I turn he's just looking at me, and then he smiles.

I didn't tell Richard, but the only Mexican restaurant I've ever been to is the taco place at the mall, and I'm pretty sure it doesn't count. The one he found on his phone seems like the real deal. There aren't even English translations on the menu.

I meant to wait until we ordered, but I find that I can't. "I got you something," I tell him.

"What do you mean?"

"You brought me a present this morning, so I got you

something back." I open my backpack and take out a plastic Harvard Bookstore bag.

"When did you get it?"

"When you went to find a bathroom." I reach in and take out a T-shirt, handing it across the table to him. Richard shakes it open and holds it up. It's crimson, with "Harvard Medical School" written over the school seal on the front. "Maybe I shouldn't have?" I ask, the thought occurring to me too late. "Is it bad luck?"

"I love it," he says.

"I mean, you're totally going to get in there, so there's nothing to jinx. I could give you an entire Harvard Med wardrobe and you'd still go."

"Thank you."

"Thank you for my shirt."

"Yeah? You like it?"

"It's great, and you had to get it specially made and everything."

"I admit, it's not something you can buy off the rack."

The waitress comes by and we place our orders. There aren't many other people in the restaurant and no one's sitting in the booths near ours. Someone is singing in Spanish, and it takes me a few moments to realize that it's one of the cooks instead of a recording.

"Can I ask you something?" Richard says, folding the shirt back up.

"Go for it."

"Why make up a school?"

"Technically, I didn't make it up."

"You know what I mean."

"Yeah, I do." I sip my ice water. "You mean, why not just tell people that I want to go to Tufts?"

"Yeah, or if for whatever reason you didn't want to share, just tell them your second-choice school."

"I don't have a second-choice school. It's Tufts or nothing."

"Because it's where your mom went."

I nod and look into my glass. "I could have just said the University of New Hampshire or something, I guess. I don't know. Grant-Covington felt like camouflage."

"Camouflage for what?"

"For the thing I actually wanted."

"I see."

I look up at him. "Do you?"

"Maybe a little. I get that there haven't been many times when you got what you wanted."

"I've done better than a lot of people," I say.

"Yeah, but I'm still imagining that you grew up wanting things and then getting hurt. You wanted your mom to get well, you wanted your sister to get herself together, maybe you wanted your father to do things a little different, too. Not that he's not a great guy."

"He could have improved in some areas."

"Sure. But I mean, it's basic conditioning. We learned about it in AP Psych. You want, you get hurt, you want, you get hurt. It builds an association. Like Pavlov's dog."

"Ah. I'm like a dog."

"A very famous Russian dog. Though actually, it's more like Little Albert. Do you know who he was?"

"Another dog? A parakeet? Squirrel? Lizard?"

"Oh, I finally found a piece of trivia that Hannah Lynn doesn't know! Little Albert was an experiment by John Watson, an early psychologist. Basically, he let this toddler named Albert play with a little white lab rat. Albert loved it, but then Watson scared the shit out of him when the rat came to play."

"How did he do that?"

"Making a loud noise behind him. He did it a few times, always when the rat came out, and after that Albert freaked whenever the rat showed up, even if there was no noise. Not only that, he got upset if there was anything white and fuzzy around."

"Sounds highly unethical."

"You see my point, though."

"Your point is that me wanting to go to Tufts is like Little Albert. It makes me scared because I'm waiting to get hurt, just like the rat made him scared because he was waiting for the loud noise."

"Right."

"You know, not many people from Evans Beach get that sort of thing."

Richard shrugs. "I don't think there's a lot of unrequited wanting in our town, but I haven't always lived in Evans Beach."

"Yeah, I know. Freeport."

"Not just Freeport. I haven't always lived in Maine. I haven't always had parents who were doctors, who had money, and took care of me. I was born in Florida and I was adopted when I was four years old."

"Really? I didn't know your parents weren't your real parents."

"They're real. More real than the people who had me and couldn't take care of me."

"I'm sorry, I didn't..."

"It's okay, I know what you meant. And you didn't know because I didn't tell you. It's not something I usually share." He smiles, reaches out, and squeezes my hand.

The waitress arrives with the nacho platter we ordered as an appetizer. I'm starving and Richard clearly is as well. We each take a plate and tear in. There's quiet for a moment, except for the cook's singing. He's pouring his heart into it; it must be some sort of love song or gospel or something like that. Something he's passionate about. I bite into a cheesy nacho, burning my tongue, and I imagine it: Richard at Harvard, me at Tufts. It took exactly eleven minutes to drive from Cambridge to Medford, not that I was keeping track. I turn the idea over in my mind and decide to risk letting myself want it, just a little bit.

"These are good," Richard says.

"Yeah, really good." I wonder whether he ever told Amity about his family. I want to ask him more about Florida and his life before Evans Beach. I want him to take my hand again.

The cook's singing swells. My cell phone rings. I pull

it from my pocket and look at the screen: Home. I glance at Richard as he tries to disentangle two cheese-drenched chips, and then I tap the screen. "Hello?"

"Hannah?"

"Henry—what is it?"

"It's Grandpa. There's something wrong with him. An ambulance is coming."

13

My father wants ice.

The machine is empty on the fifth floor so I go up to six, stepping off the elevator and facing a pair of metal doors. I yank on one, but it's locked. There's an intercom on the wall to the right and I push the button. "Yes?" a voice says after a moment.

"Yeah," I say, "I'm looking for ice."

"Ice?"

"Ice, ice," I say, shaking the empty plastic water pitcher I'm holding. "Frozen water, H2O in a solid state. Ice."

There's silence for a long moment. Then: "This is inpatient psychiatry."

"Well," I reply, "do you have any damn ice in there?"

"Try the third floor," the disembodied voice says.

"I am not going to the fucking third floor," I mutter as I turn away and jab the down button on the elevator. I step in and press the button for two. The third floor is medical oncology and I absolutely refuse to go there for all the ice in the world.

The second floor turns out to be pediatrics. I look around the brightly lit hall. There's a mural with kids in race cars. I'm trying to find evidence of a kitchenette or a nurse who might point me in the right direction but instead I see a couple coming toward me. The man is very tall and he's holding a child in his arms, close against his chest. The kid might be two or maybe three and he has a plastic hospital band around one chubby ankle. The woman is hurrying alongside, trying to keep pace with the man's long strides, and she looks absolutely terrified. "Where is ultrasound?" she asks me.

"Ultrasound?"

"The ultrasound department. They said we should bring her up here for an ultrasound."

"I'm sorry," I tell her, "I don't work here. I don't know."

The little family hurries by me.

Dad didn't announce that he was having a stroke. He complained of a headache and of ringing in his ears but it wasn't until his words started getting jumbled that Henry called for help. I watch the little family turn the corner at the far end of the hall and think that kids are basically the same as any other emergency: they're catastrophes that don't come with instruction manuals.

The ice machine turns out to be in the other direction, between two vending machines at the end of a dead-end hall. It belches a bit into my pitcher and then there's a rumbling deep within as I hit the button again and again. "Give it time," a voice says beside me. A woman in nurse's scrubs is feeding coins into one of the other machines. "It's old. It can only kick out a little bit at once."

I lean forward and listen to the rumble, closing my eyes. It's been four days. I've visited Dad every one of them. I made it to work twice and to school once, though I slept most of that time in the nurse's office. I got the boys to school, their counseling appointments, and Simon to his art class because it seemed like a bad time to disrupt their schedules. But by the time I drove those circuits, made dinner (still adhering to the menu on the dry erase), helped them with homework, and put in a token effort at fighting back against the tide of laundry and dirty dishes, there was nothing left in me. Which is unfortunate, because there is now less than one month until my early decision application is due for Tufts.

"I'm so fucking tired," I say.

"This is a hospital," the nurse says. "Everyone's tired." She takes her soda and turns away.

The machine finally gives up enough ice to fill the pitcher and I take the elevator back up to the fourth floor. Dad is in good spirits when I get there.

"Hannah, give me the thing...the little one, the box, the rectangle that you point." He gestures toward the TV suspended in the corner of the room.

"The remote?"

"Yes!"

I hand it to him. He turns the TV on and leans back

in the hospital bed. I slide a stool across the floor and sit beside him. The Celtics are losing to the Knicks. "I got you some ice."

His smile is crooked. He reaches out with his good arm and pats my knee. "I'm good for now."

Great. By the time he wants it again, it will be melted. I set the pitcher down on a table. I could move from the stool to the chair, but then I would fall asleep immediately and I can't do that. The boys will be here any minute. "You feeling okay?" I ask.

"Hundred percent. They're sending me home tomorrow."

"No, that's not what the doctor said."

"Sure it is."

"I was here, Dad. He said that if you keep improving, you'll be discharged in no time. He didn't say tomorrow, and you're going to have to do rehab."

He snorts. "I knew a guy who got sent to rehab when I was playing minor league ball. Had a taste for coke. It didn't do squat for him."

"That might have been a different kind of rehab."

"Foul!" Dad barks at the TV, but one side of his mouth isn't pulling its weight and the word comes out slurred. He sounds drunk, or old, or both. I lean forward, resting my elbows on my knees, closing my eyes and rubbing my temples. I think about the list of rehab services the doctor went through earlier: PT, OT, speech, cardiac. All weekly at least (the doc said twice a week would be ideal), and Dad won't be able to drive. I might have to break down and call Reverend Jim to see if someone from church can help. Even if they can, though, it won't be enough.

"Grandpa!"

My head jerks up. I had been starting to drift. Now Simon is bounding into the room, hurrying to the bedside, Henry trailing behind.

"Boys!" Dad's voice has some of its old boom and he spreads his good arm out, gathering both of them into a hug.

"I made you a picture," Simon says.

"Let's see it."

"I left it at school."

"Oh, that's all right."

"I drew the whole family at Sol's. You, me, Henry, and Hannah."

"Dad," I say, "are you all right if the boys stay here for a while? I have to go do something."

"Sure," he says. "The nurses won't kick them out. We can watch the game."

I give Henry some money. "If you get hungry you can go down to the cafeteria and get a snack for you and your brother."

Henry nods, stepping closer to Simon. I look at them for another moment, then walk out of the room and down the hall to the visitor's lounge. There's only one person there. "Thank you for bringing them," I say.

Richard looks up from his phone. "Not a problem."

"You could have come in. Dad likes you."

"I wanted to give you all some space."

My car failed to start when I tried to go pick the boys up from school. It's sitting in the hospital parking lot now, needing a tow, though I'm feeling like it might have finally reached the end of the line. "Oh, also your mom came by before to check in. She was nice."

He nods.

"I hate asking for favors."

"It's okay…"

"No, I mean I really, really hate it. I hate owing anyone anything, but I need to ask for another. I need you to take me someplace."

Richard studies my face. "Well," he finally says, "I'm parked out front and you won't have to owe me anything."

I nod, offer what is likely a hideous effort at a smile, turn, and walk toward the elevator.

I explain where we're going and why, give Richard the address, lean back with my head against the passenger side window, and close my eyes. The next thing I know he's gently shaking my arm. "Hannah. We're here."

I sit up and look around. We're parked on the side of the street. The number on the building beside us matches the one Dad gave me. I nod, rub my eyes, and get out of the car. Richard comes around, surveying the run-down five-story building. "You can wait in the car if you want," I say.

"I should come in with you. This isn't the best part of town."

I appreciate the offer but I don't want him to see whatever's inside. "I'd rather go in myself, Richard. I think I need to talk to her one-on-one."

"All right," he says, though he doesn't seem happy about it. "Text if you want me to come up."

"Lynn" is written on a piece of masking tape below a mailbox labeled apartment 12. The elevator is broken, so I take the stairs.

The first two times I called Pauline, on the ride back from Tufts, I got her voicemail. She didn't respond to those messages and she didn't respond to any of my texts. When I called again, later that night from the hospital, her voicemail was full and the next morning her phone didn't even ring, it just went straight to the notification informing me that I could not leave a message.

Pauline's never done Facebook or any other social media, so I had to resort to email. I wrote her a message from Dad's bedside, reiterating and updating what I'd told her in the messages I'd been able to leave: our father was at Maine Medical Center, he'd had a stroke, he was okay but he was going to need a lot of rehab and wouldn't be able to drive for a while, and she needed to ask her caseworker for permission to do more with the boys. At a minimum, to give them some rides while she's working her way back through the reunification plan.

There has been no response.

I exit the stairwell on the fourth floor. Apartment ten is on my left, eleven is on my right. There's music playing behind the door. Twelve is straight ahead. I walk over, press the buzzer and, not hearing anything, knock. A moment passes. I knock again. "Pauline!" I call. I knock one more time and then, frustrated, kick the door.

"Hey!"

I turn. The door to apartment eleven is open; a woman is peering out, music playing behind her.

"Are you looking for Pauline?"

"Yeah."

"Are you family?"

"I'm her sister."

"Hold on a minute." She closes the door. A moment later she's back, holding out an envelope. "She left this for you."

I step forward and take the envelope from the woman's hand. "Do you know Pauline?"

"Just as her neighbor. She moved."

"When?"

"She stopped by yesterday. Gave me her key and that letter. She said I could take whatever she'd left in the apartment. I went in and looked around but I didn't want anything."

"Did she say where she was going?"

"She said she was going with that guy, they're going to move in together, back near where he's from. Dan? Dave? It started with a D. You know him?"

"Doug." From the car registration.

"He's been around a lot."

Of course he has. There's always a guy. "Where's Doug from?" I ask.

"Milwaukee."

"Seriously?"

The woman shrugs. "I've never been to Milwaukee. Don't know why you'd want to go there."

"Cheese," I say absently, looking at the envelope in my hand. There's nothing written on the outside. "She left this for me?"

"She said she was leaving it for family. She said someone would probably come by, either family or her caseworker, and if it was the caseworker, he would give it to her family. So yeah, it's for you."

Another moment passes while the woman looks at me and I look at the letter. Then I turn and head for the stairs. "You're welcome," she calls after me.

I walk down one flight, then another, and then when there's only one flight left, I stop by a dirty window and tear the envelope open with my little finger. I unfold the paper and, holding it up in the dimness of the stairwell, I read it twice through. Then I fold it again, stuff it back into the envelope, and go down the final flight and outside.

Richard is leaning against his car, waiting for me. His sunglasses are on against the autumn sun and a breeze is stirring his thick, black hair. His arms are crossed on his chest and he's looking up at me, eyebrows raised. He is, if I'm being totally honest, gorgeous. He's also completely incongruous. He doesn't belong in this neighborhood. He doesn't belong in this life. I walk toward him.

"Well," he asks, "is she coming?"

I shake my head, open my mouth, and find that I can't speak.

"Hannah?"

"Here," I manage, thrusting the note toward him.

"Are you crying?"

"Just take the goddamn letter," I say.

"What happened?"

"Just read it. I'm going to walk around the block."

Pauline was kind to me, once. It's one of my first memories. On the night Mom died she let me sleep next to her in bed. I don't remember much about the days around Mom's death and I don't know where Dad was that night but I remember being alone, changing into my pajamas and realizing no one was going to come and tuck me in. I guess the church ladies hadn't descended yet. Pauline had already moved in with Marcus and baby Henry in Portland; she must have come back for the night, leaving Henry with his father. I remember her bringing me into her old room and we lay side by side, arms around each other, and felt each other crying. I eventually slept, and I know that I would not have if my sister hadn't been there with me.

I don't know what happened to that kindness. I don't know if the world wore it away or if it got covered up and it's still in there, somewhere. I do know that there's none of it left for me, or for her boys.

I rub my face and look up. My steps have led me to a 7-Eleven and I'm standing in front of a sign offering a slushy for ninety-nine cents. I contemplate it for a long moment. How is that even possible? Don't the ingredients for one of those monstrosities cost more than ninety-nine cents? They must buy in such high volume, and sell such a large quantity, that it all works out for the 7-Eleven shareholders. Amazing.

There's a familiar honk behind me. Two quick, one longer. Precisely tapped out on a German-engineered horn. The engine shuts off, a door opens and closes, and then Richard is standing beside me. "You want a slushy?" he asks.

"Not really."

"My parents never let me have one."

"Yeah, well, they're both doctors. Abstaining is probably a prudent medical decision." I turn and sit on the crumbling concrete parking block at the head of the empty space next to Richard's BMW. He sits beside me. "You know they can make these things out of rubber?" I ask. "Parking blocks. It's more durable. More expensive, but over the life of a parking lot you'll save." I pick up a handful of concrete chips. "I mean, look at this shit."

"Hannah…"

"The stuff you learn working for the DPW, right? Hang out with me long enough and you'll learn everything you never wanted to know about roads and parking lots and…"

"Hannah, I read the letter. What are you going to do?"

I shouldn't be here; I need to get back to Maine Med. The boys can't stay at the hospital with Dad. We're supposed to be doing brussels sprouts with chicken breasts and whole wheat rolls tonight, and I don't think we have the sprouts. Henry has some sort of project for social studies. Simon has to do his math homework. "I don't know," I say. "I have no fucking idea."

Pauline's letter, in all its cramped, barely legible glory—she managed to misspell the word "stroke"—made one thing abundantly clear: she is gone. She is gone, and she does not intend to come back. She gave her reasons, ranging from her love for Doug, to what she sees as the impossibility of staying sober around all her old friends in Portland, to her belief—infuriating in its accuracy—that her boys will be better off without her as their mother. In the end, the reasons don't matter. Neither do the apologies, one addressed to Henry and one to Simon and one to Dad but apparently none for me, even though I'm the one who hasn't slept and has to pick up the brussels sprouts. She's probably halfway to Milwaukee by now.

"You're crying again," Richard says softly.

"Am not."

"Apparently you don't know when you're crying."

"That's what my dad says." I rub my face with a sleeve. "You should have taken the cats."

"What cats?"

"The cats, the fucking sick cats. You should have done your community service requirement with them instead of with me. Then you wouldn't be sitting in a parking lot with a crazy girl who can never tell whether she's crying or not."

"I really do hate cats," Richard says.

"Allergic, right?"

He nods. "Very allergic."

"I have to go," I say. "I have to get brussels sprouts. Preferably organic."

"We'll stop at Whole Foods on the way back to the hospital."

"And I have to help Henry with a social studies project."

"I could come over and help. I love projects. Poster-board is my medium."

I again wipe my face with a sleeve. Richard gets up and goes into the 7-Eleven, returning with a wad of napkins. I blow my nose. "You're not a bad guy," I tell him.

"I try not to be."

"I didn't like you much, at first."

"Oh."

"Yeah. For a while, actually."

"When did you change your mind?"

"Fairly recently."

"Was it the T-shirt?"

"It didn't hurt."

He sits, looks at the parking lot, then back at me. "I'd like to kiss you," he says.

I freeze, used napkin still in hand. Richard is looking at me expectantly, like he's hoping he didn't just say the wrong thing, and I want to tell him that he didn't but that I'm scared and I'm lost and half of me wants him to kiss me, and half of me wants to get up and run out of this parking lot, and half of me wants to stay frozen on this concrete block forever. But that is not the way fractions, or moments, work. I twist around and I kiss him.

"I'm sorry," he says when we stop. "Maybe I shouldn't have done that."

"Why not?"

"Well…you're sort of in a vulnerable moment."

"That's been going on for a while," I say, "and if you wait for it to end, then we're never going to get anywhere."

Richard looks like he wants to say something else, but before he can get the words out I push everything—brussels sprouts, my father and his rehab, Pauline and her letter and her kids—far out of my mind so that I can focus on resuming what is, though it feels absurd to admit and is not something I am willing to say out loud, my first kiss.

14

Just until Pauline was back on her feet. That was the plan.
Maybe three months. Now we're about a month away from
the one-year anniversary of the boys' arrival and this is the
situation: my sister is in Wisconsin, my father is mildly
aphasic and on disability, and Ms. Harper is dressed up as
a fucking elf. She's standing on our front steps holding a
sack, and she's shivering. "Can I help you?" I ask.

"May I come in?"

There doesn't seem to be any other way. I move aside.

"Thank you," she says, stepping into the front hall.
"These tights aren't insulated, you know."

"That's...rough."

"But," she says brightly, "that is not the point. The point
is that I have a delivery for the boys. Well, not me specifi-
cally, but the Rotary, and today I am the delivery elf!"

"I didn't know there was a delivery elf."

"Santa is busy. Christmas is only sixteen days away!"

"We don't need charity, Ms. Harper."

"Oh, this isn't charity, it's just…well, it's a program. Your father put the boys' names down for the giving tree."

"Yeah, well, he had a bit of a stroke, so he's been making some poor decisions…"

"Is that Henrietta Harper I hear?" Dad's voice booms from the other room. Henrietta. Jesus. What kind of sadists name their child Henrietta when their last name is Harper?

"Hello, Larry, I didn't know you were…" Ms. Harper steps out of the front hall into the living room and stops in her tracks. "Oh," she says. "You're busy."

Dad is hanging upside down. His rack is set up directly in the middle of the room and he is dangling, shirtless, with his baggy old Red Sox shorts offering a healthy glimpse of thigh. "Not a bit!" he says. "Always time for a friend. Henry, how much time is left on the clock?"

"Forty-three seconds, Grandpa."

"Great. See if you can get that shoulder back a couple more degrees."

Henry, who is stretched out on a floor mat, rolls slightly to his left and groans. Simon looks over at him, brow furrowed in concern. He loses control of the rubber ball he is passing from one hand to another between his legs and it flies across the room, straight into Ms. Harper's forehead. "Oh," she says again.

"Yes," I say. "Oh."

Dad's rehabilitation went faster than expected, especially because Reverend Jim and people at church pitched in to drive so he was able to get there as often as the doctor wanted. The therapists, of course, all loved him. Despite what the psychologist told us about the possibility of persistent memory deficits, he learned all of their kids' names, what sports they played, what positions, and their teams' records.

The problem was that he didn't think he was done when they told him he was done. The idea of deficits that might not be "fully remediated," in the words of his PT, was not acceptable to him. He turned to the internet, watching YouTube videos in which stroke patients attested to the value of various programs and devices, including the inversion rack on which he is presently hanging. The boys, of course, were not to be left out. Dad devised programs for them to do in parallel with his own. Henry is strengthening and stretching the shoulder of his throwing arm during the offseason, and Simon is following a system purported to increase "interhemispheric cerebral transfer" for students with learning problems.

A timer goes off and Henry stands and pulls a lever on the rack. Dad slowly rotates upright until he is facing away from us. He takes a few deep breaths and then unbuckles himself. "Simon," he says, "shirt." Simon hands Dad his XXXL undershirt. He pulls it over his head, settles it on his frame, and then turns to face us, the soul of dignity. "Henrietta," he says, "thanks for coming by."

"Of course. I wanted to drop off the presents." She holds out the bag.

"Great! We're getting the tree this weekend and they'll go underneath. Hannah, will you put those somewhere safe?"

"Yup," I say, taking the bag.

"We've missed you at church, Larry," Ms. Harper says. "You're looking well."

"Thanks," he says. "The kids are taking good care of me. I expect that I'll be back at church this coming weekend, or if not then at least by Christmas services."

She smiles at the boys, then turns her attention to the far wall. "Oh, whose are these?"

"Mine," Simon says.

"May I take a closer look?" He nods. She walks across the living room, circling the inversion rack and the floor mat to examine the artwork. A half dozen of Simon's drawings are displayed in black plastic frames. Dad switches them up every couple of weeks as new work comes back from the art class. There are a few nature scenes but it's mostly people: Dad, Henry, me, teachers from school. Occasionally Pauline makes an appearance but not often, and Dad always takes her down after a few days.

"These are wonderful," Ms. Harper says. Simon and Dad both beam.

The thing about Simon's drawings is that they tell stories. They're full of emotion. I usually don't know what he's thinking or feeling until I see him draw. Ask Simon how his day was or whether he likes school or is making any friends and you're likely to get a long stare and fumbling for words. Look at his painting of a sunset or sketch of his brother and you'll get your answers, though. It's all in there: sadness, frustration, loneliness, determination.

"Your use of form and color is really bold and interesting," she says. "Are you taking classes?"

Simon nods again and tells her the name of his art school.

"That's lovely. When you're ready, I'd be happy to introduce you to a client of mine who used to teach at the Massachusetts College of Art and Design."

"Really?" Dad asks. "That would be outstanding."

"I'm in a show," Simon says.

"It's through the art school," Dad explains. "They picked three of Simon's pieces. It's next Thursday afternoon."

"I'll try to make it," Ms. Harper says.

I carry the bag of presents downstairs to Pauline's old room. Dad and I have decided to start clearing it out for the boys so that they can have a better setup than the couch and air mattress in the family room, which feels perpetually temporary.

Dad took the news about Pauline surprisingly well. We spoke about it in the privacy of his hospital room and even he, with his powers of denial, didn't say anything about her maybe coming back.

I was more worried about telling the boys; we waited a few days, until Dad was back home. During that time, they didn't ask where their mom was or why she hadn't visited their grandfather at the hospital. They've grown used to her absence. When we did tell them, sitting on the couch in the living room, they sat side by side and listened without expression, though Simon quietly reached out and held Henry's arm and that made me so sad and angry that I wanted to track my sister down in Wisconsin and kill her with my bare hands. Simon asked where Milwaukee was and we showed him on a map. Henry didn't have any questions.

I tuck the bag behind an old fan. I don't particularly want to go back to the living room before Ms. Harper leaves, but I have to get to a four o'clock meeting, so I return to the front hall and dig around for my boots as quietly as I can.

"How is senior year going, Hannah?" Ms. Harper asks.

"Fine. Great. How's Jessie?"

"Oh, she's wonderful. Did you hear? She was accepted early decision to Northwestern."

"No, I didn't hear. Good for her."

"Where's that?" Dad asks.

"Outside of Chicago," Ms. Harper tells him.

"I played in Chicago," Dad says. "Two at bats in a three-game set against the White Sox."

"Did you get any hits?" Henry asks.

"A single and a fly-out to shallow center."

I find one boot and shove my foot into it.

"Where are you applying, Hannah?" Ms. Harper asks.

"Uh, well, Tufts."

"Oh, that's where your mother went!"

"I know." There's the other boot, underneath Henry's duffel bag.

"Jumbo the Elephant, isn't it?"

"Right, Jumbo."

"Who's Jumbo?" Simon asks.

"This guy named P. T. Barnum, who started a circus, gave the school a stuffed elephant."

"Like, a real one?" Henry asks.

"Yeah. I mean, it was dead, but it had been a real elephant. And it sort of became a thing, a school mascot."

"Can we see it if you go there?"

"No, it burned in a fire. I think they have some of the ashes in a jar and people rub it for luck before big games."

"So," Henry says, "it's basically a dead elephant that got cremated."

"Uh—yeah."

"Cool."

I grab my "Simon" folder from the front-hall table.

"Hannah."

"Yeah, Daddy?"

"You're sure you don't want me to come to this meeting?"

"These meetings aren't good for your blood pressure. Don't worry about it."

He chuckles and looks at Ms. Harper. "I never worry about things when Hannah's involved. She hasn't needed me since she was five years old."

I go out the door, not stopping for a coat, untied boot laces flapping around my ankles. I need to get away from the ridiculous elf woman and my bat-father. I get into Dad's truck and look back, through the living room window. Ms. Harper is saying something to Dad. I turn the key and the engine coughs, then dies. Dammit. I try again. Same result. Now Ms. Harper is looking out the window at me, Dad beside her. Another moment and she'll be out here, offering me a fucking ride, giving me the third degree about college apps.

I've only told one person about the letter that came from Tufts yesterday, and Richard is sworn to secrecy. It's the total opposite of his reaction to the Harvard letter;

within an hour Richard's parents had notified the bulk of the greater Portland area that he was in.

I take a deep breath, turn the key one more time, and the engine comes to life. I throw it into reverse, back up, and speed away toward the school.

𝄞

My life has become a series of sealed compartments.

There's the one where I deal with Dad's health and I know that 23 percent of people who suffer a stroke will have a second one.

There's the one where I'm almost a second-semester high school senior and I have a spot in next year's incoming class at Tufts and a scholarship that will make it possible, no matter how much we chip away at the college fund.

There's the one where I've locked Pauline and her letter.

There's the one I visit with Richard during the evenings we have at his house on Marshall Street while his parents are working their evening shifts at Maine Med. Apparently 98 percent of high-school couples will break up in college, although I find that number suspect and anyway, fuck statistics.

There's one where Henry is making progress day by day, helping out more around the house, watching the clips of the '80s Red Sox online, asking Dad endless questions about the games.

And then there's this compartment, for Simon. I pull into the school lot and park. I'm ten minutes early, which gives me time to review the psychologist's report one more time.

I asked Dad to do the one thing I never ask him to do, the thing I am almost always opposed to: spend money. I'd found, by asking Simon's therapist and joining an online forum for parents of children with disabilities, the name of a psychologist who specializes in learning disorders in Falmouth who would figure out exactly what was wrong with Simon and tell the school what to do about it. He cost $3000 and, like the therapist, he didn't take insurance. A month before Dad's stroke we drove Simon down to get tested. He had to go a few times and then Dad and I went for our review meeting.

The psychologist was an older guy. He frowned at some papers with Simon's test scores and then pushed his reading glasses up to the very top of his head. He squinted at us. "Simon's a lovely boy," he said. "He has some wonderful strengths. He's very socially motivated."

"Right," I said. "He likes people."

The man nodded knowingly, as though a person liking other people represented a major breakthrough in psychological science. "He also has some very substantial challenges. Simon struggles with multiple aspects of language; structural, functional, phonological. His pragmatics are quite weak. In terms of attention and executive functioning, well, he couldn't really access any of those tests, even though they are designed for younger children. And his performance on memory testing..." He raised his eyebrows and shook his head as he studied the sheet of apparently dismal numbers.

"The school told us he has attention problems," Dad said, "and that he was pretty far behind."

"Simon's challenges go far beyond attention," the psychologist said. "He has a complex and severe learning disorder."

"Is he going to catch up in school?" I ask.

"He can make stronger progress with the right help. Much more than he's getting now; academics are very challenging for him and if he doesn't transition to a more intensive program, I'm concerned that his prognosis will not be good. He is a student at high risk."

"High risk for what?"

"Frankly, at high risk for everything. For not having the literacy or mathematical skills to hold a job. For not having the social skills to keep himself safe from exploitation."

Dad looked down at his huge work boots, sticking out of his nice khakis and said, "He draws. He draws really well. Paints, even."

"Sometimes people with these disabilities have strengths in other areas. They're called 'splinter skills.' It's good that Simon is an artist; it probably helps him express himself."

"Look, what do we do about this?" Dad asked, cracking his neck and then placing a notebook on his knee and brandishing a pencil. "If a guy is weak in baseball we give him extra coaching, right? So, where's the coaching for Simon?"

The psychologist told us about a program in South Portland for kids in kindergarten through high school with disabilities like Simon's. He said that school districts don't like to place students in it because it costs so much, but with the evidence from his testing, the Evans Beach Public Schools would find it unavoidable. I scan the last page of his report:

"In sum, Simon is a sweet, engaged, highly cooperative fifth grader. As he has grown older, and in spite of special education interventions at school, Simon's cognitive and academic functioning has increasingly deviated from that of peers. His math and his reading skills are both strikingly below grade expectations and if he is to make progress, he requires placement in an appropriate, specialized program such as the CARES program in South Portland."

I rub my eyes, try to force as many details as possible into my mind, and head for the building.

The secretary greets me with a wary, unwelcoming nod and waves me toward the back. "Thanks," I say, stopping at the coffee maker to help myself to a cup just because she hasn't offered me one. Then I proceed to the conference room.

The rest of the group is assembled up and down a long table with Mary Kelly, the Director of Special Education for Elementary and Middle School Students in Evans Beach, at one end. I sit at the other, dropping Simon's folder next to my coffee and nodding hello to no one in particular. There's an occupational therapist and a school psychologist and a special education teacher. There's a speech-language pathologist and a reading specialist and an inclusion consultant. They all stare at me, a thin film of bland indifference subtly shimmering over the frustration of people who have been called to a meeting after school hours.

"Just you today, Hannah?" Ms. Kelly asks.

"Yup. Dad's still on the mend and he's watching his blood pressure."

There's almost an audible sigh as tension drains out of the room. This is the fifth meeting we've had about Simon. Dad went to the first one alone and it did not go well. He asked me to come to the next one, and the one after that. By the fourth, which was before his stroke in September, I was doing all the talking while he sat beside me, arms crossed, simmering like a volcano about to erupt. "I know that he finds the process frustrating," Ms. Kelly says.

"Any sentient being finds this process frustrating," I tell her.

"Well," Ms. Kelly says, "in that case we had better get underway."

Getting underway implies going somewhere, which is what these meetings strive not to do. We begin, as always, circling the table with each participant reciting observations about Simon's outstanding progress from their highly specific vantage point. I glance up at the clock; it's already been fifteen minutes and they made a point of saying that we only have an hour. God, they can run the time down effectively. The occupational therapist is explaining that Simon's penmanship has improved a little bit with the exercises they've been working on but that she's planning to move him over to working on a keyboard anyway and that she'd like to get a consult from an assistive technology specialist to determine what sort of device will be best suited to him when I find that I can't take it anymore.

"Excuse me," I say, setting my pen down. "This is all great, and I don't want to be rude, but this isn't what I came here to talk about."

The OT stops, blinks, and turns to Ms. Kelly, who leans forward on her folded arms and smiles patiently. "And what did you come here to talk about, Hannah?"

"What do you think? I came here to talk about the report I forwarded to you. We need to talk about Simon's total lack of progress and how he's not going anywhere..." I look down at my copy of the report. "See, here, it says that he needs a different program. He should go to the CARES program in South Portland." I shuffle through the pages, trying to find the one with the passage I want to read them.

Ms. Kelly nods. "I understand your frustration, Hannah. Students like Simon are challenging. Change is very incremental."

"Change isn't happening because he's not getting enough help."

"Ms. Shaw was just explaining that change is happening..."

"Do you have any idea how well Simon can draw?

The problem with his writing isn't the handwriting, it's whether he can figure out what to say and how to say it. What about reading? What about math? Do you know he still gets confused about money? Last week he got a sandwich for $7.99 and he needed to check with me and make sure a ten-dollar bill would cover it."

"When he reaches high school," Ms. Kelly says, totally unfazed, "we will consider adding a life-skills goal to address those needs. If he is still with us in Evans Beach, that is."

"Jack Coburn didn't wait until high school."

"Excuse me?"

"Jack Coburn. He got a ticket to CARES when he was Simon's age. All paid for, bused from his house every day."

"How do you...I can't talk about another student, it's completely inappropriate."

"So don't talk, just listen. Dad is friends with Jack's family and they told him all about it. They say he gets picked up and driven to South Portland and goes to that program, and since starting there he's gone up something like three grade levels in reading and is doing math they never thought he'd do."

"Every child is different, Hannah."

"Yeah, they're all absolute snowflakes. But you know the key difference between Jack and Simon? Jack was born in Evans Beach, and so was his mother, and his dad works for Morgan Stanley. Simon, on the other hand, didn't grow up here and he doesn't count as one of you, does he?"

"You grew up in Evans Beach, Hannah," Ms. Kelly says evenly. "So did your father. And frankly you're being a bit hypocritical. Your sister got a lot of second chances for being Larry Lynn's little girl. You get a lot of leeway, too."

"I'm not anyone's little girl," I say. I open my folder and take out a piece of paper. "You're not sending him to CARES?"

"We are not prepared to make that placement, no."

"That's what I was expecting." I hand the paper to the woman sitting next to me. "Would you send that down to Ms. Kelly, please?"

The woman hands it to the person next to her and it is passed down the long conference table until it reaches the other end. Ms. Kelly takes it, puts her glasses on, and starts to read. The room is quiet. "What is this, Hannah?" she finally asks.

"My application essay for Tufts University."

"It's very well written."

"Thanks. I worked hard on it."

"I hope the admissions office approves."

"I believe they did. So did the op-ed guy at the *Press Herald*."

"Excuse me?"

"The *Portland Press Herald?*"

"I know what the *Press Herald* is. You sent them this essay?"

"Yes."

Ms. Kelly's lips go tight against her face. She looks down the table at me, then returns her gaze to the paper and reads aloud: "I used to think that I was poor. It's not hard, when you have a single parent working a blue-collar job and you live in a town like Evans Beach. Other kids went on vacations involving airplanes and nice hotels; we got away for day trips to Old Orchard Beach." The assembled teachers and therapists look at me, then back at her. She flips to the second page, then the third, and continues: "The thing about privilege is that it's a negative space. You can't see your own unless it's bounded on both sides. I was always acutely aware of those who had more than me, but I couldn't see how much I had until Mary Kelly and her team showed me, and for that I owe them a debt of gratitude. The way that 'Jack C.' is treated, as a child of Evans Beach; the way I have been treated, regardless of my family's affluence or lack thereof, stands in stark and defining contrast to the lack of care received by my nephew. This is privilege that money can't buy. This is the privilege of belonging, and Ms. Kelly's readiness to discard a child who does not belong has been a greater education than anything I have learned in an Evans Beach classroom."

She reads on silently for another moment, then folds the essay in half and sets it on the table in front of her. "This is going to be published?"

"They want to publish it. I haven't signed the agreement yet."

"Are you actually trying to blackmail me?"

"I'm just saying that it wouldn't make sense to publish the piece if it were no longer true. The argument is based on Simon and Jack being treated differently. If the two boys were treated the same, then the whole argument would collapse and the essay would have to be shelved as irrelevant."

Ms. Kelly stares at me.

"I'd like it to be irrelevant," I say. "I'm supposed to get back to the editor next week." I stand and look at the clock. "Look at us," I say to the room. "Wrapping up five minutes early." Then I take my coffee, turn, and leave.

My phone buzzes as I cross the parking lot.

Richard: did it work?

Me: dk...I think maybe?

Richard: It will. You're amazing

Me: aw shucks

Richard: you're going to crush it at Tufts

Me: Go Jumbos

Come next fall, Dad will have to go Simon's meetings on his own, though hopefully they'll be at the new program. By that time, he'll have his blood pressure down. He'll take his medicine every day and he'll have practiced the deep-breathing exercises they prescribed in his rehab program. As I walk away from the school, though, I'm surprised to find that I'm not looking forward to that day. I'm relishing this moment. I fought for Simon, and I think—I don't know for sure, but I think—that I won. I took care of him.

It feels fucking great.

15

"Do you think Grandpa is feeling better?"

"He's fine," I tell Simon. "I'll check in, but he probably just has a cold. I'm going to make him something to eat; you go catch up on homework."

Henry and Simon kick off their shoes and go downstairs. I linger in the living room, inspecting the Christmas tree and shifting a few ornaments around, and then walk into the kitchen to look for a can of soup. Dad was sorry to miss the art show but I have pictures and video on my phone, plus something better: the notice that came from the Evans Beach Public Schools in today's mail. They've agreed to place Simon in the CARES program, fully funded, with transportation and summer services. He'll start in January.

I've been waiting to tell Dad about Tufts. Every day that goes by seems a little bit harder. Thank God he never clued in to the early decision timeline. Tonight, though, is the right moment. I can tell him about the art show, tell him how Henry stood beside Simon's work, beaming with pride at his little brother, and that they didn't fight, even a little bit—even when Simon called shotgun on the way home and touched the car door first. I'll tell him that Simon seems to have some friends in his art class and that a cute girl named Olivia came to the show and orbited Henry all night long. I'll tell him that Ms. Harper also came and that she made an embarrassing fuss over Simon's work but that it was actually kind of nice of her to show up.

I'll tell him that the school finally did right by Simon.

Then, I'll finally tell him that I'm leaving next fall, heading to Massachusetts, and I'll watch him tell me how proud and happy he is, and I'll believe the first part but not the second.

The chicken noodle soup is simmering. I pour it from the pot into a bowl, grab a spoon and a napkin, and walk into his room. Dad is in bed, blanket pulled up. The Patriots are playing on the TV; Tom Brady takes the snap, fades into the pocket, takes his time scanning for receivers, then fires. Incomplete. I wait for Dad to bellow "HOLDING" at the onscreen ref, but there's silence. I set the bowl down on the one clear spot on his desk.

"You asleep? Daddy?" He doesn't stir. I run my hand through my hair, tugging at my ponytail. I look down at my Docs, perfect replicas of the ones Mom was wearing in a photo of the two of us taken at Portland Head Light the summer before she was diagnosed. "Daddy?" I say again. Then I reach out and touch his shoulder.

For all I eventually learned about Depression and Dengue Fever, I avoided volume D for a long time. Appropriately enough, I dawdled. Even when I started, I took my time. Gave Marcel Déat much more attention than he deserved, particularly considering his cowardly collaboration with the Nazis.

Death, when I came to it, was surprisingly simple. The total and permanent cessation of life processes that, the text calmly noted, "eventually occurs in all living organisms." The article held none of the grief and terror I associated with the topic after watching my mother waste away. It detailed the biology of death, the various mythological and religious systems that have evolved around it, and assorted definitional challenges. The author was identified as a neurologist and I found her discussion strangely comforting. She discussed death as a scientific problem to be cordoned off with words and numbers, carefully defined and relentlessly analyzed. Nowhere did she hint at the false promise of victory over her subject, but neither did she allow space for the grief of a bereaved child. I wished that I had encountered it sooner.

I think about that article as I stand over my father's bed. I think about its careful, precise descriptions; its detailing of medical, cultural, and historical fact; its almost obsessive curation of religious narratives. I hold on to those words and facts, wanting them to accomplish what they did all those years before: to crowd out grief.

They do, for a moment. Then the space opens anyway, and for once I know that I'm crying.

From: Hannah Lynn <hlynn123@gmail.com>
To: Alessandra Lynn <alessandra.lynn@gmail.com>
Subject:

I wish I thought you were together. The same part of me that wishes you were sitting on a cloud, looking down at my life, maybe once in a while putting in a good word for me with the big guy, also wants to imagine Dad arriving on said cloud, bursting in with all the exuberance he brought to a big dinner at Sol's. I imagine that he'd show up with his stupid coat draped over his wings (I'm assuming wings in this scenario) and his beat-up old hat with the ear flaps sticking out. He'd come tramping across the cloud you were sitting on, somehow spilling something along the way, and he'd give you a huge bear hug, and then you'd settle in together to watch the show down here on Earth.

The show on Christmas was pretty damn depressing. I dug around in Dad's closet and found the stuff we already had for the boys, wrapped it, added it to the donations from the Rotary Club, and put it all under the tree the night before. That morning Simon unwrapped a set of pastels and Henry got a new baseball glove; he opened it and then went downstairs to the family room so we wouldn't see him cry. Richard came over with food and helped with the boys.

School break is almost over. I have no idea what I'm supposed to do. I make meals. I clean up (sort of). I take Simon to his art class and Henry to the winter baseball clinic at town rec. I keep things normal. Isn't that the thing to do? It's what Dad tried to do for me when we lost you, though he failed at it.

Dad left a mess. He always left a mess. A well-meaning, big-hearted, completely oblivious mess. That's what they should have put in his obituary. That's what should be carved on your shared gravestone, right next to where it calls you my beloved mother.

I called Pauline. I called and called until she finally picked up. I told her. And do you know what she did? She started laughing. She laughed and laughed and couldn't stop and eventually a guy, I'm assuming Doug, took the phone and I had to repeat the news and then he hung up and they have not called back, nor do I want them to, nor do I expect them to.

We had a funeral at the church, of course. Reverend Jim took care of it. It's what Dad would have wanted. I stood there beside the boys and I did not say a word: not a prayer, not a single amen. But Pauline leaving our lives forever? That's a prayer I can get behind. A-fucking-men.

Dad is gone. Pauline is gone. You're gone. And late at night, after I've checked to make sure Henry and Simon are asleep and I've run out of tears and maybe brushed my teeth, though usually not, I lie in bed, inside my tent, and there's no word for the loneliness that I feel.

People care. They want to help. Amity sent a card. Sonya came by with a tub of clam chowder from Sol's. Richard keeps calling. Reverend Jim drops off food from the church. None of them can reach me. None of them can help with the thing Dad left me here to do, the one thing he never wanted to happen.

He left me here, alone, to send the boys away.

16

"Ben?" I ask, standing in the doorway and squinting into the blinding snow-reflected light.

"Ben Strickland," the man says. "We've met. I'm sorry to drop in like this. I tried to call, but you didn't pick up and your voicemail is full."

I nod and step back to let him in. He sets his briefcase down, wipes his feet on the mat, and takes his coat off, setting it on a hook by the door. I lead him into the living room.

Henry and Simon haven't asked any questions about what's going to happen next. They don't know about Tufts; like Dad, they had no clue I was expecting an early decision letter. I've been trying not to think about it, taking it one day at a time, assuming that Ben would show up sooner or later and tell us where they are going to go and when. It turns out that sooner or later is today.

He looks around our living room. I glance around, too, seeing it with an outsider's eyes. The Christmas tree, still up the day after New Year's, drying out and starting to drop needles. Dirty Tupperware that once contained lasagna sent by sympathetic people from the church. Dad's inversion rack pushed into the gap where the third couch, still down in my room, used to be. I notice that some of Simon's pastels are ground into the carpet near the TV.

"I'm sorry about your father."

"So's everyone."

"I mean it. He was a good man."

"Yes."

Ben looks around again. "Do you mind if we sit?"

"Sure." The couch nearest us is stained on the center cushion. I drop onto one end and he sits at the other. I'm tired. Very, very tired. Henry's night terrors have come back in full force since Dad died and I haven't slept for more than a few hours at a stretch.

"Where are the boys?" Ben asks.

"Out for a walk. Simon was supposed to start CARES today, but the paperwork got messed up so it'll be tomorrow. I let Henry come home early to hang out with him."

"That's nice. They should get out."

"Yeah."

"Where do they go?"

"Just around. Up and down the street, the woods across the way. They have their boots and gloves on."

"Sure, of course. Do they ever walk in the cemetery?"

"I don't think so. I like to, though."

"I grew up next to a cemetery in New Jersey. It was nice to walk there sometimes, especially in the winter." There's an awkward silence as he gathers his thoughts.

"Ms. Lynn," he finally says, "We need to talk. We need to make some decisions."

"I figured. I didn't want to tell them anything until I knew what the timeline was, and exactly where they'd be going." I take a deep breath. "They have real bags now, you know. Backpacks and duffels, so they won't have to use trash bags this time." It seems like so little to offer.

Ben stares at me for a moment and then shakes his head. "I don't think you understand. I'm not here to take Henry and Simon." He places the briefcase on his lap and flips it open, withdrawing a file. "Maybe it would help if we reviewed the situation. Your father, of course, was the boy's grandfather, and this was a kinship placement, but legally he was also their foster parent, their resource parent."

"Okay."

"You are aware that their mother is formally relinquishing custody?"

"Sounds about right."

"Have you spoken to her?"

"Not at length."

"She contacted our office the day after Christmas. She does not intend to return to the state of Maine."

"That's pretty much what I expected."

"And their father, Marcus, is not an option because of his record, and he has no family we can turn to." Ben sorts through the papers in the file. "Clearly it is in the interest of the children to continue to participate in a kinship placement and to remain together. But where we are, Ms.

Lynn, is, well, you are the sole eligible kin. I understand that there are no grandparents?"

"Dad was their grandfather. My mother died a long time ago."

"Sorry, I mean you. You have no living grandparents."

"Oh. That's right, yeah."

"No aunts and uncles, correct?"

"Mom had a brother but they didn't get along. He lives in Oregon. Dad was an only child."

"So, it's only you."

"What are you saying?"

He hesitates.

"You don't seriously expect me to take over the kinship placement, do you?"

"I'm saying that it's an option."

"I'm in the twelfth grade."

"According to my notes, you turned eighteen last October. You're legally an adult."

I stare at him. Ben opens his mouth, closes it, looks at his hands. "I don't care if it's legal," I finally say. "It's insane that you want to permanently leave two kids with someone who's still in high school."

He looks up. "What does that tell you?"

"It tells me you don't have a lot of options."

"There are options, but not a lot of good ones. At the moment there are none, actually. I have children living in motels with caseworkers rotating in and out to monitor them. Last month, a child I was responsible for, a boy who was placed in a group home..." He pauses.

I don't want to hear about the group home. "When you knocked on the door," I say, "I thought you were somebody bringing us another casserole."

"Are you waiting for..."

"No, I mean people have been coming by. This one woman, Ms. Harper, she's brought us dinner three times. I didn't answer the door for the last one, but she just left it on the stoop. People come up to me in the grocery store, on the street. They all knew my dad. They all say the same thing: that he was generous."

"Yes," Ben says, "I suppose that is what they would say."

"They say it because it was true. I don't think I can give as much as he did. I don't think it's fair of you to ask."

"He may have been generous. I always felt that he was. Maybe that was why he did what he did, maybe he had other reasons. Even if it was, in my experience someone always pays the price for generosity."

"So, you think it's wrong to be generous?"

"I think it's beautiful to be generous. I think it's wrong to pretend that there isn't a cost."

Silence descends on the living room. I look out the window and see movement in the trees across the street. The boys are returning from their hike. I study them as they step out onto the cracked and salt-stained asphalt. Their faces are red and Henry is smiling for the first time I've seen since Dad died. It's hard to believe he's the same kid who arrived with a half-filled trash bag. Who licked the pizza he wanted to save, who knocked holes in the wall and peed in one of them. Now he's a baseball player and he has someone who looks sort of like she could become a girlfriend. And Simon—his art is still on the wall, the last pieces Dad framed. He's scheduled to start at the CARES program tomorrow.

"Could I visit them?" I ask.

"At a new placement? Maybe. If they were in a group home, then it would partly be up to me, and my assessment of what was in their best interest, and partly up to the workers at the facility. If they were with a family, then they would have a say, and if they wound up being adopted then it would be entirely up to the adoptive parents."

Will they hold on to anything my father gave them? Or will they sink right back to the place they were when they walked through our front door a year ago, their past coming out when they no longer have meal schedules and art classes and baseball practice to keep it at bay? That past is still inside. I see it sometimes. Henry's clenched jaw. Simon melting down over basic math. One or the other of them tucking leftover food in their pocket or backpack, no doubt to be hidden someplace downstairs and contribute to the ongoing mouse problem. They struggle; they still struggle, and a piece of me believes that without my father they're going to sink anyway, even if they stayed right here, and that they'd pull me down with them.

"They can stay for now," I say. "But not forever. Just until you find something good. I can't keep them. I'm not a parent. I have my own life; I'm going to college in the fall."

"I need to make an entry in the file," Ben says. "I can

say I'm in the process of identifying alternate placements. It won't happen right away."

"I want them to be together. It needs to be a...a..."

"Joint placement."

"Right."

"That will be harder."

"How long?"

A snowball flies past the window. Simon shouts something.

"It depends. Joint is tough, especially if one is a teenager, and especially if one has special needs. I'll do my best."

Out in the yard, Henry is helping Simon roll the foundation for a snowman. Ben turns and looks out the window again. "I need to check in with them," he says.

"Don't tell them. Not until we have something definite."

"Have they asked what's going to happen?"

"They already knew Pauline was gone, and they never ask about their father. I think they just assume they're going to stay. Is that strange?"

"Kids who have the kind of history they do can have a truncated sense of the future. They may not be looking very far ahead. That's one explanation, anyway."

"What's another?"

"That they've come to identify this as their home, that they're secure, and that they don't expect to relocate again."

I clasp my hands together to keep them from shaking, open my mouth to speak, find that I cannot.

Ben stands. "I'll do a wellness check. And I'll let you know when I have something."

"All right," I whisper. "Do that." I get up, go to the front door, and open it. The boys have built half a snowman in the front yard. "Henry, Simon," I manage to call, "Ben is here. He wants to talk to you."

Henry looks at Ben's car, looks back at me, and nods. He starts toward the house, Simon following. I turn and walk away, and by the time I hear them kicking their boots off in the entryway I am closing the door to my room and heading to the closet, reaching for something of my mother's that I can hold on to.

⟞ 17 ⟞

I can't feel my hands. The warming packs I brought along have long since lost their heat and my gloves are proving inadequate. I stick the shovel in the snow, hold my hands to my mouth, and try to blow warm air in around my wrists. Useless. The only solution will be to finish this job, get back in the truck, and blast the heat on the drive back to the DPW. Simon has another two hours of after-school care at his new program and Henry will walk home and meet him when he gets off the bus, but they're counting on me to bring dinner. There's not much sunlight left at this time of year, anyway. I grab the shovel and dig in.

This pass-through is technically a town route, even though it hasn't been used in years. It is not, unfortunately, accessible to plows, at least not without damaging the thick trees on either side, and it's not even realistic to wrestle a snowblower up the trail. Every time it snows someone has to drive out here and shovel it clear by hand; we're on a rotation, and it's my turn. The guys offered to do it for me, Art Miller almost insisted, but I wanted to take care of it myself.

The work always makes me feel better. The shovel biting into the snow. The freezing cold air in my lungs. The good pain in my arms and back as the mound in front of me gets smaller. I don't know what I'll do when I get to Tufts and no one needs me to do shit like this anymore. Maybe I can get a job with the grounds crew or something.

My own breathing is loud in my ears, and I don't hear the footsteps crunching through the snow until she's almost on top of me. I swing around, raising the shovel. Amity steps back and holds up her arms in defense. "It's just me, Hannah!"

I lower the shovel. "Jesus, Amity, don't sneak up on me like that."

"I wasn't trying to sneak up on you."

I'm panting, my exhalations forming little bursts in the air in front of me. "What are you doing?" I ask.

"Looking for you. I went to the DPW and they told me you were out here clearing snow." She looks past me. "There's a lot of it."

I turn and look. It is a lot. Possibly more than I can handle by sundown.

"Do you want help?" she asks.

"I only have the one shovel."

"I have one in my car!" Amity spins and bounds off, back down the trail toward the road. I watch her go. A work buddy is not what I wanted today. I wanted to be alone. I turn back to the snow.

Amity is back by my side five minutes later. She's holding a lightweight aluminum handle and is screwing a blade onto the end. "What the hell is that?" I ask.

"My shovel."

"That's not a shovel."

"Sure it is! It's an emergency shovel my dad makes me carry in the trunk in case I get caught in a storm. He's overprotective."

The shovel is maybe a third the size of mine. It might be useful for clearing snow from under the tires of her Mercedes in a parking lot, but it's not going to do a lot out here. Still, Amity digs in with vigor, flinging snow into the woods. I watch for a moment and then set in beside her. "Why were you looking for me?" I ask.

"Because of Richard."

"What about him?"

"He's having a hard time."

"With what?"

"With you."

I straighten my back. "What about me?"

Amity also stops. Her hair is tousled and I see myself reflected in her sunglasses. "He doesn't know how to get through to you, Hannah."

"Get through to me? What's hard about getting through to me?"

"You've been a little...uh, could you not point that shovel at my face? Thanks. You've been a little distant. Actually, that's an understatement. You've been ignoring him."

"It's been a bit of a time. Maybe you heard, my dad died just a hair over a month ago."

"I know. I'm sorry."

"I'm sick of hearing that. Everyone's sorry."

"Yeah, everyone is. Richard especially. He wants to be there for you."

"Well, I'm having a tough time with that right now," I say.

"Why?"

There are three very good reasons why I have not returned Richard's calls, texts, or emails for the last three weeks; why I've been giving him the cold shoulder at school; and why, when he recently showed up at the door with Lucy, I pretended not to be home.

First, I'm extremely busy taking care of two boys who, unbeknownst to them, will be leaving for parts unknown just as soon as Ben Strickland can engineer it.

Second, I'm not letting Richard in because I do not fucking know how. He came over on Christmas morning. He drew with Simon and coaxed Henry out of the family room and into the yard for a game of catch in the snow. He fed us macaroni and cheese. He took care of us on a day when we needed taking care of and instead of gratitude, instead of affection, all I could feel was intensely, acutely uncomfortable. You can't just show up and start taking care of someone who's not used to it. It feels like being asked to jump off of something that's a bit too high without anyone being there to catch you.

And third, letting Richard do what he so plainly wants to

do—comfort me—risks making what's happened become a little bit too real.

"Hannah?" Amity says.

"Yeah?"

"You know what I think?"

"No. What do you think?"

"I think you're scared."

"Really."

"Yes, I do."

"Of what, exactly?"

She pauses for a moment. "Let me tell you a story."

"Oh, for fuck's sake. I don't have time for a story, Amity, I have to get this snow cleared and the sun is going down. If I don't, then someone has to come back first thing tomorrow. It's actually state law."

"I'll help, I can tell you the story while we dig."

I close my eyes and shake my head, then start back in. Amity does the same beside me. "When I was six years old," she says, "I had a dog."

"Huh."

"His name was Pickles."

I want to hit her with the shovel. Not the flat side, either.

"I loved Pickles very much."

"I bet you did."

"I was an only child, you know?"

"Consider yourself lucky. Sisterhood hasn't worked out great for me."

"Well, I was lonely. Pickles was a black Lab; we'd had

221

him since I was a baby and I think he sort of thought that I was his."

"Uh-huh." I'm shoveling harder now, cutting into the snow pile, throwing it out of the way. Amity is keeping pace, but unfortunately she's in great shape and still has air to talk.

"Pickles followed me everywhere. He would be waiting by the front door when I came home from school. He slept at the foot of my bed. His food bowl was right next to my place at the table."

"Let me guess," I say, "Pickles died. This is a parable about death and loss."

"He did die," she says. "All of a sudden. One day he was there, and the next day he wasn't. I came home and my mom and dad, who are not religious and do not believe in lying about these things, told me about it and said we were going to bury him in the backyard."

"Cool." At least they didn't contact the DPW. We get a certain number of those calls every year and have to explain that pet disposal is not one of the services we provide.

"My dad dug a hole and we wrapped him in his favorite blanket and put him in and covered him up and then, because we are atheists, instead of saying a prayer or something about Pickles being in a better place, we went inside and ordered Chinese food."

"Sounds perfect."

"And then, later on that night when Mom and Dad were asleep, I went back outside and dug Pickles up."

I stop working and turn to face Amity. "You did what?"

222

"I dug him up."

"Um..."

"It was a full moon, plus we have these floodlights. I was really little, so it took me a while but, as you can see, I am a talented digger."

I look at the snow in front of Amity and have to admit that she's made progress, even with her ridiculous little shovel. "This story cannot possibly have a good ending," I say.

"The ending," Amity says, "is that the sun came up the next morning and my parents found me sitting in a hole in the backyard, covered in dirt, holding a very stiff dog in my lap. Keep digging, Hannah."

I go back to digging. We're silent for a few moments. "Amity," I finally say, "why in the fucking hell did you tell me that story?"

"Like you said, it's a parable about death."

"Are you comparing the loss of my father to the loss of a dog named Pickles?"

"Look," she says, "I'm terrible at this. I understand that. I'm planning to be an engineer, okay? I do not do well with people and their feelings. My point, though, and I think that I left this out, has to do with the reason I dug Pickles back up."

"Which was?"

"Which was that I was not prepared to deal with the forward progression of time. If I had eaten my Chinese food and gone to sleep with the spot at the foot of the bed empty and then woken up the next morning and gone to school, then I would have been admitting that life was moving on without Pickles in it. Digging him up was a way of trying, in my little kid way, to step outside of events. To climb up on the riverbank and watch the water flow by without being carried along in it. And I wonder, Hannah, whether that is what you are trying to do by ignoring Richard and shutting him out? Sitting on the riverbank while the rest of us are being swept along past in the water."

"That's a pretty heavy thought, for an engineer."

"I might minor in psychology."

"Still."

"The thing is, Hannah, no one gets to climb out of the river, and if you try you just wind up covered in dirt, holding a dead dog."

"The metaphor may be breaking down," I say, "but I take your point." I attack the snow in front of me. I think I'm actually going to make it by sundown, and with Amity's help on the mound to my right, I won't have to come back tomorrow. "Thanks for helping," I say after a minute.

"Sure, I'm happy to." She finally sounds out of breath.

"I'm sorry about your dog."

"I'm sorry about your father."

We go on, shoveling the snow in the fading winter light.

It's a short drive from the cut-through to Marshall Street, but I sit outside the house for a good five minutes. The feeling is still coming back to my extremities and I'm in no hurry to get back out into the cold. Still, I can't stay long.

Richard answers when I ring the bell. "Hannah," he says, "what are you doing here?"

"First things first," I say. "You already gave your condolences, so don't say anything else about my father or I'll punch you between the eyes."

He blinks. "Okay. Do you want to come inside?"

I look over his shoulder. "No, I'm on my way to get dinner."

"All right." Richard steps out onto the front stoop, closing the door behind him. He's dressed in jeans and a checkered button-down, and he wraps his arms around himself for warmth. "What's up?"

"I need your notes."

"My notes? From what class?"

"Phys...history."

"Fistory?"

"History, dumb ass. We don't have physics together. I've missed a couple of classes."

"I've noticed. Sure, I can copy my notes. Just let me know what dates."

"Yeah. I'll do that." I look back, studying the street. We resurfaced it two years ago. "This probably could've been a text, huh?"

"Are you still doing those?"

"About that. I'm sorry I haven't been replying much. Or at all, lately."

We stand in silence for another moment, our breath clouding the air between us.

"You sure you don't want to come inside?" he asks.

"Yes. The thing is, Amity had a dog named Pickles."

"Pickles?"

"It was a long time ago, before you knew her. Before you moved to Evans Beach. The point is this: Pickles died and she dug him up and held him, with rigor mortis and everything, until the sun came up because she wanted to sit on the bank of the river of time."

"Hannah, have you been drinking?"

"No, I've been digging. And thinking."

"Okay..."

"Just shut up a minute."

"I'm not saying anything."

"Good. I have to think some more." I push my hair back and retie my ponytail. "The thing is, Richard, the thing is that you're a great guy. You're great with the boys, and I know you want to help, but it's hard for me. It's hard to get help. It's hard to let someone else take care of things. And I'll tell you something else, too. The boys aren't going to be staying with me. They don't know it yet but as soon as the caseworker can find a home that will take them both, they're going. I don't know how you feel about that, being adopted yourself. Maybe you don't feel good about it. But if you tell me that, if you make me feel like I'm being self-ish or making the wrong decision, I swear to God I do not know what I will do. So. I felt like I owed you an explana-tion and now you have one. A few, actually." I turn to go.

"Hannah."

"Yeah?"

"Will you look at me?"

I've taken a few steps down the front walk, and I turn and look back. Richard is shivering. Snow is starting to dust his shoulders and his jet-black hair. "Hannah, I'm just going to promise you one thing. It's not that I'm going to say all the right things, or that I know how to make this easier for you. But I will promise that if you let yourself want something for us, then I will do everything I can not to hurt you."

I think about that for a long moment. "If I say something, will you shut up and listen?" I ask. "And then not say anything about it after I get done? Just let me say it?"

"If that's what you want."

"That's what I need."

"All right."

I walk back to him and take his hand. "I'll never be able to tell you how much I miss my father. It's like dreaming in black and white. It's like eating sand. It's like swimming in mud. It's empty and exhausting and it's the worst thing I've ever felt and it's also nothing at all. The end. Do you like lo mein?"

"Yeah," Richard says. "Lo mein is good."

"Good," I say. "Get your coat. I'll share mine with you."

18

Six weeks go by. The March wind still stings my face most mornings, although southern Maine is making tentative efforts to edge out of winter with the occasional sunny afternoon. I don't hear much from Ben Strickland. He hasn't found a placement. Simon is in his new program. Henry has taken Olivia to the movies twice. For my part, second semester of senior year makes very few demands. I go by the DPW when I can, though it's mostly to see the guys since it turned out Dad had some life insurance through work (almost certainly something Mom opted into on his behalf many years ago) and getting hours is less of an imperative. Richard comes around to help the boys with their homework and sometimes to cook, which is good because my efforts in that department have trailed off and the meal-planning board has been entirely neglected. On nights when he can't come, we usually order out.

"Pizza," I command. "Someone call it in."

"We've had pizza twice already this week," Henry says.

"We'll get it with pepperoni this time."

"Pepperoni isn't good for you," Simon tells me.

"Fine," I say, "get it with broccoli or something."

"I liked it when we used to cook," Simon says.

"I used to cook," I tell him. "Me and Grandpa. And now it's just me, and I don't feel like cooking."

Henry grabs the cordless phone from Simon's hand. "Let me fucking have it," he says. He punches in the number for House of Pizza and orders two pies, one plain and one with pepperoni. "A little pepperoni won't kill you," he tells his brother, "and it tastes good."

There has been definite backsliding on the profanity.

"What if I start cooking?" Simon asks.

"That would be good, I guess." I was looking through the Tufts course catalog earlier and I text my latest idea to Richard.

Me: *could do Intro Ecology plus Soc 101, and then ind study on sociology of climate change in the spring*

Richard: *ooh sounds interesting!!!*

It's embarrassing how much he gets off on course selection and it's embarrassing how much I like it. He doesn't get many choices for himself; Richard is going to be pre-med, which means the path is pretty prescribed for him. I, on the other hand, am developing my own major. I've already been emailing the advisor the college assigned me, a biology professor who seems inclined to let me do anything I want so long as I don't take up too much of her time. It works for me, and I've been constructing a series of courses in biology, sociology, and communications all geared toward understanding climate threats and per-suading people to do something about them.

Richard: *might want to do the ind study next summer to get more faculty attention, u know? Maybe take your communication and social psych classes in the spring*

I tap a thumbs-up.

Richard: *love u*

I pause, then text me2. He's said it a few times now, trying it out, but it doesn't feel comfortable, to me at least. It's like a shoe I really like but that doesn't quite fit.

"I need tip money for when the pizza guy comes," Henry says. "What are you doing, Simon?"

"Making a shopping list."

Henry looks over his shoulder. "Pasta, sauce, juice. That's not how you spell sauce."

"I'm doing my best."

Henry shrugs. "I know you like pasta, but you need to come up with some other ideas."

Simon nods and chews on his pencil. "What's the pasta I like?"

"How should I know?" his brother asks.

"It's the stuff Mom used to get."

Henry and I look at each other.

"It looks like little pipes."

"Penne?" I ask.

"Yeah, that's it. How do you spell it?"

"P-e-n-n-e," I say. Pauline rarely comes up. Basically never.

"Is that the kind you guys had when you were kids?" Simon asks me.

"I don't know. Why?"

"Mom always got it. Maybe it's what Grandpa got you guys when you were little."

"It's probably what was cheap," Henry says. "That's probably why Mom got it."

"Why would it be cheaper than pasta in another shape?" Simon asks.

"Good question," I tell him. "And I don't know. Grandpa honestly didn't do a ton of shopping and cooking when I was little."

"He didn't?"

"No."

"He was always doing it for us."

"That was a more recent development. When I was young...not so much."

"Was Grandma still alive when you were young?" Simon asks. "Did she cook?"

"I was four when she died," I say. "I don't really remember."

"Do you remember her?" Simon asks Henry.

"No."

"You met her," I tell Henry. "When you were first born. There's a picture of her holding you in one of the photo albums. I don't like looking at it because she's very sick, she died less than a month later, but she's smiling at you in the picture."

Henry nods. It's quiet in the kitchen. Then Simon looks up from his list. "Someday, when we have kids, we'll tell them about you, Hannah."

"Yeah," I say, "I guess you will." Those will be great stories, all about how I dumped them in a random school hallway and then later sent them off to live with some family Downeast or in central Maine or up on the Canadian border or wherever Ben Strickland can find a spot. Their wonderful aunt Hannah. I think that I might throw up. "I'm gonna go out back," I tell them. "I just have to check on a few things. Yell when the pizza comes, there's money on the front table."

"What do you have to check on?" Henry asks.

"Just stuff. I think there was a coyote a night or two ago. I'm going to look around, make sure nothing is taking up residence in Vine Cottage."

"You want me to come?"

"I'm good. Help Simon with his list."

The ground is frozen again after a weird warm spell melted most of the snow. I walk across the lawn, the grass crunching beneath my feet, until I reach what remains of the crumbling structure.

Dad built Vine Cottage for Pauline. It was a little house, neatly put together and painted, and by the time I came along it was starting to fall apart but I would still sit inside and have cookies and lemonade and pretend to be someone else in another place. Now one of the walls is caving in and the roof is listing at a precarious slant. The water has been getting in for years and the interior is full of decomposing leaves.

I tap one corner of the cottage with the tip of my boot, feeling the lack of integrity in the wood, and look around. Henry and Dad did a lot of work cleaning up dead leaves and branches and mowing the grass. They broke the old swing set down and hauled the pieces away. It looked better than it had in years, and when they were done Dad stood out here with Henry for hours, throwing him line drives and pop flies, rolling him ground balls. They maintained the grass at an inch and a quarter, the same as at Fenway Park, and a few weeks ago Henry came out and raked in preparation for springtime. It made me feel like the worst person in the world.

My phone vibrates. Richard: *check this out—florida state program on climate communication, might use it as a model.* There's a link to an FSU website. I stare at it for a moment, then turn my phone off and put it back in my pocket.

What would happen if I kept them? I push the thought away but it lurks in a corner, nagging at me. They're my parents' grandsons. I don't know what my mom would tell me to do, but if she were alive she would care for them herself. She was a mother. She knew how to do it. She would have already raised me and Pauline; all she would be doing was shifting from us to them.

I'm not a mother. My life is still my own. That is the truth, and I can tell it to the empty cottage: "They are not mine," I say out loud. "They are not mine."

"Hannah!" Henry's voice comes from the kitchen window. "Pizza."

"Coming," I shout. I look around at the yard once more, better maintained in the late Maine winter than in any season of my childhood. Then I walk back to the house.

19

A bit over a week and three pizza nights later, Ben finally did it. He found a placement. I sit at my father's desk, laptop open in front of me, and try to feel excited, or relieved, or something other than what I'm actually feeling.

A 62 percent graduation rate is abysmal.

I click on another link. College matriculation rate. Teen pregnancy. Drug-related convictions.

The state of Maine should shut the fucking place down. They took the kids from Pauline because she couldn't take care of them. One mom with serious problems and the caseworkers swoop in. A whole school district and they're cool with it.

I crack my knuckles one at a time and take in the stats on infrastructure spending. The Evans Beach DPW spends more on maintaining playgrounds than this town does on its entire high school complex.

The door opens behind me and I quickly minimize the screen, clicking over to online payment for the phone bill.

It's Richard. "You want a grilled cheese?" he asks.

"Yeah, sure. Thanks." I reopen the window.

"Still researching?" he asks.

"Yeah. I'll be right out."

He closes the door.

There's not much more to see. I scan the town on Google maps. There aren't exactly busy roads that far north but a county highway runs through. I don't see any playgrounds to speak of, but I do find the town library. It looks small, though it's hard to tell. I close the window, erase the browser history, and look around Dad's room.

Its half cleaned up. I've been working on it in fits and starts, sorting through piles of papers and clothes. The last scraps of baseball memorabilia are still in the glass case. I've given up on Pauline's old room downstairs; now that the boys are going, there's no point making it into something more permanent. I turn off the light and close the door.

The boys are sitting at the table eating grilled cheese sandwiches. "Did you say thank you to Richard?" I ask.

"Thank you," Henry and Simon intone.

"No problem," Richard says, emerging from the kitchen and handing me a plate. "We need fuel for skating."

"You're skating?"

"Yeah, is that cool? I thought I'd take them down to the town rink. They said they've never been ice skating. It's a travesty."

"We're gonna fall on our asses," Henry mutters into his sandwich.

"Hence the need for fuel," Richard says. "Every time you fall, you have to get back up. Want another sandwich, Henry?"

Henry nods and says something that sounds like "yes, please."

"Are you coming to the rink, Hannah?" Simon asks.

"No, I have work to do around the house."

"Can Richard come back for dinner?"

"Richard can come if he wants, but he probably has things he needs to do too."

"Nah, not really," Richard says as he comes back with another plate of sandwiches. "What are you making for dinner, Simon?"

Simon frowns. "Pasta?"

"That's all you know how to make," Henry says.

"Simon's pasta is the best," Richard says. "You sure you're not part Italian, Simon?"

Simon shrugs. "I don't know what I am."

"Well, whatever it is, you got the cooking genes. Pasta for dinner. I'll make salad. Now, eat up, the rink gets crowded in the afternoon."

The boys devour their sandwiches and hurry off to get ready. Richard and I put away the bread and cheese. "How much butter did you use?" I ask, looking at what used to be a full tub.

"That's the secret ingredient. It's what makes it so good. They'll burn it all off this afternoon."

"Butter's expensive. And how much is admission to the rink?"

"My treat."

"You don't have to do that."

"I know I don't have to. I want to."

I pass a wet cloth over the counter and avoid looking up at the dry erase board, still displaying the meals planned for the week of Dad's death over three months ago.

"So?" Richard asks, peeking back into the dining area to make sure neither of the boys are nearby. "What do you think?"

I shrug. "I'm not impressed."

"Not impressed enough to say 'no'?"

"I'm not sure yet. It's way up north. All the statistics suck. But they're just statistics, you know? The family could be great."

"There are always outliers."

"There are, though not many. That's why they're called outliers."

"You could say no," he says. "Right? You could tell the caseworker to look for another place."

"I could, but who knows when another one will come along? It's taken months to get one that would take both of them, and Ben said he was surprised he found it so soon."

"Do you want me to try and get more info about the place? Maybe one of the social workers my parents work with at Maine Med would know something."

"I can figure this out," I tell him. "I can do it on my own."

"You don't have to."

"Actually, yeah, I do."

"Hannah, I'm standing right here next to you."

"You are, but you're just visiting."

"What's that supposed to mean?"

"It means you're a tourist."

"I am not a tourist. I know more about this shit than anyone."

"Why? Because you were adopted?"

"That's right, because I was adopted. And you want to know what my single biggest fear was when I was a kid? My biggest fear was that they would send me back."

"I don't need this shit, Richard..."

"I'm serious, Hannah. You don't know what it's like to know you have been lost and then were somehow found. You don't know the fear that it's going to happen again. I want to help you to do this the right way, the best way for..."

"Shut the fuck up." I reach out with one hand and shove him, hard, in the middle of the chest. "I mean it," I say. "Go. You don't know what you're talking about. You don't have a clue."

"So, tell me."

"This was supposed to be just until Pauline pulled it all together," I say. "And then she screwed up and it was just until the second chance panned out, and of course that didn't happen either. Then it was just until college, just until I left Dad with the two of them, and now it's just until Ben Strickland finds a double placement and I am fucking out of just untils."

Richard stares at me. He doesn't say anything. I look at the countertop, already wiped clean twice.

"Richard, we're ready!"

Richard opens his mouth to say something, then closes it.

I turn, grab him by both shoulders, and shove him toward the door. "Go," I say. "Now."

"Here I come," he calls. His eyes are still on mine. Then he turns and walks away. There's a moment of controlled chaos in the front hall as everyone pulls on their coats and boots. Then the door closes.

I wait to hear Richard's car start up and the engine fade away down the road. I stand still for a long time. There are a million things to be done, the lunch dishes among them, but instead I stand in the middle of the kitchen and think that Richard Greene, for all his brilliance, was only half right. I do know how it feels to be lost; I just don't know how it feels to be found.

Minutes go by and then I go into Dad's room, sit down at the computer, and send a short email telling Ben Strickland that I can keep the boys for a little while longer and that I want him to find a different placement.

I don't drink, not really, but now there are nights when I open one of Dad's beers and pour it into his Red Sox stein and force the foul-tasting stuff down because the smell reminds me of him and because it eventually makes me feel better. I tell myself that once the case he had in the pantry is done then I will be, too.

There were fifteen bottles before tonight. Now there

are eleven. I lean against the back of the house, the hard ground freezing my ass, and watch my breath disappear in the light of the moon. I try to conjure a photo of Mom, sorting through my mental supply. The beer is making them hazy. I take another sip.

"Henry said he thought you were out here." Richard approaches from the driveway side of the yard. Beyond him, in the dark, the cemetery is silent.

"Dinner's done?" I ask.

"All done. They're having a movie night. I made popcorn."

I hiccup.

Richard sits next to me. I don't look at him. We let it be silent for several minutes. I want to apologize for what happened earlier, but somehow the words are hard to find. I sink deeper into my jacket and shiver.

"I'm sorry," Richard says. "I didn't mean to make you feel guilty. It's just that I want so bad to help you, to help them, to try and make this whole thing be okay. I want them to wind up like me, with people who love them, in a situation that will be all right. That will be good."

I want to tell him what it's like for me, too, but it occurs to me that I think he knows, so instead I lean over and kiss him. "You taste like beer," he says.

"I'm sorry I shoved you."

"It's okay."

"It's not." I kiss him again.

"How much have you had to drink?"

"Just one beer," I lie. "How much time is left in the boys' movie?"

"They were starting the sequel."

"I'm cold."

"Me too."

"Where's your car?"

"Driveway."

I struggle to my feet. "Let's go."

"Where?"

"To the car. We can sit in it, it will be warm. Warmer, at least."

Richard looks up at me. "Hannah?"

"Yeah?"

"I definitely love you."

I burp, bringing some sort of acidic substance up into my mouth. "K."

"You realize you never say it back? You're always like 'me too,' or 'thanks!' It's a little…disheartening."

I sway on my feet and spit to one side. "You're an idiot," I say. "You're going to Harvard."

"What does Harvard have to do with anything?"

"You're going to meet tons of girls at Harvard. Amazing girls."

"You're an amazing girl."

"Yeah," I say, "sure. Amazing."

"You are."

I burp again and stumble this time, putting one arm out to lean against the side of the house.

"You sure you only had one beer?" Richard asks.

"No."

"I didn't think so."

"I don't feel great."

"Maybe you should go to bed instead of my car."

I crouch back down.

"You need help?"

"No. Maybe. I feel all wobbly. Are you going to pick me up and carry me in?"

"Do you want me to?"

"Well, Richard, first of all there is a non-trivial chance that I am going to vomit all over your face if you try to pick me up. And second, if you really want to help, then what I need is for the two loads of laundry in front of the washing machine to be done and for someone to stay up with the boys and make sure they eventually go to sleep."

"Uh...I think I'd rather take you to bed."

"I bet you would." I pat his cheek. Then I grab Dad's empty beer mug, rise, and stumble inside, making my way to my room. A moment later I hear Richard calling to Simon and Henry. I shed my coat and kick off my boots, then crawl into my bed tent and wrap myself in a blanket, and just before closing my eyes I whisper: "I love you, too."

20

Simon is eating what appear to be raw potatoes. I hear the crunch when he bites into them from across the room. "Stop it," I say. "Those will make you sick."

Simon looks up unhappily from his plate. "It's okay with ketchup."

"Why didn't you cook them?"

"I tried, but the first one blew up in the microwave."

Shit. "I thought Henry was going to cook dinner?"

"He didn't want to cook."

"What do you mean, he didn't want to cook? Where is he?"

"I think he's outside," Simon says. "He's feeling sad."

"Why do you think Henry's sad?"

"Henry cries. At night, when he thinks I'm asleep."

"How long has that been going on?" I ask.

Simon shrugs.

"Since Grandpa died?"

"Not that long."

"And you think Henry went out?"

He nods.

"Okay." I stand, walk to the back window, and look at the yard. Dusk is falling and it's cold. Winter came back with one more snowfall, leaving an inch on the ground. "Where do you think he went?"

"Maybe out walking?"

"Well, it's getting dark" I say. "I'm going to look for him. You stay here, and make PB&J sandwiches for us."

"Chips and Fluff?"

"No chips or Fluff." I pull my coat on and go outside. It's even colder than I thought. I walk across the front yard and look both ways, up and down the road. No Henry. Where would he go? I decide to circle the house and walk toward the gas station side first, my footsteps crunching in the thin crust of new snow. The vacant lot is overgrown but much of the underbrush has died back and I can see all the way across. There's no sign of life. I continue down the hill into the backyard, past Vine Cottage, scanning the woods behind the house before rounding the corner to the cluster of old lawnmowers, and it's there that I see the footprints. They begin under the family room window and lead directly away from the house, into the graveyard. I pull my jacket tight and follow them.

Dad is buried in the new cemetery, on the other side of town, next to Mom. I wrote out what I wanted on his stone and wished that it could have been something similar to the couple I like to visit out here, the ones who claim to have had it all, but that wasn't my parents' story.

I thought for a while and then I jotted down: "Larry Lynn: husband, father, grandfather, second baseman for the 1980 Red Sox," and I handed it to the engraver along with a check.

Henry's footprints head deeper into the graveyard. I follow as they wind between gravestones and around mausoleums. It's been a while since I walked in this old section, and things aren't holding up well. Some of the stones are tipped over.

The tracks end in a patch behind a family crypt. I walk in a circle, trying to pick them up again. I'm standing by a rickety gravestone for a husband, a wife, and a young child who all died of something on the same date 150 years ago.

Where is he? I open my mouth to call, but worry that he'd run. Then a thought occurs to me and I walk back over to the crypt. Someone told me that they don't lock these things, the theory being that when people rise up on Judgment Day they need to be able to get out. It's as asinine as every other religious idea I've ever heard. God can raise the dead but he can't unlock the door? I tug on the metal handle and it swings open.

Henry is sitting at the far end, his back against the wall, his knees pulled up against his chest. The inside is all marble, and there are drawers with names carved in them on both sides.

"Are you doing drugs?" I ask.

"I'm not doing drugs."

"So, what the hell are you doing in there?"

"It's cold."

"Of course it's cold. You know where it's not cold? At home."

He stares at me.

"For real," I say. "I paid the heating oil bill and everything. Come on back."

"I don't feel like it."

"Well, at least come out. I don't like it in here. Plus, it's probably trespassing or something."

Henry pushes himself to his feet, sliding up the smooth marble wall, walks toward me, and steps outside. I close the door behind him. "Who do you think owns it anyway?" I ask. "You think the family just pays outright when it gets built? I mean, you can't really do an installment plan. What a waste of money, right?"

Henry shrugs.

"You going to talk to me?"

"What do you want to talk about?"

"I don't know, maybe why you're sitting in some random family's mausoleum, in the freezing cold, at dusk?"

Henry sits on a gravestone. He studies the ground at his feet.

"I'm worried that you're depressed, Henry. I mean, it would be sort of normal, but I've read about depression. Grandpa was depressed for a long time after Grandma died. One thing about it was that he lost interest in what he used to like. It's called anhedonia. I see it in you. I mean, I reminded you to sign up for spring baseball about a dozen times. Coach called today, he left a message on my phone. You still haven't done it."

"And you think I've lost interest in baseball."

"Have you?"

"You think you're so smart, Hannah. Worse than that, you don't think anyone else has any brains of their own. You think you have everyone figured out, and you don't think other people can figure things out for themselves."

I stare at him for a moment. "What have you figured out?" I ask, a pit opening in my stomach.

"The bank account. Grandpa always left the file open on his computer with all the passwords in it."

"So...you've been checking the statement online? Why would you do that?" Even as I ask, I can see myself as a kid, rooting through the mail for the bank statements and the credit card bill. There's no better way to keep an eye on what's going on in a family.

Henry doesn't answer. He raises his eyes but stares past me into the fading light.

"There's nothing interesting on there," I say. "There are no secrets. What, you think I'm paying too much for groceries?"

"The art lessons."

"Simon's art lessons?"

"Yeah."

"What about them?"

"They're month-to-month. You used to pay six months ahead for a five percent discount. In February you went to monthly."

The pit widens.

"There's one reason you would do that," he continues.

"Simon loves those classes. The only reason to change it is if you think we're not going to be here."

I want to sink into the stone behind me. I want to melt into the ground, down among the graves with the bones of the little three-person family.

"You want me to sign up for baseball?" Henry asks. "Am I going to be here at the end of the season?"

"Henry..."

"Tell me it's not true."

"Does your brother know?"

"No."

"I was going to talk to you when there was something concrete. Nothing's definite yet."

Henry doesn't respond and I finally force myself to look at him. "What do you want to ask me? I'll tell you what I can."

Henry stands, brushing snow off the back of his pants. I know the look on his face. I can feel it on my own. The jaw set, the lips drawn. "You better not be thinking of separating us," he says. "Putting Simon somewhere different from me. Because that is not going to happen."

I ignore the catch in his voice and try to keep my own steady. "No," I say, "that's not going to happen." I pause. "I know you must be thinking about Olivia."

"I don't have any other questions." He turns his back and starts to walk away.

"Henry."

He stops. "What?"

"Don't tell Simon. Not yet."

"Actually, I do have a question."

"What is it?"

"Why can't we stay?"

"Because with Dad gone, I'm alone. I can't do this alone."

"You're not alone. You have me, I'm old enough to help."

"I have to leave, Henry. I have to go to college. I'm going to Tufts in the fall. I have to live my life."

"What are you doing now? Isn't this your life?"

"This is the life I was given. It's not the life I chose." I want to say something more, but anything else wouldn't be true. Dad tried to make it my choice when he asked for my permission that very first night at Sol's, but it never was. I didn't have any more choice than I've had in anything else. Everyone else gets to make their own choices: Richard, Amity, even Dad and Pauline; he chose to be here and she chose to walk away. Why not me?

Henry is still for another moment, listening to the wind. I watch him and I feel a strange sense of pride. He's smart; he figured things out, just like I used to. At fourteen he looks so grown-up, so self-contained. I want to tell him something about that, tell him that no matter what happens I know he'll be able to handle it.

Henry looks around, shrugs, and walks in the direction of the house. I watch him go, waiting until he's too far to hear, and then I turn away and I kick the gravestone behind me, again and again, teeth clenched to muffle the sobs welling up from my chest. I hate Dad, I hate Pauline, and I hate myself. I give the stone one final, furious kick and it breaks free of the frozen earth and falls. I look down at the marker for the family of three. Whatever took them—some nineteenth-century illness, an accident, a fire, an act of violence—took them all at the same time, on the same day, leaving no one behind to deal with the mess.

I'll come back in the spring, I tell myself, when the ground is soft, before I leave for Tufts, and I'll fix their grave. I turn, drying my eyes, and follow Henry home.

21

They told me to elevate my leg, but it's hard. It's hot. Way hotter than it's supposed to be in April, and sweat gets underneath the bandages and it itches. If it hadn't been warm and wet, then the grass wouldn't have grown so damn quickly and I wouldn't have been out in the backyard a week ago feeling too guilty to ask Henry or Simon to mow, feeling even guiltier if I let the grass grow long, stepping in a newly dug rabbit hole and turning my ankle.

Something crashes in the kitchen.

"Hannah!"

"What, Simon?"

"There are so many dishes in the sink that I can't wash them!"

I close my eyes and slowly count to five. "Take half the dirty dishes out of the sink, set them on the counter, wash the first batch, then wash the others."

A moment of silence. Then: "I'm hungry."

"Wash the dishes, Simon, and then you can make yourself a PB&J."

There's the clank of dishes and silverware. I rest my head against the back of the couch and listen to a truck rumble down the road. It sounds like one of the diesels from DPW, but I don't twist around to look.

"Hannah, I'm super hungry."

"Fine! Eat something and then wash the dishes."

"Can you help me find the penne?"

I wiggle off the couch, stand on one foot, and brace myself against a crutch. "Coming." I hobble into the kitchen where Simon is standing in front of an open cabinet. "There's pasta right in front of you," I say, even though I know what his response will be.

"I want penne."

I push boxes of farfalle out of the way. "It all tastes the same," I tell him for the thousandth time, yanking a half-full box of penne from the back and handing it over.

"Thank you. I'll do all the dishes after."

I eye the overflowing sink. "You do that. I have to be off my feet." I make my way back into the living room and drop onto the couch, setting the crutch on the floor, slowly rolling my neck in a circle to crack the joints in my vertebrae.

My phone buzzes. Richard: hows it feel?

I tap a reply: better today.

Bubbles as he composes something, then a pause, then an apparently modified single word response: really??

I can't help but smile. He can always tell when I'm

bullshitting, even when he's out of town visiting a friend who was a year ahead of us in school and is already at Harvard. I send back an eye-roll emoji.

Offer stands, he texts. Said offer, proffered a number of times via phone, text, and email, is for a house call by one of his parents on their way home from work later on today. Richard doesn't trust the urgent care place in the mall.

Thank u, I text back. Ill call them if its not way better in a few days.

Thought it was better?

Better not way better.

I shift uncomfortably on the couch, punch a cushion in an effort to make it a shape that it's not, and close my eyes, trying to think about anything other than what I've been thinking about for the last week.

The placement is perfect. They'll take both boys. A single-family home. Ben said it was a minor miracle that a second option opened up so soon. I know he's been working overtime to make something work for the boys. He gave me some family details: Mom is a retired teacher, Dad is an oral surgeon. They've raised three boys of their own. They have a labradoodle. The town has an active baseball league, and their school system has a 96-percent graduation rate and a specialized program comparable to CARES. Ben ticked these points off on the phone, sounding tired like he always does, and with each piece of information my stomach sank lower and lower. "I'll think about it," I told him. "I just hurt my ankle and they gave me some pain meds and I'm having a tough time focusing."

"All right," he said, "just don't take too long. I have other candidates for this placement."

I was lying about the meds; they gave me a vial with some pills at urgent care but I flushed them down the toilet as soon as I got home. I was telling the truth about not thinking straight, though. The placement is everything I've held out for, so why don't I want it?

I open my eyes and roll over. I'm hungry. Maybe there will be extra penne. I get up and hobble across the room, pausing to sort through a pile of papers on a side table. I need to get this place cleaned up. I need to decide what I'm going to do with it; if I'm at Tufts and the boys are in a new home, then there's no reason not to sell.

The papers are a random assortment of junk mail and condolence notes from a few months ago, some stained with the sauce of casseroles and lasagnas they accompanied. I flip a few open, absently scanning them, before one catches my eye. It's from Ms. Harper, written to me, expressing her sorrow at Dad's passing and her availability to help in any way she can. It's not what the note says that catches my eye, though, it's the way it's written. The handwriting. There's something about it. I know it would click if I wasn't so tired. I tap the card against my chin, thinking.

Simon's scream shatters the silence in the house. It's a long, terrified wail, an inchoate combination of syllables with my name buried somewhere inside of it.

"Simon!"

He screams again, and this time my name is clear. "Hannah!"

I frantically hop toward the kitchen. "Simon, what happened? Simon!"

I round the corner. Simon is standing half turned from me, his arms spread wide and flexed as though holding a giant beach ball. The colander is balanced on the edge of the cluttered sink. The pot is next to it. The cooked pasta is on the floor. The front of his shirt is soaking wet, and there's steam rising from it. Rising from him.

Simon doesn't move, but his eyes find me. "Hannah..."

"Oh God, Simon, don't move, don't move..." I hobble to him, my ankle crying out, and grab his shirt. The fabric burns my hands; I can't pull it over his face. "Hold on." I take kitchen shears from the knife rack and cut from the neck hole, splitting his T-shirt down the middle and peeling it back from his torso. I take one look at his skin, and now it's my turn to scream: "Henry!"

Henry was in the yard, filling in the rabbit hole. The back door bangs downstairs, and then feet on the steps. "What's going on?" Henry bursts into the kitchen and freezes, staring at his little brother. Tears are streaming down Simon's face and he's hopping from one foot to the other as though he wants out of his own burnt skin. "Holy shit!"

"Call 911," I say, pulling the cut shirt off of Simon, who for the moment is strangely silent. Henry grabs the kitchen phone and dials. I stare at Simon's chest. I hear Henry speaking into the phone, giving our address and Simon's age and telling them to hurry. "Oh, Simon," I say. I don't know what to do.

"You were supposed to be watching him!"

"What?"

"You were supposed to be watching him," Henry repeats, his voice rising, phone still gripped in his hand. "Why weren't you watching him?"

"I...he was...the sink was too full..."

"He spilled boiling fucking water right down—"

It's then that Simon starts to really scream. His first cries had been of shock and outrage, the way you scream when something has just happened and you think that, maybe if you object forcefully enough, the universe will go ahead and roll the spool of time back a few moments, just this once. This scream is different. It's as though a million nerve endings jumped to life inside of him and he can't contain the pain.

"We need to put ice on him!" Henry cries. He yanks the freezer door open and starts tearing things out, dumping them on the floor: frozen green beans, cans of orange juice concentrate, a turkey thigh left over from the holidays and covered in freezer burn inside a ziplock bag. I stand, staring, wondering whether ice is, in fact, the thing to do. Why don't I know what to do? I know a million useless facts but I don't know how to fix this.

A siren sounds from far down the road. "Go to the door," I tell Henry. He runs out of the room. "Simon," I say, my voice hoarse, "it's gonna be okay. We're going to take you to the hospital and take care of that nasty burn, and then..." And then what? I have no idea about "and then."

Simon isn't listening to me anyway. He's still screaming when, after what seems like an eternity, Henry leads two EMTs into the kitchen and the bigger of the two, a guy with a thick mustache and a mole on the bridge of his nose, looks at him, looks at me, and asks, "Where are the parents?"

"Not…here," I manage.

"You're the big sister?"

"No…"

The man turns away and helps position a stretcher next to Simon. A police officer comes in to help. "She's just the babysitter," the EMT with the mustache tells him. "It's a pretty bad burn. No parents, but we have to transport anyway."

The policeman nods without glancing at me. I don't try to correct them; "aunt" doesn't seem like it will have much more status in this situation than "babysitter." I give Simon's name and my phone number to the smaller EMT, who jots them in a notepad along with our address.

Simon is crying when they lie him down, and when they strap him in, and when they push him out of the kitchen and out of the house, and I, momentarily forgetting about my ankle, rush to follow and go sprawling on the floor, my ankle singing in pain.

"Henry! Bring me the crutch."

Henry, thankfully past criticism and into compliance mode, hurries to the living room, returns with the crutch, and helps me to my feet. I wrap one arm over his shoulder and we stumble to the door like the saddest three-legged race in history, just in time to see them loading Simon into the ambulance. The policeman is already gone. The

EMT with the mustache looks back. "Let his parents know we're going to Maine Med," he calls across the yard. He climbs inside, slams the door, and the sirens sound again as the ambulance pulls away from the curb and drives past the cemetery, around the bend, toward Route 77.

Henry and I are left standing in the open door. "Fuck," I say. "Fuck fuck fuck fuck fuck."

"Let's go," Henry says.

"I can't drive, Henry." I grope for my phone. "You know I can't work the fucking clutch with my ankle." My car is long gone; I've been driving Dad's old truck—which is a manual—for months. Richard had to come over and take me to urgent care when I got hurt, and he's been giving us rides when we he can, but right now he's in Cambridge. We're stranded.

"I'll drive! I've seen you do it a million times."

"That's not how it works." I desperately scroll through my contacts, looking for someone who could come right away, someone who could pick me up. A taxi would take too long to come from Portland.

"Come on, Hannah!"

"All right. Just do exactly what I say." I jam the keys into his hand and hop furiously to the truck, pulling the passenger door open and sliding inside, shoving the crutch over my shoulder and into the back seat. Henry runs to the other side of the car and gets into the driver's seat. "Work the clutch like I tell you to," I say. "I'll work the gearshift."

Henry turns the truck on. I try to explain how he

needs to press down on the clutch gently every time we shift gears in what is doubtless the world's fastest and least effective tutorial on operating a manual transmission. "Now, do it," I conclude. He does, and I drop into reverse. We roll out of the driveway, Henry pulling on the wheel to turn in the direction the ambulance went. He slams on the brake and my head slaps the back of the seat as we come to a shuddering, stalled stop. "Let's go again, but easy. Remember the clutch." I wait for him to comply and then shift into first gear. "Now, hit the gas."

Henry hits it a little too hard. The engine races. I desperately try to upshift, my left foot reaching for a pedal that isn't there. "Clutch, clutch," I say, "we need to get out of first." The truck bucks hard and the engine stalls. "Fuck!"

Henry shakes his head, his jaw set. "Let's try again."

I put the transmission in neutral. "Push the clutch, then let go gently." This time we stall out harder, the truck shuddering.

"I can do this," Henry mutters. He's holding the wheel so tight that his knuckles look like bones protruding from the back of his hand.

We try again. I pay closer attention to his timing, waiting to shift. Again, the truck shakes but this time it doesn't stall. "Keep going," I say as we get to the end of our street, "don't stop." Henry blows through the stop sign and onto Route 77 like stopping was the last thing on his mind, and we finally hit third gear. The truck would be happier in fourth, but I'm not pushing this lesson or our luck any further. I call Richard's cell and he picks up on the second ring. "Richard," I say, "I need you to call one of your parents."

"Hannah? What's the matter?"

"It's Simon. He burned himself, really bad. The sink was full of fucking dirty dishes and he was making pasta and he was trying to hurry because, well, because I'm such an asshole and he tried to balance the goddamned colander…"

"Hannah, slow down. Stop. Where are you?"

"I'm going to the hospital!" I shout. "I'm going to Maine Med! They took him in an ambulance and he's going to show up in the ER looking like some street kid and they're going to know that he has Medicaid and some fucking med student is going to kill him unless one of your parents meets him there…"

"Hannah, stop it, stop. That's not how it works. They'll get a burn specialist, there's a team…"

"Richard," I say, "please, please call your mom or dad and tell them to meet me in the ER as soon as they can." I hang up.

There's hardly any traffic and our path is mostly clear, largely because Henry bears down on every car ahead of us while leaning on the horn and they wisely pull out of our way. I have to assume that half the Evans Beach Police Department will be out looking for us before we make it to the Casco Bay Bridge, but we reach the Portland city line without being stopped. "We need to bear right up ahead," I tell Henry. "We need to avoid the hill."

He shakes his head. "The hill's faster."

"Hills are hard in a manual. You're not ready for a hill. Just go right..."

He bears left. He's just as pigheaded and stubborn as his grandpa was. "Fine," I say, "be an asshole, but we have to shift. Now. Clutch." I drop us into second. We turn up the hill on what is, to be fair, the straightest path to the hospital.

"Dammit," Henry says. Cars are stopped at a light up ahead. He brakes without hitting the clutch, and we come to a jerking stop.

"All right," I say, "getting started on a hill is tricky. You have to do exactly what I say."

"Green, Hannah."

The cars are starting to move. "Very gently, I want you to..."

Henry takes his foot off the brake and jams the clutch and the gas at the same time, but we're still in second. We roll back, engine revving uselessly. "Damnit!" Henry yells, grabbing the gearshift out of my hand and trying to throw us into first. The truck stutters for a moment, then stalls. I take the gear back and speak as calmly and steadily as I can: "Ignore the traffic, take a breath, press the clutch... now release it, and press the gas." Henry does it flawlessly this time, and we move up the hill.

Traffic cleared out in the time we were struggling with the transmission and there's a stretch of open pavement. Henry gets us to thirty, thirty-five, as we finally seem to master our collaborative shifting. "Take a right up here," I tell him.

"Okay."

"Don't slow down too much."

He doesn't. "I'm sorry I yelled at you," Henry says.

"I'm sorry I left him alone."

We don't say anything else until we get to Maine Med, park, and Henry helps me to the sliding doors for the ER. "Hey," I call to the nurse at the desk as we enter, "we're meeting an ambulance coming from Evans Beach with a kid who was burned."

The nurse studies the screen in front of her. "They're en route."

"What do you mean, en route?"

"They're about four minutes out."

"We beat them here?" Henry asks. "What the fuck kind of ambulance is that?"

The nurse stares at us, then looks back to her monitor. "Three minutes," she says.

"Just show us where they're going to arrive," I say.

The nurse looks back up at me. "You can't go to the ambulance bay. You need to wait until a doctor comes out."

"Wait where?"

The nurse gestures at the space behind us. "The waiting area."

"No—look, I need to be there when the ambulance pulls in, in—what, two minutes now?"

She shakes her head. "Staff only in the ambulance bay."

"You're not listening to me," I say, limping toward the counter. "Can you call Dr. Greene? Either one of them? She's the head of her department, I think. Nephrology. Call one of them down here."

The nurse looks at me doubtfully. "The treating doctor will be out once the patient is stabilized. Until then…"

"Would you let his mother in?" Henry asks. "He's a little kid. Would you let his mom go back?"

"In many situations we do allow parents of young children to be bedside, yes."

"Well then, let us in, because Hannah is basically his mother. She's the closest thing he has. She's his aunt and like, a resource parent, or whatever it's called. I don't know what to call her, all I know is that Simon needs her to be waiting for him when he gets here."

The nurse looks at me quizzically, sizing me up. "You're responsible for him? You look about seventeen, honey."

"I'm eighteen. I'm his aunt. I have to be there."

The nurse sighs and rubs her eyes. I wonder how long she's been on this shift. She stands, steps out from behind her desk, walks over to a double door, and punches in a code. It swings open. "I'll let you go in," she says, "but if we have any problems, security will show you right out."

"Thank you," I say, limping past. There's a flurry of activity at the end of the hall, another set of doors opening, this one to the outside, and I put my arm around Henry's shoulder for balance. He helps me toward it.

We're right behind the medical team when they wheel Simon in. I crane my neck to see him. His eyes are closed and he's pale. They have him wrapped in a blanket. A doctor is calling out orders, something about an IV.

"Is he okay?" Henry says. "Is he? Can you see?"

I watch as they transfer Simon to a gurney and push

him toward a room where more staff is waiting. They pause, and there's a discussion between two of the people at the front of the crowd. Simon turns his head and opens his eyes, and I think that he sees me. I move toward him, hobbling on my crutch, feeling like even my good leg is made of rubber. I reach out and run my fingers along the side of his palm. His eyes are closed again. There are too many things I want to say: *This shouldn't have happened, I should have been there, this is my fault. I'm sorry.*

His fingers flutter against mine. "Simon," I say, "I love you. I'm here."

The doctors and nurses make some sort of decision and then they're moving again, Simon's hand is pulled out from under mine, and I'm left standing alone in the middle of an empty hall. I don't know who to talk to. I don't know what I would say if I could. I can't breathe, and I think that I might fall.

Henry appears at my side. He puts one arm around my waist, keeping me up. "I think he's going to be all right," he says.

Ben Strickland picks up on the third ring. "It's Hannah Lynn," I say. "There's been an incident. I'm supposed to report incidents, right?"

"An incident with who?" he asks.

"Simon."

"What happened?"

Simon has second-degree burns on his torso and they'll

keep him overnight to start topical treatment, make sure he's hydrated, and get him going with preventative antibiotics—but he will, as Henry predicted, be all right.

Ben listens to the story. "Got it," he says. "I'll make a note in the file. Thanks for calling."

"Is that all you ever do?" I ask, exhausted and exasperated at him in the absence of anyone besides myself to be pissed at. "Make notes in their files?"

"I do more than that, Hannah. I found a potential placement. Two, actually."

I'm silent.

"Do you need anything?" he finally asks.

"What, now?"

"Yes."

I look around the hospital room. Both of Richard's parents did show up in the ER. They spoke to the doctor in that confident "we're all in the same club" way that doctors speak to each other, and after that the people caring for Simon treated me like I was a real person and not some neglectful lowlife who let the kid I was responsible for pour boiling water down his front. They also moved us to a nice room. "We're good, thanks," I tell Ben.

"All right. Call back if…"

"Wait, before you get off the phone, I have a question."

There's silence on the line. "Yeah?"

"I mean, you've seen these situations play out, right? Situations like mine. What I want to know is, do you think, if I keep them with me, the boys…do you think it will be worth it?"

"Worth it how?"

"Will it change things for them? Ten years, twenty years from now. Looking back, will it have been worth it? When I'm, like, forty years old?"

"I don't think that's the right question. I think the question has to be whether it's worth it today."

"What kind of an answer is that?"

"It's not an answer. But I think the fact that you're asking me this question might be the answer you need."

I close my eyes.

"I'll keep holding that placement for as long as I can," he says, "but you have to let me know soon. And let me know how Simon does."

"Right. Fine. Thanks." I set the phone down. Henry went to the cafeteria to find some food. Simon is sleeping with the help of painkillers and a sedative. I stand, stretch, and hobble out into the hall.

"There you are."

I turn and see Richard hurrying toward me. "What are you doing here?" I ask.

"Mom and Dad spoke to Simon's doctor. It sounds like he's going to be okay?"

"Yeah. You're supposed to be in Cambridge. How did you get here?"

"How do you think? I drove. Fast. Are you all right?"

"I...uh..." I don't know how to answer. "I didn't do the dishes," I finally say. "So the sink was way too full." I start to cry, standing in the middle of the hall, with nurses passing by pretending they don't see. Richard spreads his arms wide and wraps them around me. "Was it hard to get here?" I finally ask into his shoulder.

"What?"

"From Cambridge."

"We've driven Cambridge to Maine together. Traffic was…"

"That's not what I mean. I mean…do you mind doing it? Maybe semi-regularly?"

"Oh. No. No, Cambridge to Evans Beach is very doable."

"That's good."

"Yeah?"

"Maybe. Yeah, maybe it is." I put my arms around Richard. After another moment we go back into the room, to be there when Simon wakes up.

22

No one wants to go by Henrietta Harper. Still, if that's your name, what do you do? A girl isn't going to make the situation better by using "Henri" or something like that. Kids can be cruel once they pick you out as being different. I should know.

"Do your close friends call you Etta?" I ask.

Ms. Harper stands in her doorway, looking at me, looking at the postcard in my hand. "Yes," she says, "as a matter of fact, they do." She leans out and looks up and down the street. "How did you get here, Hannah?"

"Richard dropped me off. He'll come back when I text."

"He's a sweet boy."

"He is."

"Would you like to come in?"

I nod and she steps aside. I hoist myself in on the crutch.

"What happened to your leg?" Ms. Harper asks.

"It's just my ankle. I stepped in a hole."

"Oh, dear. Let me get you some tea."

"I don't want to bother you."

"It's no bother. Come on." She leads me into the living room and then departs for the kitchen.

A heavy wood chest, covered in framed photos, covers the length of one wall. I study them. Jessie Harper stares out of preschool and kindergarten portraits, youth soccer action shots, and then morphs, farther down the line, into the high school years. Varsity soccer. Junior prom. Apart from one picture of Ms. Harper at some sort of work party, holding a plaque and smiling, all the images are of her and Jessie and no one else.

"Here we are." She comes back into the room carrying two steaming mugs. "Come sit."

I cross to a padded leather armchair and set the crutch on the floor, then lower myself to sit. I'm very careful with the tea. I don't want to spill. This is a rare day on which I'm wearing one of Mom's original shirts, a worn button-down. I felt like I was going to need it.

Ms. Harper sits across from me. "What do you have there?" she asks.

I hand over the postcard from Cape May, the one written to my mother years ago, the one from the elusive "E." The handwriting matched Kevin's name tag from some long-ago children's party, one Ms. Harper must have helped facilitate, and it matched the note that came with the casserole. "You and my mother were friends," I say.

"Of course we were."

"No, I mean, not just church friends. You were good friends."

Ms. Harper nods and looks down into her mug. "I considered her to be my best friend."

"Why didn't I know that?"

Ms. Harper looks up and smiles. "It's no secret, Hannah. I was barely forty when Alessandra died. I was a single mother with a four-year-old but I did everything I could to help your father. You spent a night or two here at this house, shortly after she passed. Do you remember that?"

"No."

"No, you were so little, and I think... well, traumatized. There's no other word for it. But I tried to step in. You got older, though, and it was harder. Frankly, you didn't want to be mothered. Do you remember the day I tried to drive you home from track?"

"I'm not sure."

"You and Jessie were in the seventh grade. You weren't close anymore, but you were both on the team. I came by to pick her up at the field and you were waiting for your father. I had been running late and all the other kids were gone. I lingered as long as I could, making small talk although you weren't much up for it, and eventually it became clear that your father wasn't coming."

"He had a tendency to be forgetful."

"Do you remember that I offered you a ride?"

I nod.

"Do you remember what you did?"

"I walked."

"You insisted on walking. It was starting to rain. There were thunderclouds. I drove alongside you for a good quarter-mile, trying to coax you into the car. You were having none of it."

"It's embarrassing, now. I'm sorry."

"Don't be. The only reason I bring it up, Hannah, is that there wasn't much opportunity, as you grew older, for us to talk. For me to explain that your mother was once my dearest friend."

"I understand." I sip my tea, look around, try to think of what to say next.

"How are the children, Hannah?"

"Okay."

"I'll be honest, I heard there was an ambulance at your house a few days ago and I was concerned. Was it for your ankle?"

"How did you hear about that?"

She smiles and shrugs. "Mom network."

"That's a thing?"

"Of course. Evans Beach Mothers is a very active Facebook group."

I shake my head. "We're all right. It wasn't my ankle, though." I tell her the story of Simon's burn.

She listens carefully. When I finish, she sets her cup on a table by her chair. "That must have been terrifying."

I nod.

"You're one hundred percent responsible for those children now, aren't you?"

"Yeah. For the time being."

"What's going to happen?"

I squint down into my mug. "Are you going to put it on Facebook?"

"What, in the group? Certainly not! I monitor that for news but almost never post. Maybe once in a while, to find a good plumber."

"I have to decide whether to keep them."

"I see."

"The caseworker has been looking for a new family. He's trying to keep them together. I told him he has to, I won't let them go if they get separated. That was really important to Dad. And he did find a place, and it sounds great, and I have to let him know about it. Soon."

"What about your plans? College?"

"I don't know. I'm just going day to day, trying to get through, putting out fires."

"Sounds like parenthood."

"Does it?"

"Sure. I used to have a mantra, when Jessie was young and I was completely exhausted, tired and overwhelmed, and I didn't know how I was going to make it through the next five minutes, let alone her entire childhood. I'd think: hold on, just until tomorrow. Just until tomorrow."

"What happened when tomorrow came?"

"I did it again."

I nod and sip the tea. It's steaming hot and tastes like lemon.

"Is there some way I can help you with this, Hannah?"

"I don't know. I don't know if anyone around here understands what this is like. Everyone my age is leaving and going someplace amazing. Richard is going to Harvard, Amity is going to Cornell. Jessie is going to Northwestern, right? No one has a life like mine."

She raises her eyebrows. "I can understand that. I wasn't born with all this, you know." She gestures at the room around us. "My father worked in a mill, and he died when I was seven years old. I was the youngest of five children and I got married to an older guy when I was nineteen. Bob was a teacher. I was pregnant on our wedding day. We didn't have much, and I didn't have anything after he left with one of his students."

"You were pregnant?"

"I lost that child, miscarried."

"Oh—I'm sorry."

"Jessie was a later-in-life decision. Her father was reportedly quite a superstar at MIT, though maybe that's what they tell everyone at the sperm bank."

"How did you wind up here?"

"I got a job at the credit union, as a teller. I went to school at night. I got promoted. Assistant branch manager, then branch manager. They brought me to Portland. I worked harder. I made VP the day before my thirty-second birthday."

"That's impressive."

She shrugs and sips her tea. I look around the room again and marvel at how quiet and still it is. The only movement is the dust, floating through the sunlight by the windows. "I feel like you're the person I need to talk to," I finally say.

"About what?'

"Advice."

She shakes her head. "No, Hannah. I learned a long time ago not to give advice, particularly on the sort of decision you're facing."

"Why not?"

"Well, for one thing, all the advice I ever received was bad. 'Marry again,' for one. 'Don't go for branch manager.' 'Don't move to Portland.' 'Don't become a single mother.' Terrible advice, all of it wrong."

"So, do better than people did for you."

"I don't know how."

"Don't say that." I grip the mug. "I feel...I feel completely alone."

"I know that feeling."

"Do you?"

"I do."

"Everyone wants me to make hard decisions. The case-worker. The boys. Richard. Even that first night, when I saw you at Sol's, Dad threw the decision onto me. I'm so sick of trying to make decisions. I'm so tired."

"Yes. And at the same time, I'm guessing that you feel like you've never really had any choices at all."

Endless decisions and no real choices. They can carve that on my gravestone. Suddenly I feel the need to get up and move. "Can we go somewhere?" I ask. "For a walk?"

"Your ankle—are you up for it?"

"I'm fine."

"I'd love a walk," Ms. Harper says. "I find that the ocean always helps." She takes the cups back to the kitchen and we set out together. I'm getting pretty fast on the crutch and keep pace easily. There's a path at the end of the street, adjacent to her yard; it leads through the trees and a small field of uncut grass, over a low rise, and then we're here, the ocean stretching out in front of me, oblivious and gray.

"Will you tell me about my mother?"

Ms. Harper nods, as though she's been expecting the question. "Will the sand be a problem for you?"

"No, I don't think so. Not if we go slow."

"Come on." Ms. Harper leads me down onto the rocky beach and we walk along the shore. She doesn't start talking right away, and I let her take her time. I want her to gather her thoughts. "Do I need to tell you she was beautiful?" she asks. "Alessandra was beautiful. You already know that she was beautiful. But she was more than that. She was gentle, and kind, but she was more than those things as well."

"Did she like having children?"

Ms. Harper thinks for a moment, bends and picks up a shell to examine. "It was hard for her. Your sister was very challenging, more or less from the time she was born."

"I know she was. She was an accident, she kept Mom from finishing college. And there's such a big gap between us, I always thought that I might have been an accident, too."

"I don't know whether you were or not. I do know that Alessandra took being a mother very seriously."

"That's not the same thing as liking it."

"It's not, but I'm not sure it's something you like or don't like. It's not a flavor of ice cream." She drops the shell and we resume walking. "Being a parent is the simplest thing in the world: you devote yourself to another human being and you remain devoted, no matter what happens, for the rest of your life. And the first thing you realize, when you take that job seriously, is how little control you have over anything. I can't think of something else where you have so much responsibility and so little control."

"I let Simon make a stupid bowl of pasta and he wound up in the hospital."

"Just wait until they start driving."

I shudder, thinking of Henry gunning our truck through the streets of Portland.

"There was a good deal your mother couldn't control," Ms. Harper continues. "Your sister, for one. And later on, the cancer. She wasn't perfect. She had regrets."

"But she tried?"

"She did. She was always reading parenting books. Going to seminars on behavior management, that sort of thing. And certainly, with her cancer, she tried everything she could. All the conventional treatments, plus special diets, vitamin supplements. She wanted to live, maybe more than anyone I've ever known."

"I guess that will only get you so far."

"Well, Hannah, what I can tell you is that she was tough and brave, but she was also very wise. She knew exactly what cards she was holding, she played them as well as she could, and when she didn't have much time left, I don't think she wasted any of it wishing she'd been dealt a different hand."

We circle a rock and cut down to the hard-packed sand where it's easier to walk. "What would my mother do, if she were me?"

"That sounds suspiciously like advice."

"I need help."

"Look," Ms. Harper says, "in my job people come to me for advice all the time and the first thing I tell them is to state the decision they are trying to make in just one sentence. What is your sentence?"

I think for a long moment, chewing on the edge of my thumbnail and then spitting it to one side. "Do I keep the boys with me, stay here and care for them, or do I let them be placed and get the hell out of Evans Beach?"

"That's quite a sentence."

"Probably not exactly what you run into at the credit union."

"No, but in a way not that different. People are facing decisions that will change the rest of their lives. Bankruptcy, debt, business closure. The thing I notice, Hannah, is that we tend to keep asking questions we've already answered."

"That sounds like something Ben said."

"Who?"

"The caseworker. He basically said that the fact I was asking him questions about what will happen if they stay meant that I'd already made a decision."

"Ah. Yes, that makes sense. That's what I see in my

work. People walking in circles, asking themselves a question they've already answered and refusing to face the one that's right in front of them. 'Should I close my business?' when they've long given up on it and what they really need to decide is when, and how."

We've reached the end of the sand, where the beach tapers off into the water and rocks rise up from the shore. It's the sort of spot where I loved to climb when I was a child. Ms. Harper runs her hands through her hair and sits on a boulder. I sit beside her. My ankle aches. Maybe the walk was too much.

"I love the sea wind," she says. "I grew up near a paper mill and the smell was awful. Honestly, it was something I never got used to. You'd think a child would stop noticing it after a while but I hated it every day. I always wanted to live by the water, where the air would be like this. I need to have the ocean close."

"You're in luck, it's going to get closer."

"Yes, that's what I understand."

"The drainage on your street has limited capacity; it will only hold up for so long."

"I'm on the board of the company that insures half the houses on my street. I know we're getting to be bad bets."

"What will you do?"

She shrugs. "Sell in a few years, I suppose. What else can I do?"

"Who will buy?"

"There's always someone who will take a chance on life by the water."

I hope so, for her sake. I look out at the ocean. A lobster boat is crawling along, maybe a hundred and fifty yards out, checking traps.

"That day at your house," Ms. Harper says, "just before Christmas, when I was in that ridiculous elf costume. Do you remember what your father said?"

"I remember your costume but not what he said."

"You were in a hurry. You were going to a school meeting for Simon and you told him not to worry about it and he said that he wasn't because you hadn't needed him since you were five years old."

"Yeah, that sounds like him."

"I know that he was mistaken."

The lobster boat is easing behind some rocks far out on the water. "Yes," I say. "He was always wrong about that. Not that it matters now."

"Maybe it matters that someone else knows he was wrong."

I shade my eyes and watch until the boat is almost completely out of sight. Then it starts to turn, heading toward another trap. "I've already decided, haven't I?" I ask.

"I think you have."

I don't know when it happened. It might have been just a few days ago, in the kitchen, looking at Simon and his burnt chest and stomach. It might have been months earlier, standing over my father, listening to the stillness in his room. Maybe it doesn't matter when a decision gets made; maybe all that matters is that you realize it is done, and stop asking questions you've already answered, and ask the right one next.

"How do I do it?"

"The 'how' questions are the hardest. You can get an answer to 'what' or 'when' or 'where,' sometimes even 'why,' but 'how'—you have to be shown how."

"Like driving a stick shift. You can't really tell someone how to do it."

"Right."

I drop my crutch into the sand and start to cry. I don't try to stop; the tears roll down my face and I let the wind off the water dry them. "I want my mother."

"I know."

"I've spent so much time trying to imagine myself into the past. Images in photos, stories from my dad. Trying to place myself in them. I even send her emails at a dummy account, telling her what's going on. But I never imagine her into my present, imagine what she would say right now."

"You could give it a try."

"I don't think I knew her well enough. I was too young."

"I think you know the important things," Ms. Harper says. "Maybe I can fill in the details. I can tell you stories about her. I'll tell you everything I remember."

I nod.

Ms. Harper puts her arm around me. I involuntarily stiffen, then rest my head against her shoulder. "I don't understand how this works," I say, wiping a tear away and watching the lobster boat continue on its rounds. "It's not fair. When do I get a chance to be young?"

I feel her draw a breath. "It is unfair," she says, "and it always will be. But you are young, and you will be young. Just not in the way that you thought."

We sit together for a while longer, looking out at the disappearing boat and the oncoming tide.

23

Henry's bag isn't that far inside the bomb shelter. He wanted to get rid of it when we didn't sign up for spring baseball. It's been shoved behind an old dresser and underneath what appears to be the remains of a Halloween decoration, or possibly a failed attempt at hay farming. I pull it out, dust it off, and bring it to the backyard, setting it down next to my crutch.

It's a warm day. It's almost May, my favorite month. The world wakes up and things begin.

I unzip the duffel and study the contents. Baseball is supposed to generate nostalgia but this just smells like dirty socks. I sort the contents, cringing as I move the jock protector out of the way, although with two boys I suppose it's the type of thing I need to get used to. Then I stand and shout as loud as I can.

"Henry!"

It reverberates off the side of the house and the trees behind me.

"Hey, Henry, come outside!"

Another moment passes and then the back door swings open and Henry pokes his head out. His hair is a mess; it looks like he's been sleeping. "What?"

"Come on out."

He steps through the door. "What's up?"

"Come here."

He slowly walks toward me, eyeing the bag at my feet. "What are you doing?"

I pick up his glove, the new one he got for Christmas, and toss it to him. "Put that on."

"Why?"

"You need practice."

"I don't play anymore."

"You think you don't play. Just because you're not on a team doesn't mean you're not a player."

"Cut it out, Hannah."

I bend over the bag and pull out the other glove. It's heavily worn and stained and scuffed, torn and restitched in places, and far too big for my hand. I slide it on anyway. There's a ball folded in the mesh pocket. "Back up."

"I said..."

"I called the coach. He's willing to add you to the roster, but you're rusty."

Henry stares at me. He doesn't say anything but I see, out of the corner of my eye, his hand slide into the glove.

"The season runs through late June," I say, "and then there's summer ball after that."

Henry moves to one side. "Simon is hungry," he says. "I was gonna make him some lunch."

"Richard's coming over and he's bringing pizza. Keep going, you need to break that glove in."

He steps back a pace, then another, moving farther to one side.

"Coach said you're a shoo-in for varsity in the fall," I say.

"Will I still be here?"

I take the ball from the mitt. "You'll be here."

I know that he doesn't quite believe it. He will, though, in time. When enough days turn to nights and then new days, and he is still here with me. When he starts playing baseball again and I come to all his games. When, later on this spring, I finally repaint the side of the mailbox with three freshly stenciled figures.

All of those moments are still to come, tomorrows stretching out ahead of us. Just until tomorrow, I think. Until the tomorrows become forever. Just until then. I whip my arm forward, the way Dad once showed me, and the ball arcs high through the early spring air.

Henry catches it.

From: Hannah Lynn <hlynn123@gmail.com>
To: Alessandra Lynn <alessandra.lynn@gmail.com>
Subject: belated life update

Time goes by too fast.

It's been a year since the April afternoon when I called Ben Strickland and told him I was in, that I was going to keep the boys with me. He didn't sound surprised, and I can't say that he sounded happy. Maybe relieved to have two fewer kids to place. He did say one thing, though, that I have kept with me: "Hannah," he said, "there are going to be days when you love that you made this decision and there are going to be days when you regret it, but one thing is for certain: this is going to be both the hardest and the most important thing you ever do."

It definitely has been hard. I got my diploma and then went to work full time at the DPW, which was basically a second job on top of taking care of the boys the way Dad did, meal lists and all. By October I was sick of it and I didn't really need the money anyway, not with Dad's life insurance and what remained of the college fund, so I applied to the Marine Ecology program at the University of Southern Maine, right over in Portland.

It's not bad. The program is only in its second year, but part of that newness is an enthusiasm for fresh ideas and the fact that this spring is my first semester didn't stop them from jumping on my plan for monitoring climate-change-related temperature and acidity fluctuations in Casco Bay. I have a lot to do; there are ten buoys with sensors mounted on them, and every other day I take a boat out for water samples and readings. My advisor says I may get to coauthor a paper with her next year if the findings pan out.

I should also tell you about Richard. Richard was right, the road from Cambridge to Evans Beach is doable. He's going to be back here in Maine this summer, volunteering at a community clinic in Portland. Henry and Simon assume that he'll come to all of their games, and Richard says he's going to teach them how to play chess. I'm planning to have some quiet time while they're all busy with each other. Maybe I'll get coffee with Amity, who is coming back from Cornell soon. She strikes me as a Sunflower Café type, but I can introduce her to Sol's.

And the boys. The boys are doing well. Henry is a freshman in high school and, of course, he's still playing ball. He's not going to go pro—I wouldn't want him to—but his coach thinks he'll play at the college level, and that makes him happy. I caught him looking at the Tufts baseball team's website the other night. Imagine that—a Jumbo!

Simon is thriving in the CARES program. His reading is coming along, and so is his math (though slowly). More important, he's making friends. His art is still the center of his life, and I think it always will be. His drawings and paintings are all over the house and are regular gifts to Ms. Harper, who makes a point of having her favorites professionally framed for her office at the credit union.

I moved the boys out of the family room and into Pauline's old bedroom. I got all new furniture and we repainted. Henry wanted to do this terrible green that he said matched the left-field wall at Fenway Park, but thankfully Simon has better taste. I was in charge of the trim and when I got to the closet door I found our old height marks. There's "Hannah," basically two feet off the ground, and "Pauline" way ahead of her. Up the doorframe we went, hopscotching over our old selves, taller and taller until time seemed to stop on the birthdays before we lost you. I looked at those pencil marks and names and dates for a long time, and then I painted over them. It's not long until Simon's birthday and I'll stand him in the closet door with his heels together and his back straight, and we'll start all over again.

Sometimes I wonder if things would have been different if the boys had come to me when I was twenty-six or twenty-eight rather than when I was so young. You probably wondered the same thing, having Pauline when you were only a junior in college. But you don't get to find things like that out, do you? You don't get to know about other versions of you. The boys are mine, and I'm doing the best I can, and I'm proud of them. Ben Strickland was right, it's hard and it's important, but there's one thing I'd add: it's also the best thing I've ever done.

Henry and Simon are sleeping downstairs. Tomorrow we're going out for breakfast and it's Simon's turn to decide where to go. He'll pick what he always picks: Sol's. He loves it there; Sonya always makes a big deal about how tall he's getting and gives him a cruller, and I always complain about the sugar and let him eat it anyway.

I didn't wind up where I thought I was going. I'm not at Tufts, and that's okay. I wanted it because it's where I thought I would find you, but I know you're not there. Your ghost doesn't haunt Carmichael Hall any more than it haunts this house. You're on a hill, by your husband's side, not far from the ocean. I can let you rest there. I even put your clothes away, your flannels and boots and your worn college T-shirt, all sealed in a box and tucked in the back of the bomb shelter. I don't need them to know the only thing that matters: that you loved me, and that I love you, and that you are still with me.

Life is getting busier. It's been a long time since I've written, and it may be a long time before I write again, but that doesn't mean I'm not thinking about you. I think about you all the time. I imagine that you can see what I see, think what I think, and I wonder what you would say and sometimes I think that I know. Ms. Harper said that I can imagine you into my now, and that's what I do. You're not looking down from above but you are looking out from inside.

I'm where I started out. It's not the same place that it was, though. Or maybe it is, and it's me that's different. I once told Dad that people don't get saved. I still don't know if we do, but I know that we can be found.

I love you, Mom.

Hannah

author's note

The Child Welfare System in the United States is less a single system than it is a quilt of federal, state, county, and city agencies along with a wide range of private contractors. At any given time, this "system" is responsible for about half a million children who experienced abuse or, more commonly, neglect in their families of origin. It screens millions of referrals annually. About a third of all American children will experience a Child Protective Services investigation prior to their eighteenth birthday.

Prior to writing this book, I had interacted with different pieces of this "system" as a pediatric psychologist and in support of loved ones navigating the challenges of a kinship placement. I may have known more than most, but I needed to keep learning in order to create this story. While researching this book I had many conversations and shared drafts of the manuscript with active caseworkers in my effort to respectfully and authentically depict the reality behind the fiction. One consistent comment was that the scale of neglect experienced by Henry and Simon would generally not, in the real world, trigger removal from the home. If children in situations such as this were routinely removed, it would far outstrip the availability of placements. My caseworker readers and interviewers repeatedly noted that Henry is a teenager. In this story, Henry and Simon may be cold, they may be hungry, they may be neglected, but they are unlikely to wind up badly injured or dead in the immediate future. In my story intervention occurs, but in reality that intervention would not take place unless there was a more imminent threat and that wasn't the story I wanted to write.

I was horrified. My response was that there needs to be more caseworkers, more placements, better funding. Ultimately, more removals. It's a natural reaction. It's not necessarily wrong, but it is limited by my personal background and perspective.

Among many other things, the Child Welfare System is an expression of state power. Families can be monitored, homes can be inspected, services can be mandated, and, as in this story, children can be removed. The ultimate power is termination of parental rights (TPR), which permanently severs physical custody and the right to communicate with a child. For most parents, it is one of the worst things we can imagine. About 1 out of every 100 American children will experience TPR.

Like the police and the structure of public-school discipline, the Child Welfare System reflects the history and underlying biases of the state wielding the power. As such, it is not surprising that Black and Native children are more than twice as likely as white children to experience TPR. As noted above, a bit more than a third of all U.S. children will experience an investigation, but among Black children that number is more than half and in some counties it approaches two-thirds.

This book provides one particular perspective on the Child Welfare System and draws its inspiration from real instances, but it does not capture the full range of realities within the Child Welfare System experience. It is written by a white author about a white family living in a state that is 94 percent white. The primary representative of the system, Ben Strickland, is everything you would want a caseworker to be: smart, thoughtful, and relentless in his pursuit of what he believes will be best for the children under his care. And in the end, the system works in the world of the story. Though it requires sacrifice (particularly on Hannah's part), Henry and Simon move from a dangerous situation in which they were being neglected to one in which they are safe, loved, and cared for and in which they may move closer to realizing their potential.

There are times when the system works in the real world, too. There are plenty of Ben Stricklands. I interviewed a number of them for this book. They care deeply about children and families. They struggle with ethical questions and face overwhelming situations with limited resources at their disposal. They are sensitive to issues of personal and institutional bias and racism. They are underpaid and overworked, and they prevent suffering and save children's lives.

There are also too many times when the system doesn't work, and it disproportionately fails to work in the lives of poor children and families, often people of color. In fact, some scholars, including Professor Dorothy Roberts of the University of Pennsylvania, argue the contrary: that the system is working the way those in power intend it to work, in the sense that its true purpose is to control and oppress those communities. She marshals sociology and history to argue that the benefits of the system are far outweighed by the costs it exacts on poor communities and that it needs to be abolished. She points out that many instances of neglect are manifestations of poverty, and that if we truly want to help children then we should direct funds to ameliorating the underlying conditions of want.

Professor Roberts makes her case in Torn Apart: How the Child Welfare System Destroys Black Families—and How Abolition Can Build a Safer World. It can be read alongside another recent book, We Were Once a Family: A Story of Love, Death, and Child Removal in America, by Roxanna Asgarian, which tells how racism and class bias in the foster care and adoption systems led to the preventable deaths of six children. Roberts' and Asgarian's books have been vital pieces of my ongoing effort to better understand "the system." They broadened my perspective. I struggle with the case for child-welfare abolition, but I recognize that my response is blinkered by my history and identity. If you struggle with these issues as I do, if you are as shocked by the above statistics as I was, then I encourage you to listen to authors such as Roberts and Asgarian with an open mind.

In the end, we face the same questions that Hannah faced: What do we do when children need care, and when those responsible for providing it are not able to respond? What is effective? What is compassionate? What is too much to ask? Hannah answers with all the wisdom and courage she can find. So do many caseworkers, kinship caregivers, birth parents, resource parents, and adoptive families, every day. We should all endeavor to do the same.

Joseph Moldover

acknowledgments

Many thanks to my agent, Adam Schear, for his ongoing collaboration and support, as well as to my editor, Margaret Ferguson, and her team at Holiday House.

Thanks to the one and only Jenna Blum and her wonderful, wild workshop including: Trisha Blanchett, Hillary Casavant, Mark Cecil, Tom Champoux, Jenn De Leon, Chuck Garabedian, Julie Gerstenblatt, Edwin Hill, Alex Hoopes, Sonya Larson, Kimberly Hensle Lowrance, Jenna Paone, Jane Roper, Whitney Scharer, Adam Stumacher, and Grace Talusan.

Thanks to Ursula DeYoung, who published a version of the first chapter of this book in her literary journal, *Embark*, and encouraged me to see it through.

My parents, Jonathan and Rebecca Moldover, remain among my best editors and advocates. At a low moment on the long trek to publishing my second book I wondered whether it was time to quit. "Sorry, honey," my mother replied, "you're a writer." Thanks, Ma.

My cousin, Ben Strick, is a brilliant and dedicated social worker. I am very proud of him and the work he does. I am also grateful that he is a skilled reader and that he always took the time to respond to my texts and calls about details of the child welfare system.

Social workers Meg O'Malley and Shannon Taylor provided outstanding feedback about the workings of child welfare in Maine and the lives of children in the system. They are knowledgeable, dedicated, thoughtful professionals and any inaccuracies in this book are entirely mine.

Love to Jacob, Nora, Nathan, and Charlotte. You make it all worthwhile.

To those in my life who shared their own experiences and allowed me to play a small, supporting role in them: thank you for trusting me to write this book. I hope that it captures some of your spirit and strength, as well as my love and appreciation.

My wife, Leah, read this manuscript many times. She shaped the story in more ways than can be described and it is, like all my other stories, for her.